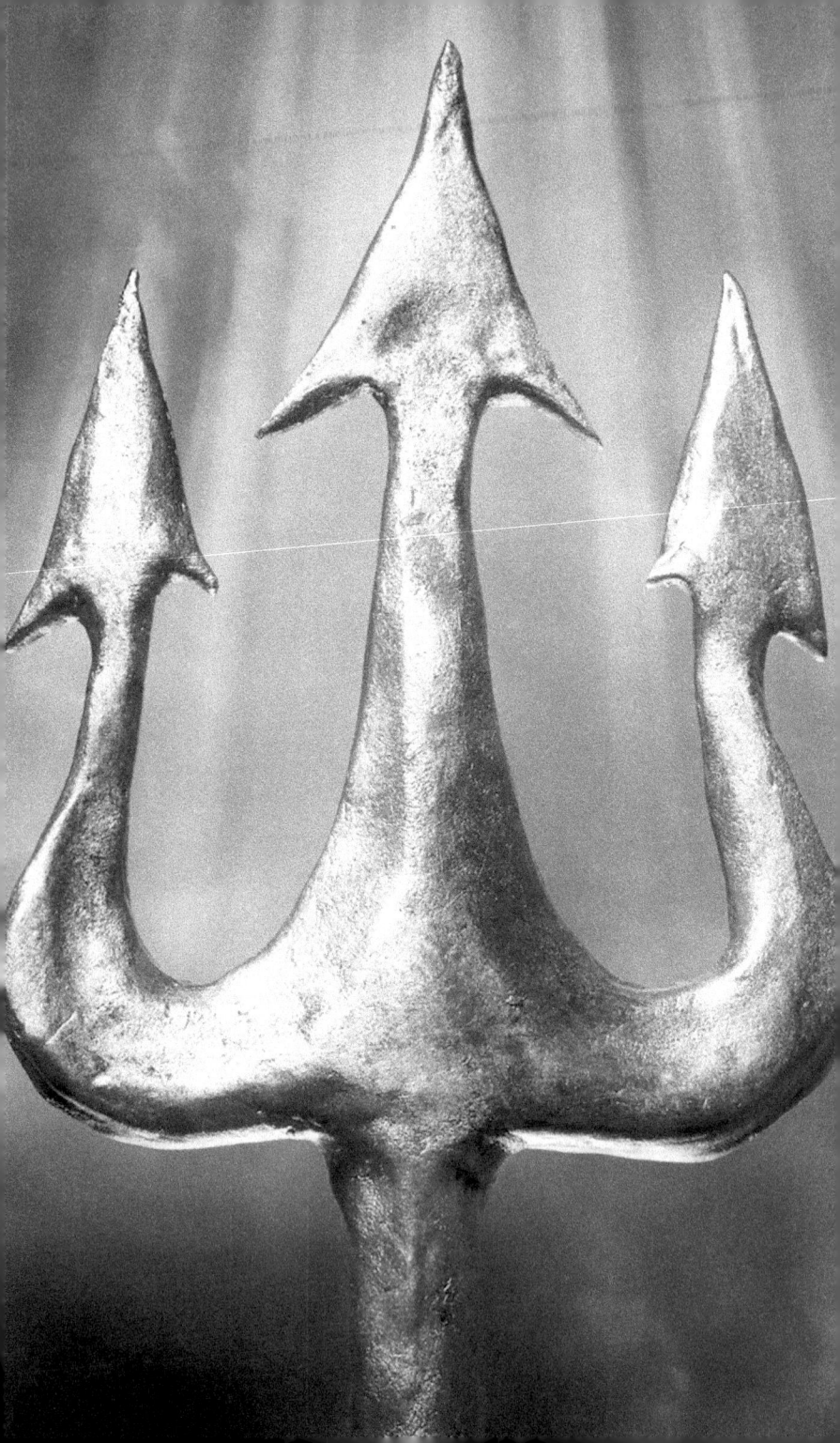

WATCHING
from the
Shadows

Trident Security Book 6

SAMANTHA COLE

To my family and friends for all their support.

ACKNOWLEDGMENTS

To my editor, Eve Arroyo, thanks for putting up with my comma handicap and all my little quirks.

To my PA, Maria, thanks for helping with all my events.
To my Beta Readers, Abby, Charla, Debbie, Felisha, Jessica, and Julie—without all of you, I would be lost. Thanks for being there every step of the way!

And to the Sexy-Six-Pack Sirens! You're the best group of readers and supporters I could ever ask for!

AUTHOR'S NOTE

The story within these pages is completely fictional but the concepts of BDSM are real. If you do choose to participate in the BDSM lifestyle, please research it carefully and take all precautions to protect yourself. Fiction is based on real life but real life is *not* based on fiction. Remember—Safe, Sane and Consensual!

Any information regarding persons or places has been used with creative literary license so there may be discrepancies between fiction and reality. The Navy SEALs missions and personal qualities within have been created to enhance the story and, again, may be exaggerated and not coincide with reality.

The author has full respect for the members of the United States military and the varied members of law enforcement and thanks them for their continuing service to making this country as safe and free as possible.

WHO'S WHO AND THE HISTORY OF TRIDENT SECURITY AND THE COVENANT

***While not every character is in every book, these are the ones with the most mentions throughout the series. This guide will help keep readers straight about who's who.

Trident Security (TS) is a private investigative and military agency, co-owned by Ian and Devon Sawyer. With governmental and civilian contracts, the company got its start when the brothers and a few of their teammates from SEAL Team Four retired to the private sector. The original six-man team is referred to as the Sexy Six-Pack, as they were dubbed by Kristen Sawyer, née Anders, or the Alpha Team. Trident had since expanded and former members of the military and law enforcement have been added to the staff. The company is located on a guarded compound, which was a former import/export company cover for a drug trafficking operation in

Tampa, Florida. Three warehouses on the property were converted into large apartments, the TS offices, gym, and bunk rooms. There also an obstacle course, a Main Street shooting gallery, a helicopter pad, and more features necessary for training and missions.

In addition to the security business, there is a fourth warehouse that now houses an elite BDSM club, co-owned by Devon, Ian, and their cousin, Mitch Sawyer, who is the manager. A lot of time and money has gone into making The Covenant the most sought after membership in the Tampa/St. Petersburg area and beyond. Members are thoroughly vetted before being granted access to the elegant club.

There are currently over fifty Doms who have been appointed Dungeon Masters (DMs), and they rotate two or three shifts each throughout the month. At least four DMs are on duty at all times at various posts in the pit, playrooms, and the new garden, with an additional one roaming around. Their job is to ensure the safety of all the submissives in the club. They step in if a sub uses their safeword and the Dom in the scene doesn't hear or heed it, and make sure the equipment used in scenes isn't harming the subs.

The Covenant's security team takes care of everything else that isn't scene-related, and provides safety for all members and are essentially the bouncers. The current total membership is just over 350. The fire marshal had approved them for 500 when the warehouse-turned-kink club first opened, but the cousins had intentionally kept that number down to maintain an elite status.

Between Trident Security and The Covenant there's plenty of romance, suspense, and steamy encounters. Come meet the Sexy Six-Pack, their friends, family, and teammates.

The Sexy Six-Pack (Alpha Team) and Their Significant Others

- Ian "Boss-man" Sawyer: Devon and Nick's brother—retired Navy SEAL—co-owner of Trident Security and The Covenant—fiancé/Dom to Angelina (Angie).
- Devon "Devil Dog" Sawyer: Ian and Nick's brother—retired Navy SEAL—co-owner of Trident Security and The Covenant—husband/Dom to Kristen.
- Ben "Boomer" Michaelson: retired Navy SEAL—explosives and ordnance specialist—son of Rick and Eileen, fiancé/Dom of Katerina (Kat).
- Jake "Reverend" Donovan: retired Navy SEAL—Dom and Whip Master at The Covenant—boyfriend/Dom to Nick.
- Brody "Egghead" Evans: retired Navy SEAL—computer specialist—Dom.
- Marco "Polo" DeAngelis: retired Navy SEAL—communications specialist and back up helicopter pilot—Dom.

- Nick Sawyer: Ian and Devon's brother—current Navy SEAL—boyfriend/submissive to Jake.
- Kristen "Ninja-girl" Sawyer: author of romance/suspense novels—wife/submissive of Devon.
- Angelina "Angie/Angel" Sawyer: graphic artist, fiancée/submissive of Ian.
- Katerina "Kat" Michaelson: dog trainer for law enforcement and private agencies—fiancée/submissive of Boomer.

Extended Family, Friends, and Associates of the Sexy Six-Pack

- Mitch Sawyer: Cousin of Ian, Devon, and Nick—co-owner/manager of The Covenant, Dom.
- T. Carter: US spy and assassin—works for covert agency Deimos—Dom.
- Shelby Christiansen: human resource clerk—two-time cancer survivor—fiancée/submissive to Parker.
- Parker Christiansen: owner of New Horizons Construction—Dom/fiancé to Shelby.
- Curt Bannerman: retired Navy SEAL—owner of Halo Customs, a motorcycle repair and detail shop.

- Jenn "Baby-girl" Mullins: college student—goddaughter of Ian—"niece" of Devon, Brody, Jake, Boomer, and Marco—father was a Navy SEAL—parents murdered.
- Mike Donovan: owner of the Irish pub, Donovan's—brother of Jake.
- Charlotte "Mistress China" Roth: Parole officer—Domme and Whip Master at The Covenant.
- Travis "Tiny" Daultry: former professional football player—head of security at The Covenant and Trident compound—occasional bodyguard for TS.
- Rick and Eileen Michaelson: Boomer's parents. Rick is a retired Navy SEAL.
- Charles "Chuck" and Marie Sawyer: Ian, Devon, and Nick's parents. Charles is a self-made real estate billionaire. Marie is a plastic surgeon involved with Operation Smile.
- Will Anders: Assistant Curator of the Tampa Museum of Art Kristen Anders's cousin.
- Dr. Roxanne London: pediatrician—Domme/wife (Mistress Roxy) of Kayla.
- Kayla London: social worker—submissive/wife of Roxanne.
- Chase Dixon: retired Marine Raider—owner of Blackhawk Security—associate of TS.
- Doug Henderson: retired Marine—bodyguard.

- Reggie Helm: lawyer for TS and The Covenant—boyfriend/Dom of Colleen.
- Colleen McKinley-Helm: office manager of TS—girlfriend/submissive of Reggie.
- Alyssa Wagner: teenager saved by Jake from an abusive father—lives with Rick and Eileen Michaelson.
- Dr. Trudy Dunbar: Psychologist.
- Carl Talbot: college professor—Dom and Whip Master at The Covenant

The Omega Team and Their Significant Others

- Cain "Shades" Foster: retired Secret Service agent.
- Tristan "Duracell" McCabe: retired Army Special Forces
- Darius "Batman" Knight: retired Navy SEAL.
- Valentino "Romeo" Mancini: retired Army Special Forces—former FBI Hostage Rescue Team (HRT) member.
- Lindsey "Costello" Abbott: retired Marine— sniper.

Trident Support Staff

- Colleen McKinley-Helm: office manager of TS—girlfriend/submissive of Reggie.

- Tempest "Babs" Van Buren: retired Air Force helicopter pilot—TS mechanic.

Members of Law Enforcement

- Larry Keon: Assistant Director of the FBI.
- Frank Stonewall: Special Agent in Charge of the Tampa FBI.
- Calvin Watts: Leader of the FBI HRT in Tampa.

The K9s of Trident

- Beau: An orphaned Lab/Pit mix, rescued by Ian. Now a trained K9 who has more than earned his spot on the Alpha Team.
- Spanky: A rescued Bullmastiff with a heart of gold, owned by Parker and Shelby.

FOREWORD

I Never Knew

Before you I felt so all alone,
Imprisoned by myself.
Secluded from the drag of time,
Un-needed and un-helped.

I'd sit and stare, I'd look at sights,
But nothing would I see.
A printed page not understood,
A beach without a sea.

But when I think of you,
It's like a gentle rain on land.
My thoughts become a symphony,
Played by a maestro's hand.

I see your figure clear and bold,
On canvas in my mind.
I dream your arms around me tight,
Embracing for all time.

When I'm with you time stands still,
Or ceases to exist.
You and I are all alone,

Enveloped in a mist.

And I can linger in your arms,
To store up memories.
For times when you're not with me, Babe,
When you're not here with me.

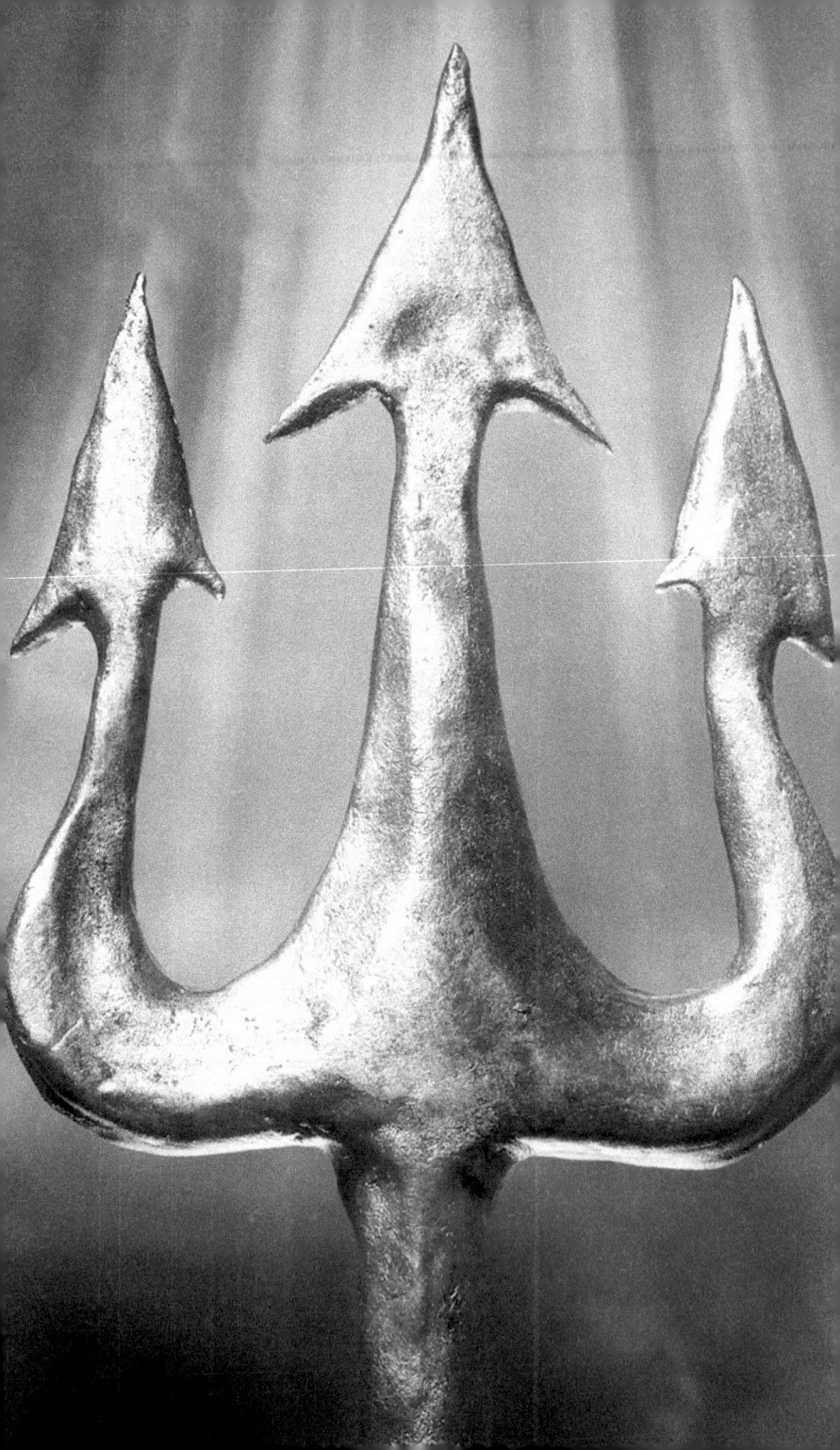

PROLOGUE

Well past midnight, the headlights of the target's truck appeared and lit up the street as he drove toward his home in a residential neighborhood of Tampa. After he passed the blue Honda Civic parked a block and a half away from his destination, the area was plunged into darkness once again. But the vehicle wasn't occupied. Its driver had crept through several backyards to the trees on the west side of the man's property. The spot had been used several times before.

Observant eyes zeroed in on the private security operative as he climbed out of his truck, dressed in black leather pants, biker boots, and a button-down white shirt with the sleeves rolled up to his elbows. With a zoom lens, several photos were taken as the man strode to his mailbox and then to his front door, unaware of the other person's presence. Or was he?

The dark-haired former Navy SEAL paused with

the key in the door lock and scanned the area surrounding his property. Sinking deeper behind the shrub coverage, the observer prayed discovery wasn't imminent. It wasn't time… soon, but not yet.

A deep breath was exhaled when the man finally entered the house and shut the door behind him. Several lights came on as he made his way through the rooms. He lived alone… had since his beloved sister passed away months before. It was a shame, but she was one less person who stood in the observer's way.

When the last light went out, the observer counted to one thousand, then slowly crept out of hiding, sticking to the shadows. Closed-circuit cameras pointed at both the front and back doors, which were expected from a man with a military and security background. But it wasn't an issue since none were pointed at the truck.

The last time the observer had left something on the vehicle—a discreet tracking device placed on the undercarriage closest to the front passenger door. Tonight's objects, though, would be left in plain sight where the homeowner was sure to see them when he left for work in the morning.

After tucking the two objects under the windshield wiper on the driver's side so they wouldn't blow away, the observer hurried back into the shadows and returned to the waiting Honda. All that was left to do tonight was print out the photos… and then wait until the time was right.

CHAPTER ONE

Across the backyard, Marco "Polo" DeAngelis watched his buddy roughhouse with four fatherless children in the newly fallen January snow. Curt Bannerman and he had flown into Fort Dodge Regional Airport the night before, then driven an hour to Stormville, Iowa, to the home of Dana Prichard—widow of their former teammate, Eric Prichard. The retired Navy SEAL had been murdered in a hit-and-run incident a little over a year ago, and the man who'd killed him had been a hired assassin, targeting specific former members of SEAL Team Four.

The SEAL community was tight-knit, and when one of them was killed or incapacitated, the others would step up and help out all they could. Shortly after Prichard's funeral, a rotating, bi-weekly schedule had been set up. Once every four months, Marco's name came up, and he traveled from his home in Tampa, Florida, to meet another team member in Iowa for the weekend. They would stay at a local motel and help Dana with anything that needed to be done around the house and yard. Landscaping, a new roof, and a bathroom renovation had been on the to-do list over the past sixteen months, among other things.

That morning, the two men had painted six-year-old Amanda's bedroom pink and purple since she'd declared she was too grown up for the old Winnie-the-Pooh décor.

If nothing pressing needed to be done at the residence, they sometimes gave Dana a weekend to herself without the kids or took the entire family on an excursion. They'd gone camping over one of the weekends Marco had been there and a trip to the Six Flags Park in Iowa City another time.

Personally, he preferred to work when his weekends came up—kids made him a little antsy. It wasn't that he disliked them—his own childhood hadn't been the greatest, and he didn't know how to relate to them as Bannerman did. Marco also had no desire to have his own children—a decision he'd made long ago.

While Marco finished stacking the firewood they'd split earlier, Bannerman and Amanda, the only girl, threw snowballs at her brothers—nine-year-old Justin, ten-year-old Taylor, and twelve-year-old Ryan. It wasn't long before Dana stuck her head out the back door. "Dinner's ready! Come and get it!"

Thank God, because he was so cold, his cock and balls were trying to crawl up into his pelvis. The temperatures had barely reached thirty degrees all day, and for a five-year resident of Florida, that felt like ten below. He had no idea how Curt was putting up with it since the man lived a few hours away from him in Daytona Beach. Before the next trip, he would invest in thermal underwear because his heavy jacket, gloves, and hat weren't warm enough.

As the kids rushed inside, Curt ambled over, brushing the snow from his blond hair. "Hand me the axes. I'll put them in the shed. You're looking a little hypothermic there, Polo."

"Ya think?" he snorted, his rarely-heard Staten Island accent coming through. "It's colder than a witch's tit out here. I knew there was a reason I moved to the Sunshine State."

Curt bent over, pulled one of the axes out of the old tree stump they'd used, and took the one Marco handed him. "I could get used to it again. You forget—I'm from Montana. This is nothing—a tropical heat wave."

"Yeah, well… why don't you stop ogling the merry widow, tell her how you feel, and then you can live in the Tropics of Iowa all year round."

Even though his cheeks were red from the cold, the six-foot-four, two-hundred-twenty-pound man blushed. "What are you fucking talking about? I'm not interested in Dana."

Crossing his arms, Marco rolled his eyes. "Please. Don't give me that. You get a goofy fucking grin on your face every time she walks into the room. Probably a fucking hard-on too, but I have no desire to confirm that by taking a look at your junk. Every time someone can't make it up here for their weekend, you've been filling in. And don't tell me it's because Eric was your best friend."

"He is... was... damn it." Scowling, Curt turned and strode toward the shed, but Marco followed on his heels. He knew the survivor guilt the guy was dealing with because he had his own ghost of Prichard. The deceased SEAL had taken Marco's place on a fact-finding mission many years ago, resulting in him being added to the assassin's hit list.

"I know he was. But you know better than I do that he'd want you to have a good life without him. The same goes for Dana. I've seen the way she looks at you sometimes. And the kids and you get along great—so, what's the problem? It's been almost a year and a half since he was killed. Get off your fucking ass before someone steps in and snatches her up."

Curt whirled around so fast Marco almost got hit in his cold cock with an ax. "Who's going to snatch her up? Someone else been eyeing her?"

He smirked. "Thought you weren't interested."

"Don't fuck with me, Polo. Who the fuck else is interested in her?"

Marco shrugged, finding amusement in the other man's fast change in attitude. "I don't know for sure, but Egghead mentioned the Sheriff seemed to be sniffing around a lot when he was up here two weeks ago." Brody "Egghead" Evans was his best friend and teammate at Trident Security and was the biggest computer geek in the world—or close to it.

"Fuck that shit."

The big man's gaze went to the rear entrance of the house, and Marco slapped him on the shoulder before taking the axes from him. "So, you gonna man up and tell her how you feel?"

Curt nodded, his eyes never leaving the backdoor. "Damn fucking straight."

"About fucking time." He watched his friend make a beeline for the house. Even though a wife and kids weren't in Marco's future, he had no problem with his buddies having them. But settling down was something he was never going to do. He'd rather cut off his left nut than walk down the aisle and have a bunch of rug rats. No way… no fucking how.

TAKING A SIP OF HIS BEER, MARCO RELAXED IN A SITTING area near the bar of the BDSM club, The Covenant, which was located on the same property as Trident Security. One couldn't ask for more than having his work and play areas within forty yards of each other, especially when he enjoyed both.

He listened to his bosses, Ian and Devon Sawyer, discuss the meeting the former had taken part in on Friday at the Pentagon in Washington D.C., about their new government contract. Their other teammate, Jake

Donovan, had met Boss-man there and then flown back to San Diego to his temporary home. Jake was currently in charge of establishing Trident Security's west coast facility there and was living with his boyfriend/submissive, Nick Sawyer, who happened to be the bosses' younger brother. Nick had just under two years left in his Navy SEAL career, stationed in California, so the set-up had worked perfectly for everyone.

At the feet of the Dominant Sawyers, their submissive women sat on pillows, chatting quietly in their club lingerie. Kristen was Devon's wife, and Angie Beckett and Ian were planning their late spring wedding. Between the older two Sawyer brothers, Jake, and their other teammate, Ben "Boomer" Michaelson, the men of Trident were dropping like flies as they'd all met the loves of their lives over the past sixteen months. The only single men left on Trident's Alpha team were Brody and Marco, and the others were betting on who was going down next. Marco felt sorry for anyone who'd bet on him because it was a losing wager.

He'd gotten home a few hours ago from Iowa, and instead of just crashing on the couch in front of his big screen TV like he wanted to, he'd ended up here for Devon's birthday. It wasn't exactly a party with presents and decorations—just another excuse for them all to get together for a few drinks and maybe some play down in the pit.

While the main second floor of the club housed the bar, offices, and a fetish store, the pit, as the members dubbed it, was the vast recreational room downstairs. It was filled with a wide assortment of BDSM equipment in both public areas and private rooms.

Even though it was still early in the evening—a little after eight-thirty—the club was bustling with activity. On Sunday nights, the place usually emptied out by eleven so people could get some sleep before starting their work week the next day. From their pillows, Kristen and Angie began giggling uncontrollably at something near the bar, and the three men turned their attention in the same direction.

"Ho-ly shit!" Devon shook his head in stunned amusement, while Marco almost fell out of his chair as laughter spilled forth and tears filled his gunmetal blue eyes. Speaking of a losing wager...

Ian's head dropped back as he groaned loudly. "Oh, crap. Is he fucking kidding me?" He glanced at Marco. "Let me guess, the Giants beat the Cowboys in today's football game."

"Yup." That was the only word he could get out as he held his six-pack abs and gasped for air.

They all stared as Brody strode toward them, good-naturedly chuckling at members' comments along the way. Dressed in his usual snug, faded jeans, T-shirt, and cowboy boots, the only thing that was out of place was the fact he had his button fly undone. And instead of his junk hanging out, it was covered by an elephant trunk and ears—the thong the loser had to wear in the bet he and Marco had made.

Every few steps, the well-built geek would stop and

wiggle his hips at some of the female submissives, causing the impressively filled trunk to flap around. By the time he reached his teammates, the entire bar area had erupted into fits of hysterical laughter.

Stopping a few feet from Marco, his best friend pointed a finger at him, unable to hide his grin. The man had no shame. "Just fucking wait, asshole. I can't wait until the next time you lose a bet."

Although he wasn't too worried, Marco knew the guy was already planning his revenge, and he might not put it off until the next wager. "Um, if I remember correctly, you were the one who swore the Cowboys would win, and the junk trunk was your idea." He wiped away a tear threatening to escape and turned his head toward Kristen and Angie. "I don't know, ladies. I think I would've filled it out better than Egghead. What do you think?"

Before either of the women could respond, one of the submissive waitresses, Cassandra, hurried over, wearing an expression of alarm. She did a double take at Brody's crotch but then directed her words to Marco. "Sir, Master Ben is in the lobby on a phone call, and he told me to come get you. He said it's an emergency."

The mirth died quickly as he leaped to his feet, followed by Ian and Devon. Brody tucked the elephant in his pants and was a step behind Marco's heels as he ran toward the lobby. Cell phones weren't allowed out on the club floor, and all calls and texts had to be taken outside—a rule that was strictly enforced. His initial thought was something had happened to Boomer's girlfriend, Kat Maier, but she was standing by her Dom's side, with worry on her pretty face, as the group hurried up to them.

"Hang on a sec." Boomer pulled the cell phone away from his face and held it out for Marco. "You remember Jake's ex on Clearwater P.D.? Drew Murdock? He's at a crime scene, and your business card was there. When he couldn't reach you, he called Trident's main number, and I'm on-call, so it got bounced to me."

While he'd never met the cop Jake had dated for a few weeks over a year ago, he knew the name. Marco took the phone and brought it to his ear. "DeAngelis."

The officer had obviously heard Boomer tell him who was on the phone. "Hey. Sorry to call like this, but I'm at a house over here in Clearwater with a home invasion, and I've got an unconscious assault victim. We haven't found her cell phone or a list of emergency contacts yet. She just moved into the neighborhood, and the house is trashed, but I found your business card on her refrigerator. Does the name Millicent Williams ring a bell?"

Marco shook his head at the unfamiliar name while his teammates and their women waited for details. "Millicent? I have no idea who that is." But something niggled his brain.

Over the phone, he could hear the squawks of police radios and the voices of other officers working the scene. "Hang on a sec. There's a diploma on the wall here in the home office. Her full name is Millicent Harper Williams—she's an attorney."

The blood drained from Marco's face, and his gut clenched as he finally made the connection to his deceased sister's best friend—the woman who invaded his dreams since their one night together thirteen months ago. "Harper? Harper Williams was assaulted?"

Around him, the men and Kristen's eyes flashed wide as they also recognized the name, but Marco held up his hand to stop anyone from asking questions he didn't have any answers to yet. "Fuck. Is she all right?"

"She got knocked on the head pretty bad. The paramedics are on their way with her to Largo Medical Center. She's still unconscious. And DeAngelis… the main reason I'm calling is… her baby is missing."

A roar equivalent to a jet engine surged through his head, and a wave of shock and confusion struck him hard. "Baby? What fucking baby?"

CHAPTER TWO

Thirteen Months Earlier

"Are you okay?"

God, he was getting sick of that fucking question. No, he wasn't fucking okay—he'd just buried his sister two hours ago—the only blood relative who'd ever been important to him. And now she was gone.

Marco regarded the well-meaning mourner, whose name he couldn't remember. The guy was one of the teachers Nina had worked with, and while the entire PTA had supported her through the fourteen-month battle against inoperable brain cancer, Marco couldn't remember who was who. "Yeah. I'm fine. Thanks for coming."

After shaking the guy's outstretched hand, he stepped away before more redundant platitudes could be spoken. The day couldn't go any slower if it tried. He knew wakes, funerals, and the after gatherings were for the living to remember the dead and to be there for the deceased's family, but he was Nina's only survivor —if he didn't count Harper, that is. His sister's best friend had been by her side, and his, throughout the entire ordeal—the woman had been a godsend.

His gaze scanned the dining area of Donovan's Pub, where the mourners had come to eat and drink a toast to his sister's memory. Jake's brother, Mike, had offered the place for the repast gathering, and between the two men, they'd told Marco the expenses were covered. While he had the finances to pay for it, he appreciated the offer since it was one less thing he had to deal with. He also knew better than to argue with one of his teammates. Jake and the four other team members may not be his blood brothers, but they were brothers of his heart, and he would do anything for them—the same as they would for him. Besides, any debts they racked up amongst each other were usually paid in full and then some at a later time. They'd all pretty much lost count over the years over who owed what.

Sidling up to the bar, he stepped into an empty space between Brody and Devon. The former clapped him lightly on the shoulder. "Another half hour and everyone will be done eating. We'll start subtly moving people out the door. Then you can either get out of here or sit and get ass-faced drunk. Your decision, and we've got your six."

Damn, he loved these guys. That was the thing about his team—they could read each other like an open book and didn't ask what needed to be done… they just did it. He accepted the bottle of Dos Equis the bartender handed him and took a swig of the cold brew. "Thanks. I don't know what I would've done without you guys these last few months."

The two men waved off his gratitude—his thanks didn't need to be verbalized. They knew it existed, and that was enough for them. He turned when Jenn Mullins touched his arm.

"Uncle Marco, did you get enough to eat? I packed some leftovers for you to take home if you get hungry later and don't want to cook. I put in enough for Harper, too—I don't think she really ate anything."

He pulled the pretty, blonde twenty-year-old into his arms and hugged her. "Thanks, Baby-girl. You think of everything, don't you? I'm good for now, but I'm sure I'll be grateful for whatever you packed up when my stomach starts growling later."

Jenn wasn't blood-related to any of the original Trident six-man team, but she called all of them "uncle," and they considered her to be their niece. After her parents had been murdered eight months ago, she'd come to live with her godfather, Ian, who'd been her father's best friend since basic training. The surrogate uncles had all been on the same SEAL Team Four as Jeff Mullins and had watched his daughter grow from a tiny infant into a beautiful young woman. Now, they ensured she was surrounded by people who loved her and would do their best to protect and care for her. She was slowly overcoming her grief, with her bubbly personality resurfacing again. When she wasn't in class at the University of Tampa, she waitressed part-time at the pub, but Mike Donovan had given her the day off to attend the funeral.

Jenn stepped away, and another well-wisher took her place, shaking his hand and telling him how much Nina would be missed—yeah, he knew that more than anyone. His sister had been the one constant, shining star in his life.

She'd been born to their flighty mother thirty-two years ago when Marco was two. At least Teresa DeAngelis knew who her daughter's father was, even though he'd been a deadbeat dad who'd left New York for parts unknown before the little girl was born. From what Marco knew, his own sperm donor hadn't even taken his pants off and ended up giving the nineteen-year-old one-night stand a false name and number—along with a baby on the way.

Since he was born, life had been a struggle for Marco, but he did everything he could to ensure his little sister was happy and felt loved, even though he was the only one providing it. As a young mother, Teresa was more interested in going out and having fun with her friends on Staten Island, NY, than taking care of two small children, who were more trouble and work than she'd expected. By the time Marco was four, she was heavily into drugs, and two days shy of his eighth birthday, she was dead of an accidental overdose. Marco had discovered her cold body on the kitchen floor of their run-down one-bedroom apartment when he woke up early that morning.

Somehow, Nina had slept through the chaos after the police and paramedics arrived, so she'd been spared the memory of their mother's lifeless body lying on the cracked linoleum floor, with a needle sticking out of her arm.

From then on, they'd lived with their grandmother, but life with her wasn't much better. Instead of drugs, Rose DeAngelis' vices included alcohol, cigarettes, lottery tickets, and hoarding. Marco had tried to keep the place from getting overwhelmed with junk, throwing things out when the woman wasn't home, but sometimes it was a losing battle. When he and Nina had returned to New York several years ago, following the woman's death, they'd ended up renting a massive dumpster just to get rid of everything. There had been very few valuables among the piles of useless keepsakes.

Someone else touched his shoulder, and Marco pivoted to accept more condolences. He groaned inwardly when he saw who it was, and over Paula Leighton's short head, he noticed Brody roll his eyes at the woman.

Paula had been the secretary at Trident Security for a few months before she'd been caught in the business' restricted access area called the war-room. It was actually Brody's office, filled with computers that the geek used to gather intel, including classified information. Aside from the data Trident received legally from the

U.S. government about their mutual contracts, Brody was a world-class hacker, and Paula had made the mistake of snooping in his domain. Her curiosity had gotten her fired with a paltry severance check. Thankfully, she couldn't access anything she wasn't supposed to see.

"Marco, I'm so sorry for your loss. If there is anything I can do…"

"Thanks, Paula, but I think everything has been covered." He tried to step away, but her grip on his arm tightened.

"Have you been eating right? I could cook a few meals for you."

Jeez. He knew the woman had a crush on him when she'd been at Trident—well, she'd actually had a crush on several of them—but he thought she would've been over it by now. She wasn't his type, even if he'd been attracted to her. She was a woman who wanted to settle down and have kids—neither of which he was inclined to do.

"Ah, no, thanks. The freezer is full of meals from Nina's PTA." He spotted Harper across the room, waving for him to join her with Nina's school principal. *Thank God.* "If you'll excuse me, I have to say goodbye to a few people."

"Sure."

He hadn't missed the disappointment in her voice, but right now, he couldn't give a fuck. He was beyond exhausted, both physically and emotionally, and just wanted this day to be over.

A half-hour later, his teammates followed through with their promise and began thanking everyone for coming, subtly indicating for them to get the fuck out. Soon, all that was left were the people he was closest to, and he took a seat at the bar. Devon's girl-friend/submissive, Kristen, sat next to him.

"I'm not going to ask if you're okay because you're probably sick of that question, but is there anything you need us to do back at the house?"

He sighed heavily. "Yesterday, hospice came to pick up the hospital bed and the rest of their stuff, so that's done. Nina gave me a list of personal things that should go to certain people, but Harper said she'd take care of it. And most of her clothes and stuff have already gone to a local women's shelter, at her request, so there's really not much left of her at the house."

He choked up on those last few words, and Kristen silently put her arm around his shoulders and gave him a sideways hug in support. It was almost as if Nina had never existed, but she had. The sharp pain in his heart was a clear reminder of that. But he would never hear anyone call him "Marky Mark" again—just like the singer-turned-actor. She'd called him that ever since they were little, and while it had been embarrassing at times, he'd loved her too much to complain.

The faint scent of a familiar perfume tickled his nose, and he knew Harper was near. He didn't know the name of the fragrant stuff, but she was the only woman he'd ever noticed wearing it. And it drove him crazy that his dick liked it too. But Harper wasn't a woman he wanted to get involved with, either. She was beautiful —fucking gorgeous if he were being honest. She was also sweet, funny, reliable, and everything else a man looked for in a life mate. Well, every man but him.

Marco needed someone who was just like him... someone who wanted a little fun with an end date. That was one of the reasons why he loved the BDSM lifestyle and its contracts. Just negotiate the terms of the relationship and agree on how temporary it would be—nothing to worry about. Harper wasn't into the lifestyle, though. But damn, her natural submissiveness had him wishing she was.

Rotating the swivel bar stool, he came face to face with her. Dressed in a simple black sheath accentuating her hourglass figure and endless legs, she tucked a strand of pale blonde hair behind her ear. The piece hadn't been long enough to stay tucked into the subdued bun she'd put her hair up in this morning. She stood five inches shorter than his six-foot-two when she wasn't wearing heels. Today, her stilettos gave her three more inches and brought them to almost eye level with each other. Her hazel eyes were filled with sadness and exhaustion as her gaze roamed his face before she pointed to his new beer bottle. "Got one of those for me?"

"Absolutely." He stood and offered her his stool, then flagged down the bartender. "Another Dos Equis, Vince, when you can, please. Thanks."

Taking his vacated seat, with her back to the bar,

Harper crossed her legs, and Marco held back a groan that almost escaped him. God, she had some of the nicest legs he'd ever seen on a woman.

Tearing his eyes away before he had a natural reaction in his crotch, he glanced up at one of the bar's TVs that'd been turned on as the funeral reception winded down. Damn, he needed to get laid... and soon. It was the only reason he could come up with why he was attracted to a woman who had shown no interest in him, other than he was her best friend's brother.

Harper and Nina had been roommates in college at the University of Virginia. His sister's major had been Elementary Education, while Harper's had been pre-law before she'd stayed there after graduation and continued her studies for her law degree. In the meantime, Nina had fallen in love with Harper's hometown of Clearwater, Florida, from their spring, summer, and winter break visits. After graduation, she received her state teaching license and moved there to get a job. A few years later, Harper also returned to Clearwater and joined a local law firm.

Marco was so happy when Nina found a friend who would become the sister she had never had. It had made his tours of duty overseas much easier on him, knowing she had someone she could count on—especially if something had happened to him.

"Marco?"

Huh? He must have zoned out and missed whatever Harper had said. Mentally shaking his head, he focused his attention on her. "I'm sorry. What did you say?"

She gave him a small smile. "I said, you look as tired as I feel. Do you mind leaving?"

Her car was at his house. Since the funeral home had given them use of their limo to the service and then the cemetery, they'd decided last night to drive there together this morning, leaving her car behind. Boomer then drove Marco's truck to Donovan's from the funeral home.

After swallowing the last of his beer, he placed the empty bottle on the bar. "Not at all. It's been a long day… and you're right, I am tired. Let me grab the food Jenn packed for us, and we'll head home."

CHAPTER THREE

Present

Sitting in the passenger seat of Brody's Ford F-150 as the geek raced them toward Clearwater, Marco tried to wrap his brain around what Murdock had told him. From the pictures in the house, the police estimated the baby girl was between four and six months old. The timeline given meant the child could be his, but they had used protection during their one night together, hadn't they?

Shit! The memories flooded his mind. The first time had been fast, furious, and up against the wall. But as soon as he'd realized he hadn't used a condom, he'd pulled out, and Harper had reassured him she'd been on the pill for years. The kid couldn't be his. So, why was his gut filled with dread?

"Is it yours?"

It didn't surprise him that his best friend would be

the first to ask the question out loud. Marco ran his hand down his face in frustration. "Honestly, Brody, I have no fucking idea. It was only one night… the night of Nina's funeral. The stress and… and grief just kinda hit us both, and it happened. Is it possible? Technically, yeah, it's possible. But Murdock isn't sure, yet, how old the kid is. Maybe it was someone she met after me. Maybe it was something she planned, like artificial insemination or something. Maybe she adopted the kid." He was reaching for straws, and they both knew it. "I don't know, man. I mean, wouldn't she have fucking told me if it was mine?"

"All right. First things first. We find the kid and make sure Harper is okay. Then we can figure out if we need to send out engraved announcements and start a college fund."

Marco groaned and threw his head back so it bounced off the cushioned headrest behind him. "Fuck! What the fuck am I going to do if it's mine? You know me. I never wanted to get married, and I sure as hell didn't want any kids."

Turning onto the street Murdock had given them, Brody pulled up behind one of the many patrol cars and crime scene vehicles, then shoved the gearshift into park. "One step at a time, brother. Let's go find out what's going on."

The two men exited the truck as Ian parked behind them and climbed out with Devon and Boomer. None of them had changed, so aside from Brody, the rest were dressed in their club leathers, drawing some stares from police officers and bystanders alike. But Marco didn't give a shit and walked straight up to one of the cops guarding the yellow-taped perimeter. "Officer Murdock called me. Can you tell him I'm here? Marco DeAngelis."

The young cop's wary eyes brightened in recognition. "Uh, yeah. Actually, it's Detective Murdock now. He got promoted a few months ago." The man lifted the yellow tape to allow them entry. "He told me to let you in and anyone you came with, but the officer at the front door will call him outside for you. They're still processing the scene."

Striding up the long driveway, Marco took in his surroundings. The house was a split-level ranch in a nice neighborhood. The landscaping had been well taken care of, and from what he could see, it didn't appear the property needed much work. The same went for the house. The siding looked new, and the roof a few years older. A fence blocked his view of the backyard, but he was sure it was just as nice. Harper had found a pleasant home for her and her child—too bad it hadn't been safe from whoever had broken in.

Stopping at the front porch, Marco waited impatiently for the detective to come out to meet them after being summoned by the officer guarding the door. The rest of his team remained silent by his side, minus Brody, who had stayed back at his truck and was covertly filming the crowd of bystanders drawn to the large police presence. The team knew there was no way this many people lived on the quiet street, and it was possible whoever was behind this was watching the activity. Once the geek finished recording, he would join them at the impromptu briefing.

A few long minutes later, a man in his early thirties strode from the house, looking like he was at the end of a twenty-four-hour shift. His sports jacket was disheveled, and his dirty blond hair was sticking up in several directions as if he'd dragged his hand through it a few times. "I'm Drew Murdock. Which one of you is DeAngelis?"

Marco held out his hand, and the detective shook it. "This is Ian and Devon Sawyer. And Boomer Michaelson. Any sign of the kid?"

"Not yet," Murdock informed them while frowning. "According to the neighbors, it's a girl named Mara. Five months old. Ms. Williams just moved into the house last week, so the neighbors have very little information on her."

"Purchased or rented?" Ian queried.

"Purchased."

"Security system?"

"Yeah, but a crappy one—wires were cut at the outside junction box." Murdock glanced down at his open notepad. "We got the call about ninety minutes ago. The neighbor across the street saw a male Caucasian—blond, mid-20s, black sweatpants and tee, otherwise nondescript. He ran from the front door, hopped into an older model silver Ford Escape, and tore out of here. The front door was left wide open, so the neighbor came over to see if everything was okay and found Ms. Williams on the floor, unconscious and bleeding from the head. Looks like it was blunt trauma. A bloody bookend was found next to the body."

Marco winced at that last word. Harper wasn't dead, but he knew Murdock was just stating the facts as he would to any other investigator. "Was the suspect carrying anything? And what about an Amber Alert?"

Stepping aside to let a crime scene tech exit the house, the detective shook his head. "Neighbor didn't see the baby with the perp at all. That's the only reason we haven't issued an Amber Alert yet. We're hoping she's with a babysitter or another family member. We're still trying to determine whether this was a random or targeted attack. How well do you know the vic? Does she have any family in the area?"

The team knew the Amber Alert system had specific criteria before an alert could be released for a missing child. Hopefully, the nationwide system wouldn't be needed.

Marco ran a hand through his short, black hair. "Her dad died when she was younger. As of a year ago, her mother was still alive and living here in Clearwater somewhere. But that could've changed. She also has a brother in Washington D.C. and a sister on the West Coast... Los Angeles, I think. I haven't spoken to Harper since my sister's funeral thirteen months ago—they were best friends. Harper's a lawyer with her own practice now, but as for her employees or other friends, I have no idea who they are."

"Detective Murdock?"

The men all turned to see a uniformed officer escorting an older woman carrying a baby wrapped in a pink blanket. Marco recognized Harper's mother from visiting Nina and the wakes and funeral. The woman had been so nice to his sister, even calling Nina her "adopted daughter."

As she approached, her face was pinched in fright. "What's wrong? What happened? Where's Harper?"

Detective Murdock stepped forward and introduced himself. "Who are you, ma'am? Are you related to Ms. Williams?"

"I'm Karen Williams. Harper's my daughter, and this is her daughter, Mara." The relief that statement brought was evident on the face of everyone present, including Brody, who walked up behind her to join the rest of them. "What happened?" she repeated. "Where is she?"

"There was a break-in. Ms. Williams was found unconscious by a neighbor who called 9-1-1. But she's alive and at the hospital now."

"Oh, my God!" The poor woman appeared not to know what to do next, but when Marco stepped forward to speak to her, her expression quickly changed from fear to loathing. "What the hell are you doing here? Did you have something to do with this?"

Shocked didn't begin to describe what he felt at her accusation, and for a moment, he was speechless. She thought he would hurt Harper? *What the fuck?*

Murdock retook control of the conversation, but his next question didn't help the churning in Marco's gut. "Ma'am, why would you think Mr. DeAngelis had something to do with the attack?"

She eyed the man in question with disgust while cradling the baby to her chest. All he could see was a tiny bit of pale blonde hair at the top of her head. The rest was covered by a blanket. "He made it perfectly clear he wanted nothing to do with Harper after she got pregnant with his child. And now, after all this time, suddenly he's here after she's attacked? Why wouldn't I think he had something to do with it?"

Marco felt the blood drain from his face, and his knees weakened. Fuck, this was going downhill fast. His child. He had a fucking child with Harper and was just finding out now? *What. The. Fuck?*

Brody pulled on Marco's arm, forcing him to step back and away from the angry woman. A natural flirt of women, young and old, the geek gave Karen a look of understanding and comfort. "Mrs. Williams, I can assure you that Marco has about a hundred witnesses to his whereabouts this evening when Harper was attacked." *Thank God for that.* "We were called here to help, and that's all we want to do. Can you think of anyone else who might have done this? Did she have any problem clients or someone who's been harassing her?"

The woman's features softened as she turned her attention to Brody. Obviously, she remembered the man who could charm the Wicked Witch of the West, and her venom was only reserved for Marco. "No, I don't. But she's helped plenty of women in abusive relationships to leave their husbands."

"Ma'am?" Drew asked. "Do you know where your daughter was tonight? It appears she had just gotten home."

"Both her secretary and paralegal had birthdays this week, so she took them out for dinner. I usually watch Mara here or at my condo, but I took her to visit my cousin in Palm Harbor for the evening. The baby was sleeping so soundly, so I stayed later than planned. Harper told me if something like this ever happened to her, I should call… oh, I don't remember her name. I have it in my purse."

She shifted the sleeping infant in her arms and tried to reach into the bag at her side. Brody held out his hands. "I can hold the baby if that would help."

Marco's mouth dropped when Harper's mother paused only for a moment before handing the child over to the hulking geek. He was further shocked when his teammate handled the little baby with practiced ease instead of like the football carry Marco was expecting. He'd never seen Brody with a baby before, but he'd apparently gotten experience somewhere. He glanced at Boomer, Dev, and Ian, who appeared just as shocked and even a bit amused.

The baby began to stir and fuss a little, but the man cuddled her closer and made little "tsking" noises to calm her. And, fuck them, it worked!

"Here it is." Everyone's attention returned to Mrs.

Williams, who had pulled out a small black address book. "Dr. Trudy Dunbar."

"Shit... um... sorry, Mrs. Williams." Dev's spat explative had almost been followed by one from Marco and the others, but they'd caught themselves in time. They knew the doctor well. She was a shrink they sent some club members to occasionally, even though she wasn't in the lifestyle. She was also very involved with Friends of Patty.

Murdock eyed Devon. "Who's that?"

"Friend of ours. She's a psychologist and is involved with a private organization that helps relocate women and children from abusive relationships. It's all done in secret."

A flash of recognition appeared on the detective's face. "I think I know the group you're talking about, but I've never personally dealt with them."

Directing his question to Marco, Ian asked, "Did you know Harper was involved with them?"

"No." Fuck, this was getting hairier by the minute, and Marco still didn't know if Harper was okay. "But you know they're like the Underground Railroad. They're all tight-lipped and know only a small portion of the others involved. It's how they keep the women safe from being tracked down. Jake ran into that problem a few months ago, remember? That organization can give the U.S. Marshals a run for their money."

Ian opened his mouth to answer, but Karen interrupted, taking the baby from Brody with her gaze aimed at Detective Murdock. "While you all are figuring out who the hell attacked my daughter, may I go to the hospital to see her?"

"Absolutely, ma'am. After I take care of things here, I'll be by to ask you some more questions." He waved over the officer who had escorted her from the end of the driveway. "Officer Carpenteri can drive or follow you—whichever you prefer."

Showing the strength Marco had seen in the woman many times when she'd been visiting with Nina during her illness, Karen squared her shoulders. "I'm fine to drive. But I will take the escort until you find out who did this and ensure my daughter and grand-daughter are no longer in danger."

With one final look of disgust in Marco's direction, the woman turned and hurried down the drive with the uniformed officer in tow. Marco stared at her retreating back until Murdock tapped his arm. "I take it from the fact you're as white as a sheet that you had no idea you had a kid."

Speechless, all he could do in response was shake his head.

As usual, Ian took charge, which was a great relief because Marco's brain was a pile of goo. "Brody…"

The geek knew what their boss would say and nodded before the rest of the order was spoken. "Got it."

He jogged after the older woman to offer to drive her car to the hospital. Since he appeared to be Mrs. Williams' favorite out of the five men present, he was the ideal person to handle her. While the Clearwater and Tampa police were good at their jobs, Harper, her daughter, and Karen were now a top priority to the Trident team. They would guard them around the clock until they found out who was responsible for the attack and why.

"Boomer, have Egghead find out Mrs. Williams' address and go make sure the place is safe. I'll send a few guys over to relieve you." Knowing the youngest man on their team knew exactly what needed to be done, Ian didn't bother waiting for an answer before turning back to Murdock. "You going to have someone watching the house for now, or do I have to leave some of my men here?"

The detective shook his head. "Don't worry. Until the crime scene is released, there will be uniforms stationed here. I'll notify you when it's released, though."

"Good. Mind if I go with you to talk to Dr. Dunbar? We have a good rapport with her."

"That's fine. I don't look any gift horses in the mouth."

Still watching the pink bundle as Karen Williams carried the child down the driveway, Marco barely heard the conversations around him.

Holy fuck. Was he really a father? And if he was, what the hell was he going to do now?

At two-thirty in the morning, Kristen Sawyer was relieved to hear the front door open, announcing Devon's return to their apartment. He'd been gone for hours but had texted her earlier to let her know things were okay, and he'd fill her in when he got home. Before he left with the others, he'd instructed her to return to their place. He didn't like her being at the club without him, which was fine with her—she tended to feel like a vital part of her was missing when he wasn't there. Ian and Boomer had given Angie and Kat the same marching orders for the same reason.

The two women had joined her for a glass of wine and the second half of a *Lifetime* movie before heading to their own homes. Kat and Boomer lived about seven minutes away, while Angie only had to walk downstairs to the apartment she and Ian shared.

She felt bad Devon's birthday night at the club had been interrupted, but the teammates always looked out for their own. They weren't just friends and co-workers. They were family—a family she adored.

The bedroom door opened, and she grinned. It'd taken her a while to get used to her husband's stealth, lack-of-even-the-slightest-noise footsteps. She swore he walked on feathers as he'd unintentionally, and sometimes intentionally, scared the living fucking shit out of her numerous times. She pulled the sheets on his side of the bed down for him as he tossed his keys and wallet on the room's high-boy dresser.

"You look beat. Is Harper okay? What happened?" She'd met the woman several times before Marco's sister passed away and then again at the wakes and funeral. Kristen thought she'd been friendly and had often wondered if Marco and Harper had ever hooked up. They would make a handsome couple, but she hadn't seen Nina DeAngelis' best friend since the funeral.

Devon toed off his black leather biker boots and sighed. "From what the police have so far, it was a home invasion. They think the guy was already inside when Harper arrived home, and she interrupted a burglary. She got clocked on the head and knocked out. They did a CT scan, and there's no fracture or major damage, just a bad concussion. The doctors put her on some meds to help with some minor swelling in her brain, which is causing the unconsciousness, and they expect it to be short-term. Marco and Brody are staying at the hospital until she wakes up."

After pulling his T-shirt over his head, he undid the laces of his club leathers and peeled them off. God, how she loved watching him do that. The man was built and hung to perfection, in her opinion. And hers was the only one that mattered. "Eyes up, Pet, unless you want to hear the rest of the story after I ravish you."

The twinkle in his eye and the lengthening of his cock said he was dead serious. "Just answer two more questions, my love, and then you can ravish me all you want." He raised an eyebrow and stroked his now almost fully erect penis. Her mouth watered as she tried to remember what else she'd wanted to ask him.

"Um… oh… the baby… is he or she okay? Is it really Marco's?"

"The little girl, Mara, is fine. She was with Harper's mother the whole time. As for her being Marco's, I'm as positive as I can be that she is, even without a DNA test. We all knew it as soon as she woke up at the hospital and flashed those gray eyes, which are the spitting image of his."

Kristen knew them well. The first time she'd met Devon's teammate, she'd compared his gentle eyes to her favorite steel-gray cashmere sweater. They were distinct and not a color she'd ever noticed on anyone before him.

"It's thrown him for a loop. Mrs. Williams has it in her head that he wanted nothing to do with the kid and even had something to do with the assault."

She gasped and sputtered, "W-what? Marco would never hurt a woman! Never!"

Climbing into bed, he laid on his side, facing her, and palmed her naked breast, brushing his thumb over the taut, pink peak, sending a jolt of electricity through her. "Calm down, Pet. That's exactly what we told her and the police. Besides, he's got an iron-clad alibi with over a hundred witnesses. There's a possibility the attack is because of her helping Friends of Patty or even just a random break-in. The place was trashed."

A moan escaped her when he leaned over and licked her other nipple, not letting up his thumb's onslaught on the first one. "*Hmmm.* I… uh… I didn't know she was involved with them."

She'd heard about the clandestine group, who helped women and children of domestic violence, a year and a half ago when Jake had needed their help for a seventeen-year-old girl and her mother to escape an abusive father/husband.

Her husband let go of the tit he'd been sucking on. "Neither did we. But then again, that's how the group operates. Anyway, hopefully, we'll know more when Harper wakes up. Mrs. Williams went to her condo with the baby to get some sleep. She'll head back to the hospital in the morning. I called McCabe, Foster, and Mancini to guard them until we find out if this was random or intentional."

His hand left her breast and slowly slid down her torso. She'd better wrap up her inquiry because playtime was about to start. Her breathing and heart rate sped up, and she almost forgot what he'd just said. "The Omega team is probably glad to do something other than training. That's mostly what they've been doing the past few months."

A new secondary team had been put together to be based out of Florida. Trident Security had developed an impeccable reputation in the past few years, and it was either form another team or start refusing cases and missions. A third team was also being developed out in San Diego, with Jake at the helm until they were up and running.

Nudging her thighs apart, Devon ran a finger over her clit and bare pussy lips, and she fought the urge to move her hips. She wanted more but knew her Dom would take his own sweet time. "The training is important, Pet. The reason the guys and I work so well together is because we've trained like that for years. These guys didn't know each other before now, and they have to get to the point where they can finish each other's sentences and know, from just a look, what the others are thinking. They have to know exactly what their teammates will do before they do it. It's how they'll stay alive and successfully complete a mission.

"Now… are you done asking questions? Because I want to fuck you silly for the next few hours. That's my birthday present to myself."

"Your birthday was over almost three hours ago."

He dipped his fingers into her wet core, and she felt the flush of arousal that eased his entry. "My birthday isn't over until I get my birthday spanks… well, you're the one who will be getting spanked, Pet. I get to give them to you. How does that sound?"

"Like a little hell before you take me to heaven, Master."

A low groan rumbled from his chest. "I like the sound of that. C'mere."

CHAPTER FOUR

Thirteen Months Ago

"I can't believe I'm saying this, but I'm starving."

Marco chuckled at Harper's declaration as he pulled his Chevy Silverado into the driveway of the three-bedroom ranch he'd bought two years ago, right before Nina had gotten sick. "I was just thinking the same thing. Those leftovers smell delicious. Thank God for Jenn." He put the truck into Park. "Come inside, and I'll reheat everything. I think I still have a bottle of that white wine you and Nina love... loved."

Harper reached over and squeezed his forearm as he swallowed the sudden lump in his throat. "It'll get better."

Nodding, he took the food bag from her lap and opened the driver's door. "I know it will. I just have to get past this feeling of being in limbo."

Not waiting for a response, he climbed out and

walked around to the passenger side to open her door for her. One of the things the Navy and being a Dom had taught him was how to be a gentleman to women of all ages. Without a father and with two poor maternal figures raising him, many simple manners had escaped him during his youth. If it hadn't been for a few good teachers in his elementary and high schools, Marco probably could have been classified as a Neanderthal when he entered basic training.

After unlocking the front door, he held it open for Harper, then followed her into the kitchen. Working together in silence, it wasn't long before they were seated at the dining room table with full, heated plates of food and glasses of Pinot Grigio.

Harper swallowed a piece of chicken marsala and picked up her wine glass. "It was so sweet of the school children to sing 'Amazing Grace' at the service. It was beautiful."

Nodding his head, he wiped his mouth with a napkin. "It was. That little girl who did the solo has some voice on her. Their music teacher said they'd been practicing it for weeks since we found out there was nothing more the doctors could do. Nina had called the principal to update him so the school could prepare for the news when she passed."

"She told me. She said that back in junior high, one of her favorite teachers was killed in a car accident, and it was so hard on many students. She didn't want the announcement to be a sudden shock to her kids like that. Nina loved them as much as they loved her. She left quite a legacy behind at that school."

A sad smile spread across his face. "That she did."

After they finished eating, they shared the chore of cleaning up. Marco returned from wiping the crumbs from the dining room table to see Harper standing still at the sink with her back to him. But she wasn't completely still—the small movement of her shoulders made him realize she was crying, although he didn't hear a sound.

Tossing the sponge on the counter, he grasped her elbow and turned her into his arms. "*Shhh.* It's okay. You've been a rock through all this, so I wondered when you would finally crack."

Harper let out an un-lady-like snort before crying harder, her sobs now audible. Wrapping his arms around her, he held her tight. She rested her head on his shoulders as the grief she'd held back for days came to the surface. "I'm... I'm s-sorry."

"*Shhh.* No apologies. Just let it all out. I've got you."

Present

THE STEADY BEEP OF HARPER'S HEART MONITOR WAS A comfort and a curse. The noise was irritating, but it also meant she was still stable. The doctors had been optimistic she would wake at some point in the next few hours, but it couldn't happen fast enough for

Marco. One, he wouldn't be convinced she would be okay until she opened those hazel eyes which changed color depending on what she wore and recognized him. And two, he wanted to hear from her lips that the baby was his, although, as soon as the little girl had woken from her nap, it was crystal clear to everyone she was his daughter. She had his eyes and his mother's nose, which he and Nina had inherited. However, his was broken in a bar fight during his early days in the Navy, and it looked nothing like it used to.

Nina. Huh! His kid sister was in the great beyond, laughing her ass off at him now... it was either that or she wanted to kick his ass. He absentmindedly rubbed the tattoo, which he'd gotten shortly after her death, on his left upper arm. Hers was the only woman's name that would ever be inked on his skin. She'd known very well how much he was against having kids of his own and his reasons why, despite her protests that he could overcome their crappy childhood and open his heart to a wife and children.

A wife and children. Holy fuck!

He dragged his hand through his hair. *Marriage? Fuck, am I going to have to marry Harper?*

While the thought of Holy Matrimony filled him with dread, things could be worse—thankfully, the two of them got along well and were obviously attracted to each other. And the sex that night had been off the charts. But what about the D/s lifestyle? It was a deep-seated part of him now. Would he be able to convince her to give it a try?

Fuck! What the hell was he thinking? He wasn't husband material—for that matter, he wasn't father material either. Marriage was not an option.

A moan had his gaze whipping to where Harper lay in the hospital bed. She stirred for a moment before falling silent again. Well, that was a good sign, he guessed. It was the first sound she'd made all night. His eyes roamed her face. God, her skin was almost as white as the sheets she was on. Who had done this to her and why?

Even if this was all a misunderstanding, and the baby wasn't his, he would still hunt down the bastard who'd dared to hurt Harper. He owed it to his sister and to her to make sure she and the baby were safe. Then he would give her whatever financial support she needed, and when she met someone who would make a good husband and father, he would step aside and let her be happy. *Fuck!*

A cup of coffee entered his line of vision, startling him. He glanced up to see Brody handing him the brew.

"You look like you could use a good cup of coffee. Unfortunately, all I could find was this sludge—it just might double the hair on your balls."

Marco snorted and took the proffered cup. "Thanks."

Tilting his head toward the bed, Brody asked, "How's she doing?"

"The doctor hasn't been in yet, but the nurses tell me her vitals are stable. She was moving and moaning a minute ago, so hopefully, she'll wake up soon."

"Good." His friend stuck his thumbs in the belt loops of his jeans and sighed heavily. "When she *does* wake up, bro, just channel the man all the subs like to bring their problems to for comfort, and don't go all pissed-off Dom on her. There's got to be a good reason why she didn't tell you about Mara *and* why her mother thinks you didn't want anything to do with them."

"Really?" He shook his head as his anger began to surface again, but his gaze stayed on the woman in question. "Maybe Harper regretted having my kid and told her mother I was the bad guy in all this. It's not like she didn't know how to fucking find me."

A frown came over his teammate's face, and his voice dropped in noticeable annoyance. "Don't give me that fucking shit. I saw and talked to her almost as much as you did during Nina's cancer. She's good people, and I refuse to believe she intentionally hid your baby from you. And stop trying to convince yourself Mara's not yours, fucktard."

Leave it to his best friend to let him know he was being an ass. Brody chose to see the best in people he met, despite seeing the worst mankind could do to each other as a SEAL and operative. But Marco couldn't get past the fact that Harper had been pregnant for nine months, and it had been five months since she'd given birth, and he was just finding out about it now.

Unable to meet the geek's irritated glare, he stared out the window. The sun had been up for about an hour or so... life was continuing as normal for so many people, and he wished like hell he was one of them. "Hey, change of subject, how the hell did you do that last night... with the baby, I mean?"

"What the fuck are you talking about? What did I do with the baby?"

He faced the other man. "You know... holding her and all that... that baby-talk shit."

A soft bark of laughter escaped Brody, and his eyes lit up in amusement. "Baby-talk shit? Oh, my friend, do you have a lot to learn. I know kids give you the heebie-jeebies, but holding a baby is a piece of cake. Now, changing diapers is something to freak out about. Especially when that shit starts to smell—it's yucky poo-poo, as my nephew, Brendan, would say."

That's when it hit Marco. Back in Texas, the geek had three sisters and two brothers. They'd started cranking out rug rats a few years ago, which was right around the time Marco had stopped visiting them with his buddy. The Evans family was close, loud, boisterous, and very, *very* big huggers. While they had always welcomed him with open arms, he tended to feel out of sorts amid the chaos that always seemed to occur with the large family.

Growing up, he and Nina never had friends over, and while he did have friends in school, their parents weren't always too keen on having him in their homes. He hadn't been a bad kid but had lacked manners and decent clothes that hadn't come from a thrift store. He'd also had a foul mouth on him, thanks to his mother's and grandmother's penchants for cursing.

Now he was comfortable in groups and one-on-one, but he still had trouble adjusting to his friends' energetic families. He preferred things to be low-key gatherings, and still felt like the outsider, waiting to be told he wasn't good enough to be invited into people's homes.

Soft sounds emanating from the bed caught both of their attention. "*Mmm. Mara... Mara...*"

Leaping from the chair, Marco hurried to Harper's side and took her hand. "Harper... Harper, sweetheart, wake up."

Her head whipped back and forth on the pillow as the beeping from the monitor increased in speed. Her arms and legs struggled to fight whoever or whatever her unconscious mind had conjured up.

She moaned louder, and the pain he heard there pierced his gut. "Brody, get a doctor in here."

"On it." The geek rushed out of the room.

Marco stroked her cheek, carefully avoiding the bruises on her face from when she'd hit the floor after being knocked down. "Harper, honey. Wake up. The baby's okay. You're okay. Come on, sweetheart. If you wake up, I'll have your mom bring the baby here, so you can see for yourself she's okay."

"Mara!" Her scream was followed by her jerking awake, and her eyes flashed open in sheer panic.

WATCHING FROM THE SHADOWS

Obviously confused, she began swinging her arms and fists at him, and he grasped her wrists so she wouldn't hurt herself... or punch his lights out. Damn, the woman could pack a wallop. He wondered what she could do if she were completely aware of her surroundings.

"Harper. *Shhh*. It's okay. It's me... Marco. Calm down."

"W-what?" She stilled as her eyes focused on him. "Marco? Where am I? Where's my b..."

He saw the moment she realized she almost said, "baby," before slamming her mouth shut again. His teeth ground against each other. Now wasn't the time to discuss why she hadn't told him he was a father—there would be plenty of time for that later. Taking his teammate's advice, he channeled his inner, gentle, understanding Dom.

Yeah, good luck with that.

"The baby's okay. She's with your mom." Her relief was evident on her face. "Do you remember what happened?"

The confused expression returned as she tugged one of her wrists from his grasp and brought it to her bandaged head. "I don't... I'm not sure. What happened?"

They were interrupted by Brody's return with a doctor and nurse behind him. Marco stepped away from the bed so they could examine her but remained close by. Vitals were checked, a light was flashed into her eyes, and a litany of questions were asked to deter-

47

mine if she knew her name, the date, and who the president was, among other things.

After the doctor said he wanted to keep her another day for observation, Harper became upset. "No! I can't. I have to get home to take care of my baby. I can't stay here."

The doctor eyed Marco, who nodded. "No worries. She's not going anywhere. Her mother is watching the baby."

"But…"

His glare told her he'd tie her to the bed if he had to. "No buts, Harper. I'll tell you everything that happened, but you'll stay here until the doctor says you can go home. End of argument."

He could see she wanted to prove him wrong and continue to argue, but she wisely kept quiet until the doctor and nurse left the room. But then, all bets and kid gloves were off.

"Who the fuck do you think you are?" she hissed.

"For now, I'm your bodyguard…" He couldn't hold back any longer. "And apparently, the father of your baby."

Her mouth opened and closed several times in shock until Brody cleared his throat, and they both turned to face him. "Should I stay and play referee, or should I step outside and keep everyone else away from the door while you two hash this out?" He grinned and shrugged his shoulders. "Personally, I'd like to stay and watch the fireworks."

"Out," they barked simultaneously.

The pain-in-the-ass sighed dramatically and headed for the door. "Fine. Just keep the decibel level down, will ya? This place is filled with sick people trying to get better and some really hot-looking nurses—especially the brunette doing paperwork at the desk. Holler if you need me—but not too loudly."

The moment the door closed, and they were alone, Harper sat up and, despite the blood draining from her face at the sudden movement, pulled the blanket off her body. When she began to swing her legs over the side, Marco growled. "Don't fucking think about it, Harper. You're not going anywhere, and you won't like what I'll do to you if you try to get out of that bed."

Instead of arguing with him, Harper's coloring changed from white to green, and she clutched her stomach. Having seen that look many times in the military and on Nina's face after her chemotherapy sessions, Marco lunged for the plastic basin on the bedside table. Throwing it into Harper's hands, he was just in time as she puked into it. The stench curled his own gut, but he fought the urge to join her while he pulled her hair out of the way as she emptied the contents of her stomach.

When the retching finally slowed, she began to sob, and Marco's heart clenched.

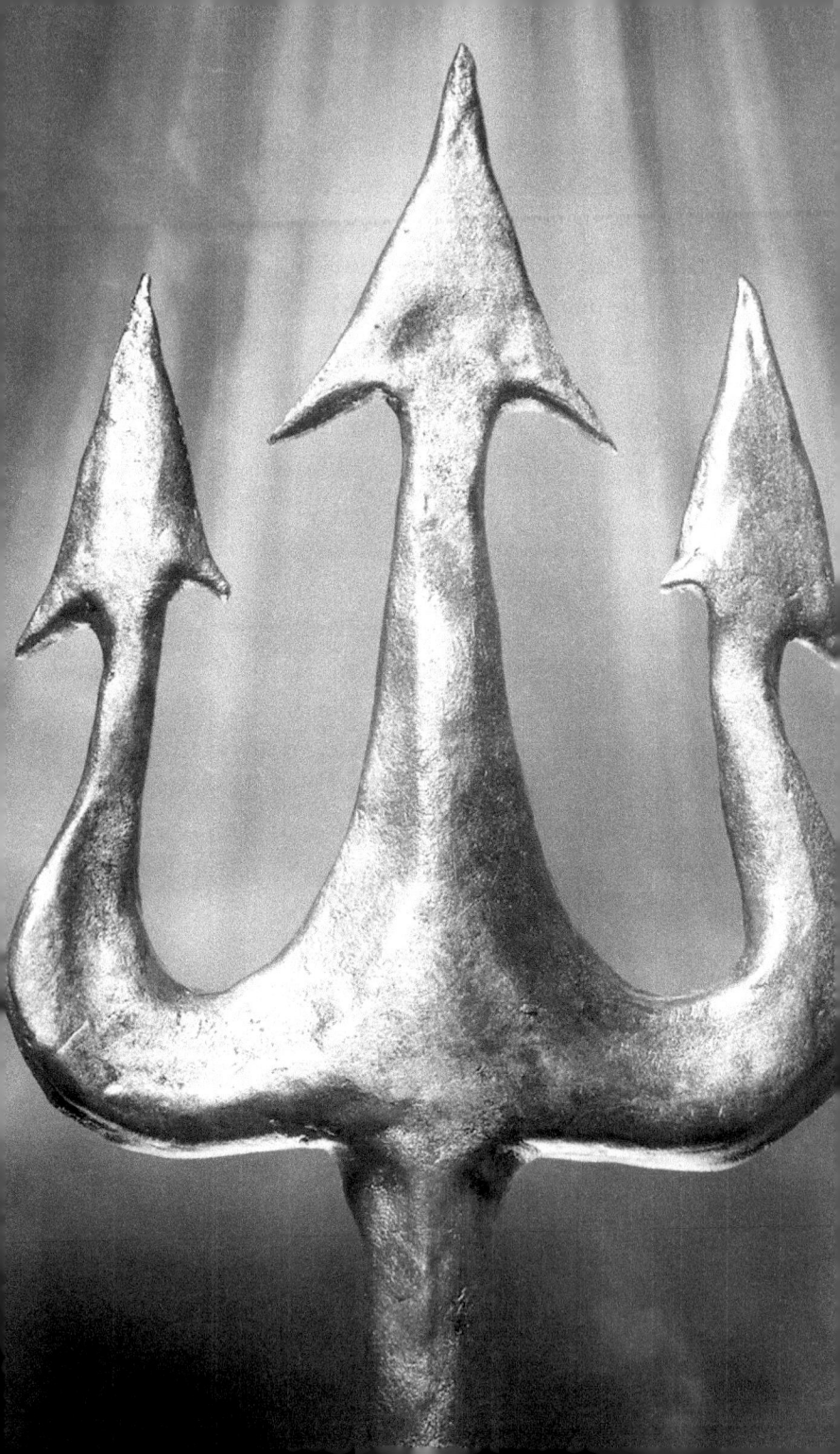

CHAPTER FIVE

Thirteen Months Ago

Harper had been trying to suppress falling apart for Marco's sake, but the past few days... hell, the past few months came crashing down around her. Nina had been closer to her than her own sister had ever been, and watching her dwindle down to ninety pounds as her life drained from her body had been heart-wrenching. They had become best friends within a week of being assigned dormitory roommates in college, and it wasn't long before they told each other their deepest darkest secrets, which they swore they'd never tell another soul.

Marco's strong arms enveloped her as she cried into his shoulder. His hands rubbed up and down her back slowly while his solid chest rumbled with his low murmurs of comfort. The heat from his body warmed the chill that had sent shivers down her spine.

Inhaling deeply, she savored the leather and citrus scent of his cologne. Nina had gotten it for him a few Christmases ago, and after smelling it on him that first time, it had become Harper's favorite scent. Unfortunately, it made her wish Marco wasn't the man he was, instead of being the man she wanted him to be. The man she could fall in love with and who would fall in love with her. The man who would marry, settle down, have children and, eventually, grandchildren with her. Nina had been after him to open up his heart to a woman he could spend a lifetime with, but he'd made it clear on several occasions that a wife and children were something he would never commit to. And Harper refused to settle.

As her sobs ebbed, she lifted her head and brushed the last few tears from her eyes. "I'm sorry. I didn't mean to lose it in front of you."

He didn't respond, nor did he release her. In fact, she swore his embrace tightened around her. The temperature of the room appeared to have spiked sometime in the last few minutes, and the air crackled with sexual electricity. She was suddenly aware of the bulge in his pants, which she couldn't ignore if she tried.

His charcoal-colored eyes pierced her own hazel ones, and she saw the heat in his stare. Not anger-heat, but—*holy hell*—lustful fuck-me-raw heat. Her tongue wet her lips, and the movement drew his gaze. His pupils flared as he moved even closer. A split-second of panic was replaced by desire, and she prayed she wasn't misreading or imagining the situation. While he wasn't a forever kind of guy, right then, she didn't need forever. She needed comfort... the kind of no-holds-barred, balls-to-the-walls comfort that would make her forget her grief—if only for a little while.

He inched closer still, and his voice dropped to a raspy, pain-filled whisper. "Tell me to stop, Harper. Tell me to let you go and not kiss you."

Her voice was just as low and hoarse from her crying. "I can't."

A groan was dragged from his lungs seconds before his mouth came down on hers. The kiss was far from gentle. Instead, it was hard, demanding, dominant, and just what Harper had hoped for. One of his hands snaked up into her hair, now down from its bun, and held her head in place as he took her breath away. The other hand at her back crept down to the swell of her ass, and she wished he would rip her dress off because she never wanted to wear the bleak reminder of her loss again.

MARCO HAD TO BE OUT OF HIS MIND, BUT HE COULDN'T stop if he tried, especially since Harper made it clear she wouldn't ask him to. He'd always found her attractive, but it was something he fought to ignore. Hooking up with your kid sister's best friend was one of those taboo things, such as hitting on a friend's current or ex-girlfriend. It only caused trouble for everyone involved. But Nina was gone, and the only other person he had to consider in this scenario was the woman whose arms were wrapped around his neck and rubbing her delectable body against his. Thankfully, his dress pants gave him plenty of room for his cock, which was now fully erect and throbbing.

Holy hell! He wanted her in the worst way. Wanted her warmth, her comfort, her submissiveness, but most of all, he wanted her to make him forget, if only for a little while. The submissiveness was something he could do without occasionally. Vanilla was okay with him as long as it was just occasionally. There was a time and place for everything, and now was the time for comforting each other. Joined by their mutual loss, for a few hours, they could help each other grieve and, hopefully, heal.

He kissed her like a man drowning in desperation. Hunger rose within him. His belly was full from their dinner, but the feast he now wanted was something altogether different. Skimming his hands down her body, he gathered the fabric of her dress and drew it upward, bunching it at her waist. His hands reversed direction again, and when they hit nothing but soft skin and lace, he withdrew from her mouth and glanced down. *Holy fuck!*

"Woman, thigh-high stockings are my all-time favorite thing a woman can wear, and you look fucking gorgeous in them."

Dropping to his knees, he reverently kissed along the lacy edges of the sheers. Placing a hand behind one of her knees, he urged her to bend it and put her leg over his shoulder. He licked and nibbled on the silky skin just above the stockings on the now-exposed inside of her thigh. Her hands went to his hair again, holding him in place as he worked his way up to her satin-covered pussy. A wet spot on the navy panties told him she was as turned on as he was. He tongued the spot, tasting her and making her even wetter.

Grabbing the lacy strings of the bikini on both hips, he glanced up at her. "I hope these aren't your favorites. If they are, I'll replace them." Not waiting for an answer, he tore them from her body.

Fuck! Another pleasant surprise. She was waxed bare—completely. Damn, the woman just kept pushing all the right buttons. He hoped like hell he hadn't hit his head and was dreaming all this as he lay in a coma because that would really suck.

Letting her leave the stockings and shoes on, he clutched her ass cheeks and held her still as he licked the soft folds of her pussy. Never had a feast tasted so incredible. He could eat her for hours and never be full. Encouraged by her moans and gasps, he plunged his tongue into her as far as it could go several times before moving to her clit. Its hood was pulled back, revealing the little pearl, and he sucked on it. Using his tongue and teeth, he tortured the bud until her breathing increased and her legs shook. "Come for me, baby. I want to hear you scream."

And she did as he thrust his tongue back into her hot, wet pussy. Her legs shook almost violently, and he held her hips to keep her from falling. The hands in his hair clenched to the point of pain in his scalp, but it didn't bother him. It was a testament to the fact they were alive. As her waves of ecstasy ebbed, he eased his assault. When her foot dropped to the floor again, he stood, grinning and licking the evidence of her orgasm from his lips and chin. She watched the movement, then leaned forward and used her tongue to help clean him up.

Damn, that was fucking hot!

Her fingers fiddled with the buttons of his shirt until, in exasperation, she yanked the two edges, sending the little fasteners flying across the room. She shoved the shirt off his shoulders and down his arms. Her frenzy fed his. Pulling her dress over her head, he dropped it and then popped the front snap of her bra. Her breasts were round, perky, and beautiful. Retaking her mouth, he flicked his thumbs over her nipples as her hands dropped to his belt. Within seconds, she had it undone, along with the button and zipper of his pants, pushing them past his knees with his boxer briefs. He toed off his shoes and, using his feet to push the material down further on his legs, managed to leave his clothing in a heap on the floor without ever taking his hands from her tits.

Bending slightly, he picked her up, turned, and backed her against the wall. Her legs wrapped around his hips, with the feel of her high heels on his ass only making him harder. The tip of his cock found her wet warmth, and his only thought was to get inside her. He shifted to line up with her slit and thrust forward without ceremony as her body yielded to him.

Harper cried out as he began to pump his hips. "Yes! Oh, shit, yes! Harder! Pleeeease, harder!"

The drag of his cock along her walls felt incredible. He buried his face in the crook of her neck as he impaled her over and over again. This time would be fast and furious, but he was more than willing to go two or three rounds with her. Slow could come later. For now, he was sprinting toward the finish line. Something niggled in his brain as a tingling started in the base of his spine. Something was wrong. What…

Crap! He withdrew from her body so fast he almost dropped her, and she yelped. Unable to stop, he came all over her abdomen. "*Fuck!* Shit, Harper. I didn't… I didn't use a fucking condom… I'm sorry… *Shit!* I—I don't know if I pulled out… in time."

"It's okay… *shhh.*" Calm hands went to his cheeks, and she looked him in the eye. "It's okay. I'm on the pill. Have been for years."

He dropped his head to her shoulder, his lungs heaving for oxygen. "Thank God. I'm clean… I've always used them… I'm sorry… I wasn't thinking."

"Same here. I was too busy feeling."

Bending his knees, he picked her up again, ignoring the mess between them, and carried her out of the kitchen toward his bedroom.

"Marco, what are you doing? Put me down," she giggled.

"Uh-uh, sweetheart. You didn't get to come when I

did that time, and I'm not satisfied with only one orgasm from you. I hope you're not too tired because it's going to be a long night."

Present

PULLING UP TO THE INTERIOR GATE OF THE TRIDENT compound, Marco rolled down his window and placed his hand on the security scanner a few minutes before noon. After the machine beeped, the chain link barrier slid open. He parked his truck next to Brody's and got out, slamming the door behind him as his best friend exited the building housing the offices.

The geek had returned from the hospital about two hours ago. "What are you doing here? I figured you'd still be with Harper."

Tucking his keys in his front pocket, Marco shrugged. "With the newbies, there were plenty of guards to watch her, so Devon told me to get lost for a while. Her mother showed up with the baby, and from the looks I was getting, the woman wanted to grab the first scalpel she saw to stab me. Between her there and Harper being allowed to go back to sleep for a few hours, I took a break. I'll go back later."

He eyed a nearby vehicle. Although he hadn't seen it in a while, he knew exactly who the sleek, black Dodge Challenger belonged to. "What's Carter doing here?"

"Drove in about an hour ago. He's crashing upstairs

for the night before heading out to parts unknown again."

The U.S. black-ops agent was known for showing up unannounced and disappearing again just as quietly. The man, who only went by one name, was also a Dom, so when he was in town, it was a sure bet he would be stopping by The Covenant for some downtime. The spare bedrooms above the offices were always available to him, but their friend's sudden appearance was the last thing Marco cared about at the moment. "Has anyone heard from Murdock?"

Brody leaned against the bed of his Ford F-150 and crossed his arms. "Boss-man just got off the phone with him. Nothing new. Doc Dunbar is contacting her people at Friends of Patty to see if any of the wife-beaters could have decided to go after Harper. From what I understand, she'd represented some women in court proceedings before they decided to disappear, so it's not that big of a stretch."

"Fucking great. The suspect pool just multiplied."

"Yup. So…" The big geek paused and seemed to weigh his words. "Um… did you get a chance to talk to Harper about Mara without ticking her off again?"

"No." He kicked a pebble on the ground in front of him. "After she finished puking, they drew more blood and then took her for another CT scan. Everything came back negative or normal, so it's just a side effect of the concussion."

"I'm sure your pissing match didn't help." There was that pause again. "So, what are you going to do? I mean, there are worse things in life than marrying a woman who's as smoking hot as Harper."

With his anger and frustration over the situation growing again, Marco growled. "Who said anything about getting fucking married?"

"You're obviously Mara's father, and if I were you, I sure as hell wouldn't mind going home to Harper in my bed every night. Hell, I even hit on her a couple of times." He shrugged unapologetically at Marco's angry glare. "What? I'd have to be dead not to. Tell me you never thought of us topping her together."

"Fuck you." It didn't matter that he and Brody had shared many women over the years. The thought of Harper in any other man's arms, even his best friend's, made his blood boil, even though he had no claim over her. "And I'm not marrying anybody. No fucking way!"

"You asshole," Brody snarled, pushing off the truck and pointing his finger at him. "You better man up and do the right fucking thing."

Tossing his hands up to the side, Marco stared at his friend. His voice got louder with every word. "What? Get fucking married just because she had my kid? I refuse to be trapped in a fucking marriage because of a stupid mistake! Stay the fuck out of this, Brody... I'll support the brat financially, but that's it!"

"You son-of-a..."

He didn't hear the rest as his jaw exploded in pain when Brody's fist connected with a right hook. As soon as the words were out of his mouth, he'd known they'd been the wrong things to say. The anger that had flared in the other man's eyes was something Marco had only seen there while in combat. But he was just as pissed off, and beating the hell out of somebody, even if it was his best friend, was something he needed right now.

Bending at the waist, he caught Brody in the gut with his shoulder, and the two of them hit the pavement—hard.

While they were the same height, the geek had about ten or fifteen more pounds on Marco and used every one of them to his advantage. The two men had sparred in the gym and given each other bloody lips and bruised ribs on the basketball court many times, but this was the first they'd ever hit each other in anger.

Grunts, growls, and curses were aplenty as they both wrestled, punched, and jabbed. And blood flowed.

Using a tactical maneuver, Brody ended up behind him, wrapping his arm around Marco's throat and squeezing. Turning his head into the crook of Brody's elbow, Marco was able to use that bit of extra space to continue getting air into his lungs as he tried to dislodge himself.

Thrusting his elbow back, he connected with hard flesh and heard a satisfying grunt, but the bastard wouldn't let go of him. Reaching over his shoulder, he managed to get a hand under Brody's chin and pushed upward. In response, his opponent rolled to the side, trying to pin the free arm to the ground.

Assorted shouts and barking reached Marco's ears, and suddenly he was free. But not for long as Ian and

Murray, the day guard, hauled his ass up and held him back from lunging at Brody again. Carter and Boomer were restraining the geek, but from the look on his face, he was ready to start round two.

Well, fucking bring it on!

"Fucking knock it off, assholes," Ian roared. "Now!"

After a few meager attempts to break free, both men reluctantly backed off, knowing there was no way their friends would let them get near each other again —at least not until they'd both cooled off. Even Beau was standing between the two of them, and a curt command from Ian cut off the trained guard dog's incessant barking.

Marco's lungs heaved for oxygen as his best friend glared at him while wiping the blood from the side of his mouth with his fist. Brody shrugged out of Carter and Boomer's grip.

"I'm good. I'm done," he said to them before pointing a finger at Marco again. "You better do the right fucking thing, man, because if you don't, I will."

"What the hell is that supposed to mean?" he spat. His jaw throbbed in pain.

"It means, fuckwad, if you don't man up and start acting like a father to Mara... a real fucking father... then I will!"

Marco scowled at Brody's retreating back as the man headed toward his truck, jumped in, and peeled out of the parking lot. Wisely, Ian, Boomer, and Murray backed off, but Carter surprised him by stepping forward, ignoring Marco's angry stare. Evidently, someone had filled the guy in. "He's right, dude. I know you're still in shock, but think about this long and hard before you walk out of that kid's life because when you're old and gray… that walk might just come back to bite you in the ass. And then, it'll be too late."

Minutes later, Marco stood all alone in the lot, licking his wounds and wondering what the fuck had just happened. Hell, even the usually friendly Beau snubbed him, having returned to the offices with the others. For the first time in years, he felt truly alone.

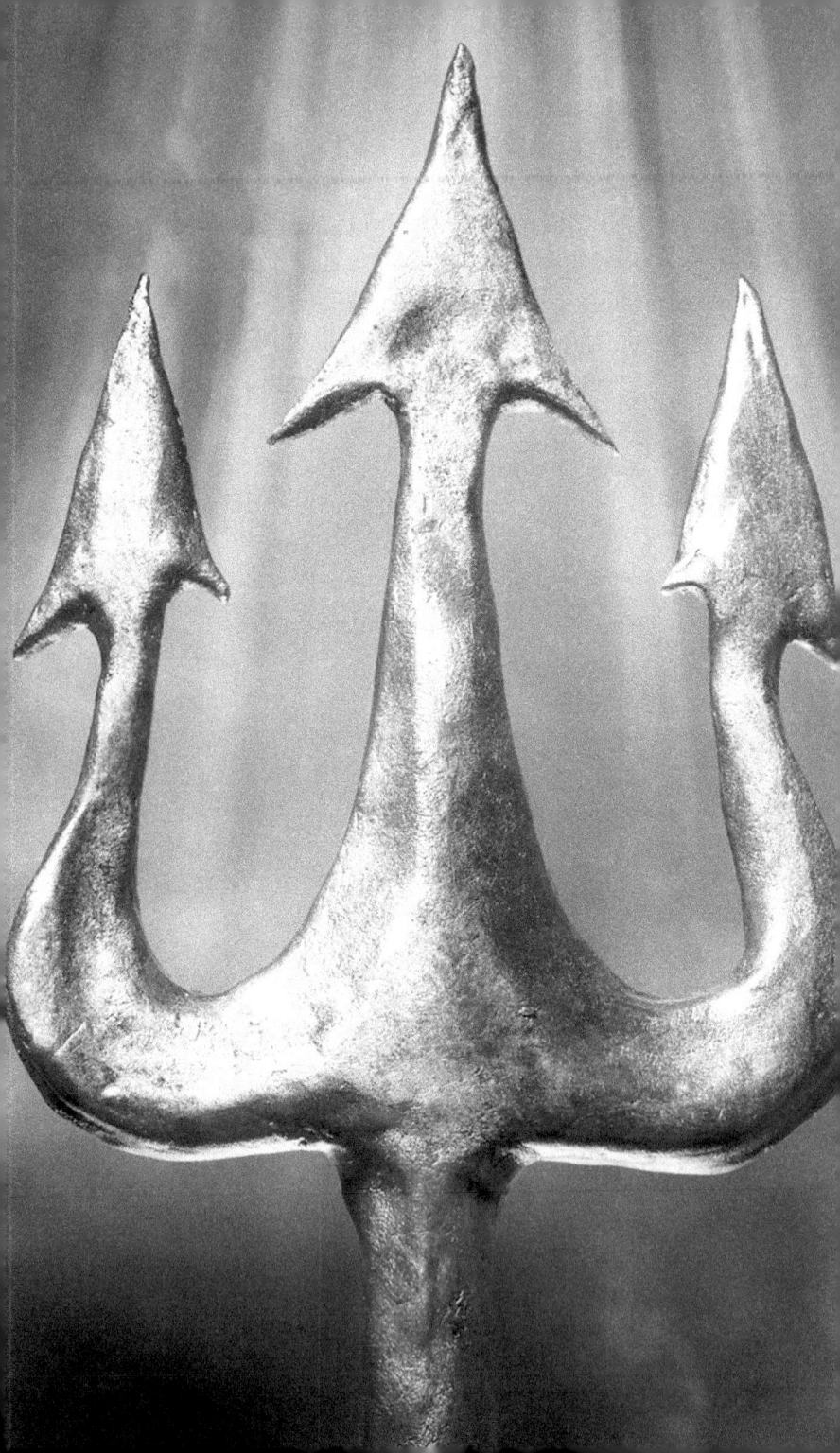

CHAPTER SIX

F ive hours later, covered in sweat, Marco pounded on the punching bag hanging from the ceiling in one of his spare bedrooms. It had become Nina's bedroom when she'd moved in with him six months before her death. After her passing, it had taken him weeks to enter the room again, even though she had given away most of her possessions after finding out her cancer was terminal. The hospice bed was long gone, so aside from a few pieces of furniture and pictures on the wall, it had been relatively empty.

A few months ago, he'd opened the door one day and decided to do something with the room. He already had an office across the hall, so a home gym seemed the perfect solution.

He'd taped his bruised knuckles from his earlier fight with Brody to prevent the abrasions from bleeding all over the leather-covered bag. They were sore, but he ignored the pain, channeling it back into his punches. Alternating between jabs, crosses, hooks, and uppercuts, followed by some knee and foot kicks, he punished the bag for its fictional crimes against humanity.

Shit! He'd actually had a knock-down, drag-out, fist fight with his best friend. What the hell had gotten into him? He couldn't blame Brody for decking him. As he thought back to the words he'd spit out seconds before the geek's fist connected with his chin, he deserved every punch thrown at him and more. His reaction to the whole fucked-up situation was… well, fucked up.

After landing a one-two combination harder than necessary, he finally hugged the bag in exhaustion. A shower, followed by something to eat, and he'd head back to the hospital. It was time for Harper and him to have a serious talk. From there, he'd figure out what to do next, but in the meantime, he would do everything he could to keep her and their daughter safe. Their daughter… *jeez.*

He'd just opened a nearby cabinet to get a towel when the *beep-beep-beep* of his security system went off. Grabbing for the pistol he kept hidden on the top shelf, he prepared to confront the intruder but heaved a sigh of relief when he heard a familiar voice bellow, "Don't fucking shoot me. I'm just here for the food."

Leaving the weapon where it was, he stepped out into the living room, wiping his dripping face with a towel, to find Carter in the adjoining dining area. The guy was sorting through several bags of takeout from Donovan's Pub, which sat on the table next to a six-pack of beer. The remark about the food was a long-standing joke between the team and the operative after he had run into Devon unexpectedly at a swanky hotel in Rio de Janeiro while on a mission many years ago. But the quip was usually stated negatively, though, and meant he couldn't talk about his current classified assignment. Apparently, right now, he was in the mood to talk. *Great.* Just what Marco fucking needed.

The super-spy glanced up and smirked. "Figured you could use a good burger and a beer or two. Jenn threw in a slice of carrot cake, too, just for you."

He grabbed the nearby remote and turned on the TV to ESPN with the volume on low. "That's 'cause she likes me best."

"Not." Carter snorted as Marco headed to the kitchen for some napkins and ketchup. "She likes me best. She packed up some fresh-out-of-the-oven chocolate chip cookies for me. The big ones I like that come with the vanilla ice cream, which she also gave me a container of."

"We'll call it a tie then." Returning to the table, he took the takeout container Carter pushed his way and sat down.

"God help us when that girl falls in love. You single guys will starve to death. Thankfully, I know how to cook."

Marco added some ketchup to his burger and fries before handing the bottle over. "By the way, the door was locked with the system armed, and you've only been here once before that I can remember. How the hell..." He stopped and rolled his eyes, knowing the man could probably get into Fort Knox if he wanted to. "Fuck, never mind. Stupid question."

"Yup, it is. Dig in."

After a few minutes of eating in silence, Carter grabbed a napkin and wiped his mouth. "So, talk to me, my friend."

"Don't want to," he mumbled through a mouthful of food.

"Then I'll talk. You just sit there, stuffing your face, and listen. I know enough about your background to know we aren't that different. But where you were raised by family members, whether they were there for you or not, I got bounced around in foster homes for years."

Stunned, Marco paused with his beer halfway to his lips. He'd been friends with the man across from him for about seven years, but he knew very little about him beyond their professional and BDSM worlds. Being a black operative for the U.S. government, Carter had always kept his background and personal life outside of Tampa as secret as his classified missions.

Ignoring his friend's look of surprise, Carter took a swig of his beer before continuing. "Do you remember what it was like back then, when you still had hopes and dreams of being part of a normal family—mother, father, siblings—in a house with a dog and a white picket fence? And don't deny it because every kid with a crummy childhood like ours has that dream until they find out there's no Santa Claus or Easter Bunny."

Placing his beer back on the table, Marco nodded. "Yeah, I remember. But like most orphans too old or not eligible for adoption, I found out it was a pipe dream."

"But even though you were technically an orphan, you still had someone. You had Nina. I only met her a few times, but she was sweet and funny... and obviously got the good looks in the family—which you missed out on."

Marco snorted but let the insult slide.

"And now you have an opportunity to have a family again. With your daughter. And with Harper. Or maybe without her, but from what I saw at the funeral, there was something between you that I don't think either of you were aware of at the time."

"You were at the funeral?" Marco hadn't seen him, but that didn't mean anything. He could be a ghost when he didn't want to be spotted.

"At the gravesite. I only had a short window of time, but I wanted to pay my respects." He leaned back in his chair, leaving only a few stray French fries in the takeout container. "But I'm getting away from the subject. Anyway, it's obvious to me you have abandonment issues, my friend."

He held up his hand when Marco opened his mouth to argue with him. "Deny it all you want, but coming from a similar background, I see it in you. But I also see a man who's overcome every obstacle life threw at him since birth to become someone on a very short list of people who I admire and I'm honored to call a friend."

Dropping his gaze to the last of his hamburger, which he no longer wanted, Marco swallowed a lump in his throat but remained quiet. He and Carter had had many meaningful conversations over the years but never anything this deep and personal. Well, as they say, there's a first time for everything.

"You turned into someone the subs adore. Not just for the orgasms you give them but for the part of you they find comfort and guidance in. I don't know where you got it—maybe from raising Nina—but it's there." He jabbed his finger on the table a few times, emphasizing his point. "Take that part of you and give it to Mara. You did a damn good job of making sure your sister became an adult who would have conquered the world if cancer hadn't taken her. She was an amazing woman, and the turnout for her funeral is a testament to that. Dude, give Mara the tools she needs to become an amazing woman like Nina. Don't *ever* let her feel like you abandoned her in any way because I know that's not the man you are."

STANDING OUTSIDE HARPER'S HOSPITAL ROOM, MARCO took a deep breath, ignoring the inquisitive looks McCabe and Foster were giving him. He was trying to psych himself up for the coming conversation.

Her mother and the baby had left an hour ago

under the watchful eyes of Boomer and Devon. The overnight shifts had been contracted out to Chase Dixon's Blackhawk Security, where Trident got their backup personnel and transportation when needed. Even with the new Omega guys, they were using six guys per shift—three on Mrs. Williams and the baby and two here outside Harper's room. The sixth man had been assigned to the security office downstairs on the first floor. Ian had called in a favor to the hospital's CEO, so they had eyes on everywhere the cameras were within the facility. The police department still had a man outside Harper's house guarding the crime scene.

"You going to stand there all night, just staring at the door?"

Not turning his head toward the man, Marco held up his middle finger. "Fuck off, Foster, or your next training session will be a twenty-mile run with a fifty-pound ruck."

The former Secret Service agent snorted but wisely kept his mouth shut.

Come on, DeAngelis, get a fucking grip. You can do this. Just walk in there and propose. How hard can it be? "Shit."

Pushing the door open, he entered and ensured it was completely shut again before directing his gaze toward Harper's bed. If she was surprised to see he'd returned, she didn't show it as she waited silently for him to say something. He cleared his throat but didn't move away from the door. "Are you feeling any better?"

"I'm done puking," she answered in a matter-of-fact

tone he didn't care for, "if that's what you're asking, but my head still feels like I got hit with a baseball bat. By the way, what *did* I get hit with? I forgot to ask the police."

"A bookend. One of those wooden elephants you have on your bookcase. You're lucky he didn't grab the cast iron or marble ones."

Harper kept an extensive book collection in her home office and had been collecting elephant book-ends from around the world since she was young. The police figured her assailant was in that room when she pulled up the drive, and he grabbed the nearest thing he could find. She had only gotten a few steps into the foyer when he struck her from his hiding spot behind the front door. Her office and bedroom had been trashed, but they would need her to look through everything to determine if anything was missing.

"Did you remember anything?"

She gestured for him to sit in the chair next to her bed, and he relaxed a little, relieved they would talk and not yell. When he sat, she shook her head slightly, mindful of her injury. "No, I didn't. The last thing I remember was stopping at the supermarket for diapers. Ian and Detective Murdock were here a little while ago and gave me the third degree about my clients and who might have a grudge against me. It could be any of my clients' husbands or boyfriends who felt I was the cause of their separation, divorce, or their wife or girlfriend's disappearance. I told the detective I would check with the bar association on

Monday to confirm what I can release to the police without breaking client/attorney privilege. But I'm always so careful that I'm not being followed, especially when I leave the office and court. And since I keep my home address and phone numbers unlisted, I really think it was a burglary with bad timing on my part."

Marco had gotten an update from Ian on the way over. While it was a possibility the attack was random, it was the general consensus among the team, who didn't believe in coincidences too often, that Harper had been targeted for some reason. According to Dr. Dunbar and Harper's office staff, she had been on the receiving end of death threats in the past from men who blamed her when their abused partners couldn't take it anymore. The local chapter of Friends of Patty would not confirm which women they had helped disappear or even how many of them there were, but Marco's guess was the number was in the hundreds. He hoped they were wrong and this was a random crime because he didn't like the thought of someone gunning for Harper.

"What happened to your neck and chin?"

Not wanting to tell her why his best friend had decked and choked him, he lied. "Sparring in the gym... got a little out of hand."

A heavy silence fell between them. Staring out the window, he mentally ran down a checklist of things that needed to be done before she was released tomorrow. He knew Ian and the team had every detail covered, but the unknown assailant could always throw them a curveball they would never see coming. So they had to expect the unexpected.

"Mara was born three and a half weeks early. You can confirm it with my doctor, but she's yours."

He almost missed her whispered confession. Swallowing hard, his gaze stayed on the darkness outside the window. "I know she is. What I don't understand is why I'm just finding this out now. Were you ever planning on telling me if I didn't find out by accident?"

Turning to look at her again, he tried hard to keep his anger in check. But what he didn't expect was the rage he saw on her face. "What are you talking about? You already knew!"

Shaking his head, his eyes narrowed in confusion. "What are *you* talking about? I didn't know anything about her!"

"Bullshit, Marco," she spat out with venom. "When I first found out, I tried to tell you. I called and called, but your cell kept saying you were unavailable. I figured you were on a mission. So I called the office and told your secretary I needed to talk to you. You didn't return a single call. Then I was all set to confront you at your house when I got your letter by messenger." The volume of her voice began to increase with every word. "By a fucking messenger, Marco! You couldn't even tell me to my face that you had already found out I was pregnant and you wanted nothing to do with me or our baby. So, fuck you! I'm raising her without you! I don't need or want your fucking help!"

Her shouting prompted Foster to open the door and stick his head in. "Um, sorry, but you might want to keep it down. I'm getting dirty looks out here from the staff."

The man didn't wait for a response and shut the door again, leaving them gaping at each other—her in anger, him in total bewilderment. When it looked like she would start laying into him again, he made a 'T' with his hands and did his best to keep his voice down. "Timeout and take a deep breath, please. I don't want you to get sick again. I'm telling you the truth, Harper. I knew nothing about any of this, and I sure as hell didn't know anything about the baby. I swear on Nina's grave."

Those last five words struck home as he'd hoped, and now it was Harper's turn to look lost. "But... but the letter. The... what... then who the hell sent me that letter? The handwriting looked like yours."

"I don't know, but it wasn't me. I swear. Do you still have it?"

Biting her bottom lip, she shook her head. "No. I was so pissed at you that I shredded it and threw it in the garbage. But what about my phone calls? Why did I keep getting a message that you couldn't be reached?"

He had a theory about the how but not the who and why. He'd have to check with Brody to find out if the idea had merit. "Again, I don't know, but I have a question for you." His mind was jumping all over the place between what was currently going on and what happened thirteen months earlier. "You said you were on the pill back then, so how did you get pregnant?"

"I *was* on the pill, but as they say, it's not one hundred percent effective. My doctor thinks with all the stress of Nina passing away and the funeral, my system was out of whack. I honestly didn't think about it until... until I was late. I was still taking the pills up to the point I realized I might be pregnant. I was terrified they would hurt her. Thankfully, that wasn't the case."

Shit. First, Nina's death. Then the pregnancy and fear the baby might have been harmed while she'd still been taking birth control. She'd gone through all that alone. Well, she'd had her mother, but he should have been there for her... whether he wanted to be there or not. Brody was right. It was time to man up.

"Marco, what the hell is going on?"

His mind was reeling, but nothing made sense to him either. "I have no idea, but I'm going to have Egghead check out a few things. In the meantime, we have other stuff we need to talk about." He took a deep breath and let it out slowly. "Marry me."

Silence filled the air as Harper's eyes widened until he couldn't take it anymore. "Say something."

"I think I need another CT scan because it sounded like you just said, 'Marry me.'"

"I did."

She snorted and pointed at his face. "You know, every girl dreams of the day some guy proposes to her, but in my dreams, the guy never looked like he just received an enema, followed by a death sentence."

Marco didn't realize he was frowning until she gestured toward his mouth with her finger. He tried to relax his features. "I'm serious—I think we should get married."

Crossing her arms, she stared at him in disbelief. "Why? Because one of your sperm took a wrong fucking turn? I don't think so." There was no mistaking the scathing sarcasm and annoyance in her voice.

"Shit, Harper." Why she was making this so difficult, he had no clue. He ran a hand through his hair in frustration. "I'm trying to do the right thing here. If we get married, you and the baby will be covered under my pension and insurance."

"Oh, please," she scoffed as her eyes rolled upward, and he squelched the urge to reprimand her. She wasn't a sub. "You can put Mara on the insurance. I don't need it. This isn't the 1950s, and no one is holding a shotgun, so there's no need for us to get married. I'll only marry someone I'm in love with and who's in love with me. Otherwise, the marriage certificate isn't worth the paper it's written on. So you're off the fucking hook."

Standing, he paced the room while she watched. Finally, he stopped at the end of her bed and tossed his hands in the air. "Fine. Then move in with me. That way, I can protect both of you. Even if this was random, you must have ex-husbands who blame you for their wives walking out."

As soon as he'd said for her to move in with him,

she'd started shaking her head and was still doing it when he stopped talking. "No. I'll take the protection Trident is willing to provide right now, and I'll pay for it." She ignored his growl and furrowing brow. "I'd be stupid not to have someone watching Mara and my mother until we figure out if the attack was random or not. But after this is over, you can go back to your house, and Mara and I will go back to ours. We'll come up with an agreeable visitation contract for you to be part of her life. I won't deny you that, but my heart and body are not part of any arrangement."

AFTER THE NURSE FINISHED CHARTING HER VITAL SIGNS, which had been normal, she quietly left Harper's room, leaving her to return to her tossing and turning. It was three a.m., and she hadn't been asleep for more than twenty minutes since Marco had left for the night. She knew two men were stationed outside her room, but her safety wasn't why sleep eluded her. It was the conversation she and Marco had earlier.

When she first found out she was pregnant, she had freaked—there was no point denying it. Knocked up and single wasn't how she imagined the next few months of her life to be. She had still been grieving over Nina's death, but each day seemed a little brighter, producing a new reason to smile with every hour that passed. She had begun to remember all the good times, and they pushed the sad ones to the side.

But once the shock of her OB/GYN's announcement had worn off, she began to relish the tiny life growing inside her. She hadn't lied to Marco. She had tried to contact him, but once she got that letter, all thoughts of a perfect, happy family had gone out the window. So, instead of breaking down, she built herself up and prepared for the birth of her daughter.

Determined to give Mara the best childhood ever, despite the lack of a father figure, she was recording every milestone in a diary she planned on giving the girl on her eighteenth birthday. Her daughter would always know what it was like to be loved.

Her mind flashed back to Marco's "marriage proposal." Oh, how she'd wanted it to have been real... and a lot more romantic. She realized why his perceived rejection of Mara and her had hurt so much back then—she was in love with the man. And had been long before Nina's death and the fateful encounter with her friend's brother, which had altered Harper's life in more ways than one.

She wished she'd told him that night she was a submissive in the lifestyle since her college days, but it wouldn't have made a difference in the long run. They might have played together a few more times, and she would have finally known what it was like to submit to Master Marco. But she was certain the end result would have been the same. Marco was never falling in love and getting married—to her or any other woman. Harper found the thought was sadder for him than for her.

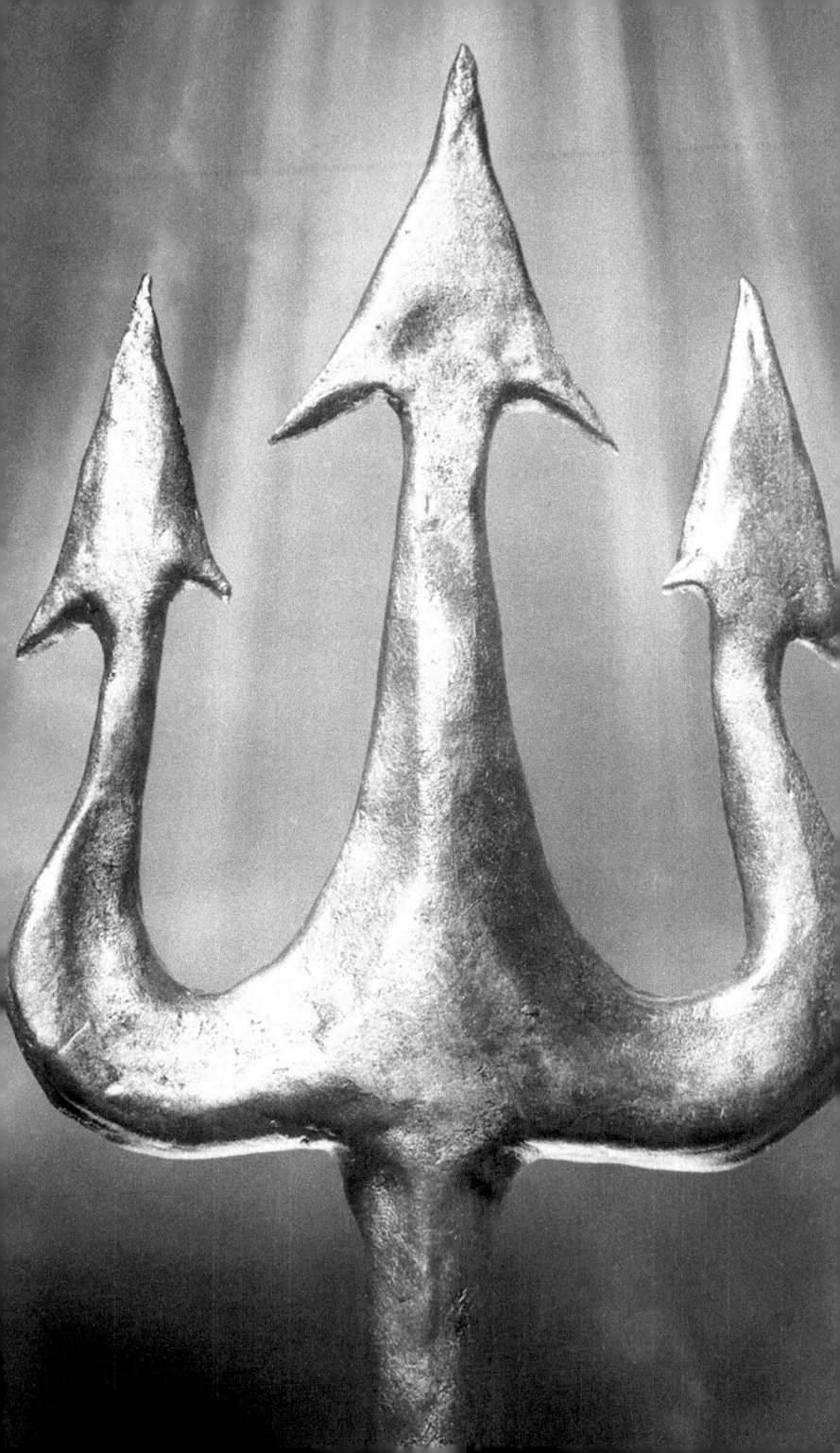

CHAPTER SEVEN

Kristen exited her doctor's office in complete disbelief. What had started as her required, routine checkup and blood work for her club member-ship, had turned into something more... something wonderful. Her mouth had dropped to the floor when the doctor congratulated her on her pregnancy. The thought that she might be pregnant never occurred to her, since her periods were back to being irregular. Devon and she had agreed she would stop taking her birth control shortly after their wedding and let nature take its course.

Holy shit-balls! She was fucking pregnant! As in having a baby. Starting a family. Something she'd always dreamed of was now coming true. She couldn't wait to tell Devon—but she would have to. She didn't want to do it over the phone or when he was so exhausted between guarding Harper and Mara and dealing with both businesses. She wanted to tell him when he was relaxed and not so many things were on his mind. For now, it was her little secret. She wasn't telling anyone until she told her husband. Thankfully, the doctor was willing to withhold the information from her medical clearance for the club. It helped that her new GYN was a member of The Covenant and knew Kristen wasn't into any play that would be harmful to the baby.

A baby! She climbed into her car and sat there for a moment, still trying to wrap her mind around the news. A fluttering in her gut was most likely butterflies taking flight, but the thought that it could be the little life developing there had a silly grin spreading across her face. The doctor had prescribed pre-natal vitamins for her, and she planned on stopping at the pharmacy after her book signing event at a little local bookstore that specialized in selling romance novels. Speaking of which, she had to hurry to make sure she wasn't late.

The publicity assistant provided by her publisher had called before Kristen went into her 10:00 a.m. appointment and informed her the line was already out the door and down the block. And that had been a little over an hour ago. *Leather & Lace* was an even bigger hit than *Satin & Sin* had been, and she was hoping her newly finished book, *Velvet Vixen*, reached similar success when it was released in a few weeks. With Devon acting as her muse again, this time for the fictional Master Zach, how could it not be?

Twenty minutes later, she parked her car behind the bookstore to avoid the throngs of fans at the front. Janice, her assistant, was waiting at the rear door, along with a man Kristen did not recognize, but based on his attire and the flowers he was carrying, she assumed he was a deliveryman. It wasn't unusual for her to receive presents from fans, and some would have them delivered if they couldn't attend the event.

As Kristen approached them, the man stepped forward. "Kristen Anders Sawyer?"

"Yes, I'm she. Janice, can you take them for me, please?" she asked, pulling off her lightweight coat and shifting her purse to the other shoulder. But instead of handing over the flowers to either one of them, the man pulled an envelope from beneath the bouquet and held it out to Kristen. Instinctively, she took it and looked at him in confusion. It was then she realized he'd called her by both her maiden and married names. "What's this?"

"A summons, Mrs. Sawyer. You've been served. Have a nice day."

———

TAKING HIS ID BACK FROM THE ARMED GUARD AT THE gate, Darius Knight followed the man's instructions to pass through the second gate and park his convertible next to the building that housed Trident Security. He had been here twice already during the Omega team's selection process, and today was his first official day on the job. He'd been thrilled to be hired by Ian and Devon Sawyer, having been on SEAL Team Four with them for a year before both men retired to the private sector. Now, five years later, he was looking forward to, once again, working with the six former SEALs who made up the original Trident team.

He was supposed to have been here earlier in the day, but Ian's secretary had called and advised him the boss was going to be delayed and Darius should arrive at noon to meet the others on his team. Climbing out of the vehicle, he stretched while taking in the surrounding compound. His buddies had done a great job with the facility, having recently added an obstacle course, similar to the SEALs' O-course, a helipad, and a training building. An outdoor "Hogan's Alley," otherwise known as a shooting gallery, had been erected using false storefronts with pop-up targets and bad guys. Instead of live guns and ammo, it utilized laser weapons, which allegedly felt, sounded, and responded like the real thing, and he couldn't wait to try them out. The high-tech toys had been obtained under a prototype trial through one of Trident's government contracts. The fictional town setup sat next to the training building on the south side of the property, while the helipad and O-course were on the north end.

From what he could see, Brody "Egghead" Evans had worked his magic with the compound's security system, and a tango, or bad guy, would be nuts to try to gain entry. As far as Darius knew, two attempts on the lives of the team members and their women had been thwarted, thanks to what some people might call extreme security measures resulting from paranoia. But in their business, paranoia was usually based on reality.

Striding toward the entrance to the offices, he froze when a large, black lab/pit mix came running full speed around the corner of the building on a mission, before sliding to a stop in front of him. The dog had been introduced to him during both his previous visits, but knowing it was a trained guard dog had him wary. He relaxed when the canine dropped a hard rubber ball covered in slobber at his feet and looked up at him expectantly, its tail wagging furiously. "Beau, isn't it?"

The dog woofed in response to his name as he sat down, his rear end still twitching.

"I thought you were supposed to be a bad-ass dog who only understands German." He picked up the ball while Beau's eyes tracked it in anticipation. "Look, I have no problem playing fetch with you, but next time, can you put on the brakes a little sooner and not two feet away from me? I thought you were about to take me down."

"*Woof.*"

Darius chuckled. With the dog's markings, it looked like he had a permanent smile, and it was infectious. "All right. You only get one throw now, otherwise, I'll be late. But you can hit me up for a game of fetch later. Agreed?"

"*Woof.*"

Rearing back, he threw the ball toward the far west end of the compound with the dog hauling ass after it. Shaking his head, he started for the offices again. Inside, he reintroduced himself to the company secretary, Colleen McKinley. The petite blonde was a pretty woman, with luscious curves, and obviously engaged with a huge diamond ring on her tiny hand. That was probably a good thing, since, although she was the typical girl-next-door he was normally attracted to, he'd be stupid to get involved with a Trident employee. He didn't play in the same sandbox where he worked.

"Hi, Darius. Nice to see you again. Welcome aboard." Smiling, she handed him a large brown envelope. "In there is your ID, insurance paperwork, tax forms for the payroll, computer passwords, which you'll need to change after signing in the first time, and a few other papers you need. Later, Brody will get your handprint scanned into the system, so you can access any locked area in the compound. If you have a seat in the conference room over there, Ian will be with you in a moment. Can I get you some coffee from the break room?"

He grinned—the woman was damn efficient. "Thanks, but I can get it myself if you point the way."

"Sure. Down the hall, last door on the right."

After helping himself to a fresh cup of gourmet coffee from the company's Keurig machine, he wandered back to the conference room and took a seat. But he immediately stood again when two men and a woman entered the room, with the lead being his old teammate and new boss.

"Hey, Batman." Ian held out his hand, and when Darius took it, pulled him into a man-hug, slapping him on the back a few times. "Glad to finally have you on board. Did you get settled in Reverend's condo?"

"Yeah. Since Jake left most of it furnished, I put my stuff in storage for now. I'll have to thank him again for renting it to me."

"When he's in town, he stays here in Nick's place now, so he was glad to rent it to someone he knew." Stepping away again, Ian gestured to the man who'd been standing behind him. "Darius Knight, Navy SEALs, this is one of your new teammates, Valentino Mancini, aka 'Romeo,' Army SF and FBI HRT."

Darius was impressed with the credentials—Special Forces and then a gig with the fed's Hostage Rescue Team. He shook the tall, dark-haired man's hand, and then turned to the woman who Ian introduced next. "And this is one of our new snipers, Lindsey Abbott, Marines, aka 'Costello.' She'll be training with your team for a bit, before starting assignments with mine. She'll be filling in for Reverend while he's getting the West Coast team up and running."

Holding out his hand, Darius gave her a nod. "Nice to meet you."

The brunette was about six inches shorter than his own height of six-foot-two, but her military training was noticeable with her straight spine, shoulders back, head up, and eyes directly focused on his. She shook his hand and smiled, which lit up her face. "Same here. Why Batman?"

It was obvious to him how the others probably got their nicknames. Abbott was "Costello" from the old comedy duo, and Valentino had most likely gotten "Romeo" due to his name being close to Valentine. However, Darius's was a little more obscure but just as amusing. "Stuck from basic training. Darius Knight... D. Knight... Dark Knight... Batman. My RDC—Recruit Division Commander—was a big fan of the movie."

The others laughed, then took seats at the table with Ian at the head. "Two of your teammates have been training with us for a few months while we've been waiting for you all to retire from your various careers. Cain Foster, Secret Service, and Tristan McCabe, also Army SF, have gone on a few assignments with us but will begin training with you this week. We'll be running you through your paces, so you can figure out each other's weaknesses and strengths. You've all trained in teams before, so I don't foresee any issues there. The rest of your team will be arriving next month, and that's when all bets will be off. We're going to be dropping you off in the wilderness somewhere until you know each other inside and out. We also have a new helicopter pilot, Tempest Van Buren, who will be reporting in a few weeks. The bird we purchased was flown in last week and will be available as soon as she inspects and clears it. In the meantime, an unexpected situation involving Marco DeAngelis has cropped up and that will take precedence over the next few days until we know more." Eyeing Mancini and Abbott, he added, "I believe you both met him already."

As they both nodded, Darius raised his brow. Although time and distance had come between them, he still knew DeAngelis pretty well, and he couldn't think of what trouble the straight-up guy might be in. "What's going on with Polo?"

Running a hand down his face, Ian sighed. "I usually don't go dropping personal shit on newbies or contract agents, but you'll need to know since we're going to be using you all on guard duty. Marco just found out he's a father to an infant. The mother, Harper Williams, is a longtime acquaintance of his, and he had no clue about all this before yesterday, but that's between them. I'm staying out of that part of it. Anyway, Harper was assaulted during a home invasion two nights ago. She's getting out of the hospital today and will need guarding until we find out if this was a random attack or not. The baby is with Harper's mother, at the moment, and that's where McCabe is right now with one of our regular bodyguards. Foster is with Boomer and Marco on Harper. We'll be rotating shifts between both teams, as well as a few contract agents from Blackhawk Security—"

"Ian? Sorry to interrupt..."

The boss didn't seem bothered by the secretary's intruding on the meeting from where she stood in the doorway, especially when it was clear from her wide eyes and frown that something was wrong. "What is it, Colleen?"

"Cain is on the phone. They're at Harper's house, and he says it's an emergency."

Grabbing the cordless handset from the landline phone in front of him, Ian stabbed the button for the blinking light. "Sit-rep."

This couldn't be good because whatever was said over the line had the usually stoic man's blood draining from his face. His voice dropped to a near-whisper. "Oh, shit."

THRILLED TO FINALLY BE DISCHARGED FROM THE hospital, Harper climbed into the passenger seat of Marco's truck. As much as she wanted to see Mara, she needed to see what was going on at her house first. She was sure she would have to clean up her office, bedroom, and foyer, between whatever the intruder had done, and what the police had to do during their investigation.

She still couldn't remember the attack or even arriving home that night. The last thing she could recall was leaving the restaurant with her secretary, Joanie, and paralegal, Monica, and stopping at the supermarket for the diapers. After that, everything was a blank until she woke up in the hospital with Marco watching over her. The doctors warned she may never remember what happened and not to get discouraged over it. The less she tried to force the memory, the better chance she had of it popping into her brain again. While her nausea was gone and her dizziness was under control as long as she didn't move too fast, she still had a pounding headache. Her neck and back were also stiff, causing her more discomfort. The doctor said that should all disappear after another day or two and would only allow her to have acetaminophen for the pain, which wasn't making much of a difference.

The police still didn't have any leads on her attacker, and as a result, she was stuck with Marco being attached to her hip for the next few days. He'd told her he would be sleeping in her spare bedroom until they determined she wasn't in any further danger. If it had just been her, she would have outright refused, but she couldn't take a chance with her mother and daughter's lives. She believed Marco was telling her the truth about not knowing about Mara, but then the big question was, who sent her that letter all those months ago and why?

"Did you find out why your phone was unavailable to me?"

Marco pulled into traffic with Boomer and Foster in a truck behind them. "Yeah. I spoke to Devon earlier. Someone called Trident's cell provider, claiming to be me, and put a block of your home, cell, and office numbers on my cell about two months after Nina's funeral. Apparently, I reported you were harassing me with phone calls. Devil Dog had them check the rest of the team's phones, and it was the same deal, so you couldn't contact any of them."

This was crazy. "Who the hell would've done that? And then send me that damn letter?"

"I don't know, but when we find out who the bastard is, I'm going to put a serious hurt on him. It could be anyone who has a grudge against me, and that list is pretty long with all the missions we've been on. Or it could be someone screwing with you. With your connections to Friends of Patty and being a lawyer specializing in divorces and family court, your list is pretty long, too."

It was. Over the past few years, she had helped about two dozen women start their lives over with new identities. Most of them had very little family and few friends after their husbands or boyfriends had isolated them during the never-ending cycle of abuse, so it was rare to have a missing person report filed. Usually, the abusers gave up looking after a while and moved on to another poor soul, who would fall victim to their initial false charm, designed to draw them in. The women who had disappeared hadn't been from Pinellas County only. Friends of Patty had contacts all over the state and country from coast to coast. There had been women leaving Florida for parts unknown to Harper, and others moving into the state to start a new life.

It wasn't long before Marco pulled into her driveway and parked next to the garage. Her keys were in her purse, which was somewhere in the house, but she had memorized the code to open her garage door.

Her wallet apparently had been missing, so with her mother's help yesterday, she'd canceled all her credit and debit cards, along with the few checks that had been left in there. The police had told her they hadn't been able to find her cell phone either, and she reported the theft to her provider, which was supposed to be overnighting a new one to her. A quick glance at her front porch showed it was empty of packages, so it hadn't come yet. Marco exited the vehicle and came around to help her out. While they still had a lot of issues to iron out between them, she knew him well enough to know he genuinely wanted to take care of her. It was in his nature, which was probably why he was a Dom in the BDSM community. It wasn't something they had ever talked about, but Nina had told Harper years ago that her brother admitted to being a Dominant. And, thankfully, her friend hadn't told Marco about Harper being a submissive in the lifestyle.

Stopping at the garage's keypad, she punched in her code and the overhead door began to slide upward. After it was halfway up, they ducked underneath and strode to the inside door, where she hit the button to close the door again. She was surprised to see a new security panel on the wall where the old one had been. "Who put that in? Brody?"

"Yeah," he answered while entering a six-digit number Brody had texted him earlier, which resulted in the red light going out, indicating the system was now unarmed. "Egghead and Boomer did some upgrades and installed a few cameras. I'll show you how to work everything after you check to see what's missing."

He held the door open for her and after she stepped into the hallway, she decided to go grab her mail and started for the foyer. She needed to do something normal before the fear of what could've happened took over and sent her into a panic attack.

CHAPTER EIGHT

"Where are you going?" Marco asked as he closed the door to the garage and tossed his car keys on a hallway table.

"I need to get my mail."

Taking hold of her arm, he stopped her in her tracks. "I'll get it."

She rolled her eyes, and, once again, he fought the impulse to reprimand her. She wasn't his submissive. Hell, she wasn't anyone's submissive, although there had been times he'd wished she was. Since their one night together, dreams of playing with Harper had been a regular occurrence which, thankfully, had faded a little with time. Until last night. He'd had one hell of an erotic dream about her which had made him take matters into his own hand for some relief.

Fuck. Don't think about it.

"It's broad daylight, Marco. I highly doubt I have anything to worry about. Besides, despite what everyone thinks, I'm sure it was a random burglar whom I surprised. I don't have any enemies, and the house and utilities are all in my first name, Millicent, so I'm not easy to locate, even if I did."

He let go of her arm as the heat of her soft skin started to burn his fingers. Damn, the electricity between them was still there after all this time. "Yeah, about that. What's with the first name, and why don't you use it? As far as I know, you've always been Harper."

"I *have* always gone by Harper. Millicent was my grandmother's name, and she died a few months before I was born. My father's family was big on naming their kids after other family members, especially right after someone died, so he insisted that my first name be Millicent. My mother only agreed to it being my legal name as long as they called me by my middle name."

Chuckling, he turned toward the door. "Well, if it helps, you look more like a Harper than a Millie or Millicent."

A sweet smile spread across her face for the first time since he'd been reunited with her. "And I thank my mother for that every time I have to put my legal name down somewhere."

"Why don't you go see if anything looks like it's missing, while I get the mail?"

She glanced around. "Who cleaned up? From what everyone told me, I figured it would be a mess."

"Kristen, Jenn, Angie, and Kat did it last night after the police released the crime scene. They came with

Brody and Boomer because they didn't want you to come home to a mess. Kristen said they put a lot of things in boxes and bags in your office for you to sort through. They were afraid to throw anything out, in case it was important or sentimental."

Reaching the new security panel in the foyer, Marco punched in the same six-digit code from the garage, then unlocked and opened the front door. A quick inspection of the front property told him nothing seemed to be amiss, and Boomer's truck was parked across the street, where he and Foster would be keeping an eye on things until their relief showed up. Taking a step out onto the wooden porch, he froze when a faint click, which was very out of place, reached his ears.

Holy shit! Please, Lord, don't let that be what I think it is.

Eyeing the long driveway, he realized his team-mates were too far away to hear him if he shouted, and he couldn't take the chance of retrieving his cell from his pocket. Using all his strength and will to keep perfectly still and not shift his weight, he called out, "Harper?"

"Yes?"

"Can you come here for a minute?" he asked through a clenched jaw. Her footsteps announced her reentry to the foyer. "Stop right there and don't come any closer. I need you to call Boomer's cell phone and tell him I need him."

"What—"

"Just do it!" He hadn't meant to bark, but there wasn't time for her questions.

"Okay." Her fear and uncertainty hung on that one word. "W-what's his number?"

Marco rattled it off, and in less than thirty seconds, he saw the two men bolt from the truck and rush up the driveway, scanning the area for whatever the problem was. When they were close enough, so he didn't have to shout, he spoke with a calmness he didn't feel. "Boomer, I need you to crawl under the porch and tell me I'm wrong."

"Huh?" His teammate's eyes first narrowed in confusion and then flashed to horror a split second later. "Oh, fuck! Don't move!"

"As if I didn't figure that out for myself, jackass." While Boomer ran to the end of the porch, Marco saw the moment Foster put two and two together. They needed to get Harper out of the house and had to assume the rear entrance was rigged as well. "Call Ian for backup. Tell him to have the team on her mother and baby move them to the compound, ASAP." When the man pulled out his cell phone and weapon, Marco turned his head slightly, so Harper could hear him. "Sweetheart, I want you to grab my keys and go back out through the garage to Cain. Don't touch anything else. He's going to put you in my truck. As soon as the rest of the team gets here, he's going to take you back to the Trident compound and keep you safe."

Her voice dropped to a frightened whisper. "Marco, what is it?"

He didn't want to scare her, but he needed her to obey him without question. "I hope I'm wrong, but I think I just stepped on a landmine."

A loud gasp was followed by the jingle of his keys and the interior garage door opening. From under the floorboards of the porch, the sounds of Boomer belly-crawling in the small space became louder until he was almost underneath where Marco stood. Terror and impatience battled for superiority within him as he awaited his friend's verdict. His gut sank when a muffled "fuck" came from below, then his life flashed before his eyes, and it wasn't pretty.

"Polo, don't fucking move. It's not a landmine, but damn fucking close. It's a homemade job with a pressure trigger. I gotta get my tools, so just hang on."

"Sure. No problem. Have someone get me a beer and a pizza, and maybe the sports section of the newspaper to make the time go faster." If they'd all learned one thing in the military, it was that wry humor tended to ease a person's panic. Most of the time. Some of the time. Oh, fuck, it wasn't helping his panic at all this time.

As Boomer crawled back out to retrieve his EOD—Explosive Ordnance Disposal—kit and protective gear from his vehicle, the overhead garage door finished sliding open, and in his peripheral vision, Marco saw Harper emerge. She was wide-eyed and pale from fright, and he wished he could be the one to comfort her right now.

Proving he knew how to protect a principal asset at

a time like this—well, he *was* a former Secret Service agent, so he'd better—Foster grabbed Harper's arm. He rushed her to the waiting truck with his gun in his other hand, ready to fire at any threat that might appear. Harper clicked the remote, unlocking the door, and with a worried glance over her shoulder at Marco, she jumped into the passenger seat at Foster's urging. Taking the keys from her, he instructed her to climb into the rear seat and lay down out of sight, before slamming the door shut. Hopping into the driver's seat, the man started the engine with a roar and sped toward the end of the driveway, away from the potential blast. While it wasn't an ideal location for her at the moment, it was better than the alternative, and Marco didn't want them heading back to Trident without reinforcements. Confident Harper was in good hands, he concentrated on staying perfectly still as beads of sweat rolled off his forehead and temples. And for the first time since Nina was alive, Marco began to pray.

Was this how it was supposed to end for him? Was fate going to be so cruel as to kill him on a beautiful sunny day, far away from the hells of war, right after he found out he was a father? Yeah, he wasn't thrilled about that, but... damn. Was his teammate going to die with him? *Jeez*, Baby Boomer had just reunited with the love of his life a few months ago, after thinking the woman had been dead for twelve years. Marco would curse the universe if he was the reason those two were separated by death once again.

He didn't know how much time had passed—it felt

like hours... eons even—before two Clearwater P.D. patrol cars with their lights flashing came screeching to a halt in front of the property, followed by several unmarked vehicles. Ian emerged from a black Suburban, barking out commands. From another SUV, Marco saw Drew Murdock climb out and give two uniformed officers their own orders. The cops split up, heading for the houses on either side of Harper's, probably to evacuate any occupants.

Following Ian's command, their new sniper, Lindsey Abbott, and the Omega Team's Mancini jumped into Marco's truck, and Foster floored it before both doors were fully shut. The rest of the crew dashed across the front lawn, with Brody and Devon skirting the house to check for more explosives. Marco didn't miss the worried look, followed by a thumbs up, that his regular ménage partner sent his way before disappearing around the corner. While they hadn't spoken since yesterday's fistfight, he knew it was his best friend's way of saying that no matter what, Brody was watching his back and always would.

"Sit-rep." Ian stopped at the bottom of the porch steps with Murdock and Darius Knight. While it was great to have the newly retired SEAL on board with them again, a proper reunion would have to wait for a bit. All three had put on bullet-proof vests as a precaution. Not that the protective gear would stop flying shrapnel from ripping them to shreds if the explosive went off, but there was no way of knowing if an ambush was planned if the bomb wasn't successful.

Ignoring his boss' request, Marco asked, "Are Harper's mother and the baby covered?"

Ian nodded. "McCabe and Tiny have them en route to the compound. No signs of trouble at their end. Boomer?"

"Down here," came the answer from under the porch. "I'm going to need someone to come in from the other end to hold this flashlight for me."

Ripping the Velcro straps of his vest open to remove it, Knight responded, "I can do that. Which is the 'other end'?"

When Marco shifted his eyes and gave his head a minuscule tilt to his right, the experienced newbie hurried over, pulled off the piece of lattice covering the crawl space, and then dropped to the ground to drag himself underneath. Marco wasn't surprised their old teammate jumped right into a fucked-up situation on his first day, and he planned on thanking him. That is, if they all survived the next fifteen minutes.

Boomer filled the newcomers in on what he'd found. "It's a homemade job, Ian, with a pressure switch. The good news is, it's a bomb any idiot can make if they have access to a Walmart and the internet. The bad news is, it's a bomb any idiot can make, and I can't guarantee this guy followed the directions to a 'T'."

A round of curses came from all of them. Brody and Devon came back from the rear of the house, and the now dirt-covered geek ducked into the garage. Just as dirty—they'd obviously crawled under the back porch

—Devon approached his brother. "All clear back there. No signs of forced entry, and there's nothing to indicate the alarm system was bypassed, but we'll do a run-through inside just in case."

By this point, the sweat on Marco's forehead rolled into his eyes and down his neck, but he didn't dare try to wipe it away. Any movement could cause him to shift his weight, and then it would be bye-bye time. "Dev, get him out. Ian, you guys have to get out of the blast range. You too, Murdock. It's bad enough Boomer and Knight are fucking toast with me if this thing blows."

"Oh, ye of little faith." Boomer was obviously a tad insulted.

A large black van, with T.P.D. Bomb Squad in large white letters on the side, pulled up to the curb in front of the house, along with two more patrol cars. Tampa PD's specialized unit also covered the smaller cities and towns in Pinellas County. Their arrival caught everyone's attention for a moment before Ian turned back to face Marco with a frown. "Fuck you, Polo. This is no different from combat. When one of our asses was on the line, the others didn't bail back then, and it's not fucking happening now either."

Marco watched as Devon also ignored his plea and headed toward the garage door, while Ian just stood at the bottom of the steps and crossed his arms. Marco knew it would be like trying to move the Hoover Dam ten feet to the left, but he had to try once more. "Boss-man, please. You've got a fiancée now. One who, I might add, won't be happy if I get you blown to smithereens."

"And you have a daughter now, so I repeat—fuck you. Besides, no one is going to get blown to smithereens. Boomer can do this shit with his eyes closed."

"Hey, how'd you know my eyes were closed?"

Usually, the inane banter in stressful situations didn't disturb Marco, but at the moment, he wanted to punch his younger teammate's lights out for shits and giggles. Shaking his head at the bad joke, Ian eyed the detective standing next to him. "You, on the other hand, have procedures to follow, so go fill your squad in."

If Murdock took offense to being ordered around, he didn't show it. In fact, Marco wasn't surprised to see a flash of relief come over the other man's face and didn't blame him. As the detective proceeded down the driveway, two bomb squad members were on their way up. After a brief conversation with Murdock midway, they approached the porch with their own equipment. Thankfully, this wouldn't turn into a pissing match, since Boomer had done some cross-training with several local law enforcement bomb squads, including T.P.D. and the F.B.I., over the past few years. There were always advantages to having government security contracts, and this was one of them. Both men had worked with the former Naval E.O.D. expert before and respected his skills as much as the Trident team-mates did.

The two-man team, Sgt. Barry Templeton and Officer Freddie Mendoza, acknowledged Marco's precarious position but wisely ignored him after that. He needed all his concentration for the task at hand—remaining perfectly still—and it was getting more difficult as the seconds ticked by. After being told Boomer was under the floorboards, Templeton raised his voice to be heard. "Boomer, how you doing down there?"

"Pretty good. I just beat Knight's straight with a full house, but I could use another beer and some buffalo wings. How you doing up there?"

Marco growled at the quip from under the porch and silently swore he would kill Boomer if they lived through this.

"Not bad. Mendoza's with me. You need us down there?"

There was an extended pause before the answer came. "Uh, yeah, actually. I can't completely remove the cover and do what I have to do without an extra set of hands. The wires are too short. The FNG came from the other end and is holding the flashlight, so you're going to have to come in from the side. Avoid the plank Polo's standing on and the two on either side of it, for a total of five."

Squatting to inspect the lattice covering the space he needed to get to, Mendoza's eyes narrowed. "Who or what's an FNG?"

Ian, Boomer, and Knight all gave the same droll response. "Fucking new guy."

"Ah. Gotcha."

Marco's torso was now as sweaty as his face, and it was starting to itch like crazy. He wished he could yell at everyone to shut the fuck up, as well as hurry the fuck up, but it would be a waste of breath. It would be done when it was done, and working any faster could kill them all. "Ian, can you check on Harper and Mara for me?"

While his boss stepped away to make the call, Marco realized it was the first time he'd said his daughter's name aloud. Up until now, he'd referred to her as "the baby," "the kid," or anything else along those lines. Carter and Brody had been right, and if Marco got out of this alive, he was going to make sure Mara knew he'd always be there for her—and not just financially. Nina would come back from her grave to haunt him if he didn't man up. An image of her holding her niece popped into his head, and the corners of his mouth ticked upward, despite the situation. Remembering how good she'd been with her school children, he knew Nina would have made an awesome aunt and mother if only things had been different.

Muffled comments came from below after Mendoza joined the party, and it seemed as if hours had passed, instead of only ten or eleven minutes, before Boomer finally announced, "We're clear! You can move, Polo."

Move? Hell, he almost dropped to the ground and kissed it. He didn't realize how tense he'd been until he sighed in relief and every muscle in his body screeched in pain as they tried to relax. From behind him, someone grabbed his shoulder and squeezed. Turning, he found Brody standing in the doorway, grinning at him.

"Glad you made it," the geek teased. "Because I'm still planning my revenge for the whole 'trunk-junk' thing, and it would really suck if you weren't around for it."

Marco held out his hand, and when his friend shook it, he pulled him in for a man hug with lots of back-slapping. "Can you wait a week before you spring it on me? Not sure my nerves could handle anything before then."

Stepping back, the man snorted. "No problem. In the meantime, we need to head back to the war-room and check out the video feeds. Hopefully, we got our bomber on film."

As Ian hung up his cell, the two teammates joined the others at the bottom of the porch steps while Boomer, Knight, and Mendoza crawled out from under it, all covered in dirt and cobwebs. Even though the bomb had been deactivated, they all moved a little further down the driveway. Marco endured some more back-slapping as he tried to get his heart rate back to normal and his knees to stop shaking. He raised a questioning eyebrow at Ian, who nodded. "They're all safe and secure. I told Foster to tell Harper you're okay and her house is still in one piece."

Well, he wasn't exactly okay, since he was now going through a massive adrenaline crash, and the shaking in his knees started to spread throughout his body. But it was far better than being dead, so he'd take it. "Thanks."

"I'm going to go talk to Doc Dunbar and see if she's come across any wife-beaters through Friends of Patty, who know a thing or two about explosives. I'll try to get some names from her if it doesn't violate the organization's rules."

Devon exited through the front door, side-stepping the planks that the explosives were still attached to, and declared, "House is clear—inside and out."

Brushing himself off, Boomer added, "I'll stay and help dispose of this thing. Once we pull it out, we'll take a closer look and see if we can find any signatures, but I'm not counting on it. It was pretty crudely made. A sixth grader could have made it as a science project."

Most experienced bombers styled their explosives a certain way, creating their own "signature" in the design. However, with bomb-making how-to sites all over the internet, wannabe bombers could easily transition to actual bombers. But they weren't usually as intelligent as the experts, so signatures were sometimes absent nowadays.

Marco lifted the bottom of his sweat-soaked shirt and wiped his face with it. Brody smacked his upper arm and pointed to his truck in the street. "Come on. I'll give you a lift to your place so you can shower and change, and then we'll head to the compound."

"No, let's go straight there. I've got clothes in my go-bag in my truck. I'll take a shower in one of the bunkrooms." He had to reassure himself that Harper and Mara were okay. After thanking his team and the others one more time, he followed his best friend down the driveway. A butterfly came out of nowhere and fluttered around his head before taking off again. Nina had mentioned once that if a butterfly did that, it was a loved one in the afterlife letting you know that everything was going to be all right.

Hmmpf.

Their roles were now reversed, and she was watching over him. Rubbing the remembrance tattoo on his left upper arm, he glanced skyward and said a silent prayer of thanks.

CHAPTER NINE

Pacing back and forth in the compound's parking lot, Harper tried to hold it together. He was safe. Ian had called and said Marco was alive and out of danger, but she wouldn't believe it until she saw him again.

Nearby, Kristen and Ian's fiancée, Angie, kept a close eye on her from the grassy "backyard" that had been created between the last two warehouses in the complex. The building to her right, she was told, housed the gym, training rooms, indoor gun range, and storage. The one to her left had been transformed into four huge apartments. Angie and Ian had the bottom one on this end, with Kristen and Devon's unit above them. The units on the other end mirrored those, and Ian's goddaughter, Jenn, had the bottom, while the youngest Sawyer brother, Nick, had the top one, with his partner, Jake. She was happy for the two men. Though she'd only met Nick once, she thought he was the perfect mate for Jake. While Marco's teammate was a Dom, she'd always gotten the feeling he needed someone as Alpha as himself outside of the bedroom.

Angie had come out of her apartment and introduced herself when Harper had arrived under guard, a short time after her mother and Mara. She had gotten the older woman and baby settled in her spare bedroom, but Harper declined the invite to rest inside. Upon Kristen's arrival, the two women did their best to ease Harper's growing anxiety. Her last panic attack had been shortly before Nina's death and thankfully hadn't been in her dying friend's presence. She'd had them a lot in her teens but had never been able to pinpoint the reasons for them. They usually popped up when she was stressed but not always. With the help of a counselor in college, she'd been able to ward them off by concentrating on something or someone she loved. Right now, she kept images of Mara laughing and playing in her mind, and hopefully, it would be enough for her not to break down and start to hyperventilate.

The compound had been sealed after her arrival, only letting in Kristen and several contract agents from Blackhawk Security. Armed men now had the gates and surrounding fence line covered. Someone was inside the offices monitoring the many cameras, and even Beau was on alert, his ears and nose twitching in search of danger to his humans.

"Miss Harper? Can I get you anything?"

She glanced up at the mountainous man, who was surprisingly quiet for someone six feet and eight inches tall. She'd never heard him approach. "Thanks, Tiny, but I'm okay for now. I just need to see that Marco is okay for myself."

Travis "Tiny" Daultry had, at one time, been a professional football player. But after an injury ended his career, he became a bodyguard. When he wasn't doing that for Trident, he was the head of security at The Covenant. Harper had never been inside the BDSM club at the other end of the compound, but she had heard it was the nicest kink club in the southeast. She'd met Tiny several times during Nina's battle with cancer, and both women had agreed he was one big teddy bear.

The sound of a vehicle approaching had them turning in the direction of the front gate, but her hopes of seeing Marco vanished with Tiny's declaration. "It's Miss Jenn."

Harper watched as the red Volkswagen Jetta was allowed entry through the far gate, then made its way past the interior one and parked a few feet away from her. Jenn barely shut off the engine before jumping out and throwing her arms around Harper. If someone who didn't know them was observing, they'd be surprised to hear the two women hadn't seen each other in over a year, the way Jenn squeezed her tight. "Oh my God! Are you okay? Uncle Ian called and told me to come straight here after my class. That something happened at your place, and he'd explain when I got here."

She returned the younger woman's hug, then took a

step back as Kristen and Angie joined them. "I'm fine. And according to Ian, everyone else is okay, too. They should be here soon. I'm sorry if we scared you."

"*Pfft*," Jenn scoffed. "You kind of get used to it around here after a while." They all chuckled because it did seem that trouble followed the men of Trident, along with their women. "Where's Kat?"

Harper hadn't met Boomer's girlfriend yet, but Marco had filled her in on the new relationships at Trident which had started in her absence. She was glad the men were settling down because everyone deserved their own happily ever after. Maybe she would find hers someday soon—with or without Marco.

"She's still at work," Angie informed her. "She can't be much safer than at the state police headquarters, training their new K9s, but we called and gave her a head's up after Ian gave the all clear. We didn't want her worrying about the bomb, since Boomer was the one taking it apart."

"Bomb?" The word came out on a screech filled with disbelief.

"*Shhh.*" Angie grimaced as she put her arm around the younger woman. "Sorry. I forgot they didn't tell you yet. There was a bomb at Harper's, and Marco stepped on it, but it didn't go off. Boomer was able to deactivate it."

Her eyes wide, Jenn gaped at them. "Holy shit! A freaking bomb! Where do these weirdoes come from? I swear, Kristen, sometimes it feels like I'm living in your book series. *Jeez.*"

The author laughed. "Where do you think I got the storyline for *Velvet Vixen*? My life has been a romance/suspense story ever since I met Devon."

After a few minutes of catching up with Harper, Jenn followed Angie to her apartment to check on Karen and Mara. Glancing around to be sure everyone else was out of earshot, Harper leaned closer to Kristen and whispered, "If you don't want anyone to know you're pregnant yet, you might want to stop touching your abdomen. I know it's hard to do, though."

Kristen gasped as she yanked her hands away from her body, her eyes darting around to see if anyone else had noticed. "Oh shit! Is it that obvious?"

Despite her worry, she couldn't help but giggle. "Only to someone who's been there before. Congratulations."

The relief on the other woman's face was palpable. "Thanks. I actually just found out this morning and haven't even told Devon yet."

"Then your secret is safe with me. I won't tell a soul. But after you tell him, feel free to come over to my place and take all the *What To Expect When You're Expecting* books from my shelves. I have over a dozen of them."

"Thanks, I will." Kristen paused. "Actually, I do have something I need to talk to you about later after all the excitement dies down. I have a legal problem. My bastard ex-husband is suing me for half my earnings as an author. This is the same man who laughed, calling it my 'little hobby,' and was surprised anyone bought my books."

It was a tale Harper had heard several times in her practice, but each one usually had its own twist. "I take it he's now claiming that he's entitled since your first books were published while you were still married to him."

The other woman rolled her eyes. "Something like that. I really didn't have a chance to read the whole subpoena and don't really understand all the legal mumbo-jumbo. I was served two minutes before I was scheduled at a book signing, and then I came home to this, so…"

Feeling guilty about her problems being forced on everyone else, Harper needed to apologize. "I'm sorry. This is all my fault."

"No, it's not." Kristen actually shook a finger at her like she was scolding a child. "And don't let Marco hear you say that. Doms get bossy when women try to put the blame on themselves where it doesn't belong. Trust me. I know from experience, and my ass has paid the price."

Harper was about to say something in response, but the sounds of several vehicles approaching had them looking up in anticipation. She recognized they belonged to Ian and Brody. *Thank God.* The vehicles parked next to the Trident office building, and when Marco emerged from the Ford F-150, she couldn't stop herself from running into his arms and hugging him.

"Thank God, you're okay! Don't ever do that to me again!"

He held her tightly and laughed quietly. "It was never my intention to do it the first time, baby, but I'll try not to scare you in the future."

Despite his shirt being soaked with sweat, she couldn't let go of him. She had been terrified from the moment he'd told her he had stepped on a landmine. As much as she'd hated to leave him, she knew her being there would be a distraction to him and everyone else, so she obeyed his orders without hesitation. It had almost killed her to do so.

His hands began to slide up and down her back in comfort, but her body decided to react differently. Now that the terror was gone, the need for comfort was being pushed aside by the need for something else. A stirring began low in her abdomen, and her nipples responded to the feeling of being crushed against his muscular chest. Worried he would notice, she tried to step back, but he refused to let her go.

"Please, not yet." His voice was hoarse and filled with emotion. "I need to feel your heart beat with mine, just for a few minutes. I've never been so scared in my life... and it wasn't for me but for you."

"And I was scared for you." Swallowing hard, Harper relaxed against him and buried her face in his neck. "Hold me as long as you want." She wanted him to hold her forever, but since that was improbable, she'd take the next few minutes and treasure them.

MARCO TOWELED OFF FROM HIS SHOWER IN ONE OF THE spare bunk rooms above the offices and pulled on a pair of cargo pants, commando style. Apparently, clean underwear was something he'd forgotten to throw into his go-bag, but it wasn't a big deal. He'd gone without it during many missions since the start of his military career and gotten used to it quickly. Besides, he no longer needed to worry about the hard-on he'd been sporting earlier. He'd jacked off in the shower since his body had still been reacting to a combination of adrenaline and Harper's body flush against his. He wasn't sure how long they'd stood there holding each other, but when they finally separated, everyone else had disappeared into the buildings or backyard. The armed guards had been walking the compound's perimeter and were focused on keeping them all safe.

For now, the women were keeping Harper and her mother company in Angie's apartment while the baby slept, so the men could plan their next steps. Pulling on a clean T-shirt, he headed downstairs to the conference room, where most of his and the Omega team had gathered, along with Tiny. The head of security would need to be aware of what was happening, just in case it affected the club. Boomer and Knight were still at Harper's house with the police and would stay there until relief showed up. In addition to the security measures, that had already been put in place, there would now be two armed guards watching the house at all times. Taking an empty seat, Marco grabbed one of the bottled waters Colleen had placed in the middle of the long table and guzzled half of it.

Ian stabbed the speaker button on the phone sitting in front of him. "Reverend, you still there?"

Of course, Jake had been kept in the loop, despite being in San Diego. "Yup. Is Polo there?"

Marco leaned forward to be heard clearly. "Yeah, I'm here. Can't get rid of me that easily."

"Thank God for that. I'm dying to hear what Egghead's junk-trunk revenge is going to be."

While the members of the Omega team looked confused, the rest of them laughed. Marco would gladly take the ribbing he was in for over the next few weeks because it meant he was alive. "Before we start— and Ian, don't tell me to fuck off again—I just wanted to thank everyone for... well, for everything. I know my team has always had my back and vice versa, but the Omega Team stepped up to the plate without hesitation. So, again, thanks." There were a round of head nods and a few murmurs. Theirs was typically a thankless career, so when gratitude did come, even from a fellow teammate, it tended to fluster them. "All right. Fill me in."

Ian nodded for Brody to start the briefing. The geek hit a button on his laptop, and the video feed from Harper's front porch appeared on a wide-screen monitor hanging on the far wall. "Jake, you should have it up on your screen, too, although there isn't much to see."

"Got it."

Brody leaned back in his chair. "Our perp showed up just after midnight. He knew the cameras were there and was wearing a Frankenstein Halloween mask, gloves, and hoodie. From the body type and language, I'm pretty sure it's a guy. Either he expected cameras or did a drive-by and saw us installing them."

Everyone watched as an indistinguishable human entered the picture, carrying a large duffel bag. The bastard had the balls to wave at the camera before going out of range again, presumably to crawl under the porch and set the bomb. Egghead fast-forwarded the recording, and about ten minutes after his arrival, the bomber reappeared and flashed his middle finger at the camera lens before jogging back down the driveway. They hadn't installed a camera at the end of the drive, but Marco knew that would be remedied sometime within the next few hours.

When the screen went blank, Marco turned his gaze to Ian's. "That could be anyone from sixteen to sixty, from this state or any other. Did Boomer find any signatures?"

The boss shook his head. "No. But they did find a partial print on a piece of electrical tape. Murdock's having it run through AFIS, so hopefully there's a match. He'll be stopping by in a little while for a copy of the video."

AFIS was the national Automated Fingerprint

Identification System. If their suspect had ever been fingerprinted for any reason, criminal or not, it should be in there. However, it could take minutes or hours for the system to kick out possible matches, and then those had to be double-checked by a technician. Even though the system was widely used across the United States, it did have a few faults. While there were millions of prints in the system, some smaller police agencies didn't have the manpower or resources to upload their prints, so some fell through the cracks or had long delays before they were entered.

The frustration Marco felt was evident in his voice. "So what the hell do we do now besides twiddle our fucking thumbs?"

It was kind of a rhetorical question since they all knew the answer, but Ian replied anyway. "We wait. And in the meantime, we keep Harper, Mara, and Mrs. Williams safe."

Jake's voice came over the speaker again. "Polo, while we were waiting for you, I called Kristen and asked if the girls could do a quick inspection of our apartment and change the sheets. You can put the baby's crib or whatever in Nick's office, and Harper and her mom can stay in the master bedroom. There's still no bed or mattress in the spare bedroom, but I asked Kristen to arrange for one to be delivered tomorrow, just in case. This way, they have the security of the compound, and it's nicer than the bunk rooms with the newbies staying up there."

His teammate was right. Marco wasn't sure what

Mara's sleep schedule was like yet, and he doubted the women would enjoy being woken up in the middle of the night if the Omega team members had to go anywhere. "Thanks. I appreciate it."

"No problem. Have the geek scan their handprints in for easy access. And, Ian, I'll contact Todd Wheeler. If there's any word on the street about a bomber, my snitch may have heard about it. Hang on a second." They waited a moment for Jake to come back on the line. "If you don't need me for anything else, my next applicant for an office assistant just walked in."

"Fine," their boss responded. "Check in later."

After the call disconnected, Marco placed his elbows on the table and leaned forward. "Okay. Now that the sleeping arrangements are settled, I think we have to get a list of the women Harper has helped through Friends of Patty."

"Absolutely not." All heads turned to the doorway where Harper stood with Dr. Trudy Dunbar behind her. And from the expression on her face, Harper was pissed at him... again. "There is no way anyone from the organization is turning over any list of names to you or anyone else—even with a federal warrant, I would fight it. So come up with another plan, because that is out of the question."

"Harper—"

"No, Marco. Just... no." She put her hands on her hips and glared at him. Damn, she was a mixture of sexy and delectable when she was mad. How come he'd never noticed that before?

Clearing his throat, Ian pointed to two empty chairs. "Ladies, please join us." As they walked toward the seats, he continued, "Teams, for those of you who haven't had the pleasure yet, this is Harper Williams, our principal target, and Dr. Trudy Dunbar, one of our consulting psychologists." He pointed at the new employees of Trident who were currently present. "This is Valentino Mancini, Lindsey Abbott, Cain Foster, and Tristan McCabe." The group acknowledged each other with either a "hello" or a nod of their head. "Now that everyone has been introduced, Harper, can you think of anyone who could be behind all this without breaking client/attorney privilege?"

Marco bit his tongue, crossed his arms, and leaned back in his chair—his gaze pinned on Harper. He wasn't going to argue with her in front of everyone, but, boy, was she in for it when he got her alone. His hand was twitching to get at her ass. *Shit.* He wished she was his submissive.

"Not off the top of my head, but it could be anyone from either my practice or the past four years I've been working with the organization. I'll have to go to my office and start looking through my files to see if anyone clicks. If there isn't an issue with confidentiality, I'll compile a list for you. But, as I said, it's not going to be a complete list. If it's a woman who we've helped disappear, I'm not going to name them under any circumstances. It would put the women and their children at risk, and then no others would trust us to help them if something happened."

If Ian hadn't sent him a "shut-up" glare, Marco would have said something that probably would have Harper pissed off at him even more than she already was. How could she put those other women over herself and their daughter? He glanced around the table and knew he had his answer. Harper was just like all the other women and men in the room. No sacrifice was too big or small when it came to protecting the lives of innocents. He sure as hell didn't like that Mara was in the middle of it all, but her mother was making sure she would be as safe as possible by putting her under the watchful eyes of the Trident teams. Harper was trusting them with her daughter's life, just as those women and children she'd helped had trusted her with their own lives.

"All right," Ian agreed. "We'll get you to your office tomorrow so you can give us something to start with. Maybe we'll get lucky between your list and the partial print." He paused. "What if this isn't work-related? Any ex-boyfriends we should be looking at? Anyone who was interested in being a boyfriend and you turned them down?"

In silence, Marco's jaw clenched at the questions, but his relief was immediate when Harper shook her head and answered, "No. I haven't dated anyone in over two years. And I can't think of anyone who I might have slighted by turning them down."

"Okay." The boss consulted some notes he'd made earlier on a yellow pad in front of him. "Back to your office for a minute. Is it possible to give your staff a couple of days off—at least until we get a better idea of what is going on? Or can they work from home?"

She nodded. "Yes, and thanks, I hadn't thought that my office could be targeted, too. I'll call my staff and make arrangements. They were able to reschedule things for the rest of the week, but I have court on Monday, if this goes on that long, and it's not a case I can hand off to anyone. I have to be there."

"No worries. We'll get you there, but we do it our way. If the team tells you to duck, you start quacking. Understood?"

"Understood."

Ian's gaze shifted to Dr. Dunbar. "Trudy, anything you'd like to add?"

The psychologist had her brunette hair pulled into a neat bun, and she pushed her glasses back to the bridge of her nose. "I came to support Harper and to see if I could help, but I'm not a criminal profiler, Ian, you know that. And even if I was, there's not much to go on yet."

"I was afraid you were going to say that, but it was worth a shot. I'll still get you copies of everything we have, though, as well as what Detective Murdock has. Maybe you'll see something we're missing." He rapped his knuckles twice on the wood table and began rattling off orders. "Okay. Here's the deal for now. Harper, Karen, and Mara will stay holed up here until we can figure out what this is all about. Devon will put together an updated schedule. I want at least six armed guards walking the compound at all times. Call Chase Dixon at Blackhawk and have his men fill in any gaps. Tiny—two armed men at the gate at all times, three during club hours. Mitch will shit a brick if we close the club again. Both gates stay shut unless letting someone through." The big man silently dipped his chin once in agreement while making a note on the pad in front of him. Devon and Ian's cousin, Mitch Sawyer, was the manager and third owner of the club but had nothing to do with the security business. "I'll call Mitch after this meeting and fill him in. Next, we'll see if the rest of the women here can keep their off-site activities to a minimum. I don't want a repeat of the past where the others became targets for some whack-job. Boomer, it's up to you about Kat. She's safe at the state PD headquarters, but if you want her escorted back and forth, let Devil Dog know. Omega Team, your training is on hold for now, but don't worry, you'll be making it up when this is over... double time."

Snorts and groans filled the room. Ian was a stickler for training, and while the newbies had a reprieve for now, they'd be sweating their asses off again soon enough.

"Cain, with your background, I want you with Marco anytime Harper has to leave the compound. McCabe, you're his partner. You'll be advised where you're going with enough time to plan escape routes if needed." The former Secret Service agent and the ex-Delta Force operative, respectively, had been training together for the past few months and made a great team. They were already able to anticipate their partner's thoughts and actions, something which would develop for the others over time. "For now, though, pull the ATVs out from the garage and make sure they're gassed up. I want the guards doing random sweeps of the woods surrounding the compound, day and night. Did I miss anything?"

Marco couldn't help but grin when Harper raised her hand like a school child. Apparently, Ian found it amusing as well because the corners of his mouth ticked upward. "You don't have to ask for permission, Harper. I don't bite anyone but my fiancée. What did we miss?"

"I need a lot of things from the house for Mara. Clothes, diapers, formula, toys, the works. And my briefcase should still be in my car."

"All right. Make a list, and Boomer and Knight can bring everything back with them. Plan for at least a few days, unless we get lucky with a suspect. Abbott and Mancini, head back to Harper's house for a few hours until Devon finishes the schedule and gets someone to relieve you." Ian stood. "Meeting adjourned. Doc, can I see you in my office for a minute? I need to talk to you about a few things."

While everyone headed out for their assignments, Marco and Harper followed Brody to his war-room where he scanned her hand into the security system. "Ask your mom to come over whenever she gets a chance, and I'll scan her in too."

"Thanks." She turned to Marco. "Can I have a pad and pen? The list is going to be long."

"Yeah. Let's go to my office. You can sit and write it out." *And I'll try to forget what it felt like to have you in my arms again.*

CHAPTER TEN

"You fucking idiot! That asshole you hired almost killed the wrong fucking person! This is twice you screwed up! How hard is it to kill that bitch and get the fucking kid? What the fuck am I paying you for?"

Randy Lairson rolled his eyes. He wouldn't risk it in person, but since the conversation was over the phone, he couldn't get in any trouble. Propping his feet on the ratty old ottoman in his apartment, he relaxed on the equally crappy sofa. Soon this would be all over and he'd get a nice payout for the job. Then he could get some nicer digs. "How was I supposed to know the kid wasn't there the other night? The lights were on in the house, and the bitch always parks in the garage. And you didn't tell me not to kill anyone else. What difference does it fucking make?"

"I don't give a crap if you kill anyone else, just not

the baby or DeAngelis. He's mine to deal with. Now, find a way to do it right and get me that fucking baby."

Before he could say anything else, the call disconnected. Lairson tossed his cell on the couch next to him and picked up the remote, turning the volume up on the TV again. There wasn't anything he could do right now. For a hundred bucks and some weed, his buddy was keeping an eye on the road to the compound where the bitch was holed up in. They couldn't get close to the place because it was heavily guarded. He'd have to wait until she went back to her office or something. Too bad the bomb hadn't worked. It would have been cool to watch the explosion from his hiding spot across the street and behind the neighbor's house. After he realized that it wasn't going to work, he'd cut through some trees and yards to a few streets over, where he'd stashed his car in the parking lot of a medical office.

His stomach growled at the same time the doorbell rang. The pizza he'd ordered arrived just as his marijuana-induced munchies were kicking in. *Life is good.*

A LITTLE AFTER SIX P.M., TWO AND A HALF HOURS AFTER the meeting was over, a human assembly line was set up to get everything upstairs to Nick and Jake's apartment. Brody had ended up driving his truck over to Harper's as well, since everything hadn't fit into Boomer's vehicle. Marco never realized how much stuff a baby needed—crib, playpen, bouncy thingy, swing, car seat, diapers, toys, monitor, food, clothes, clothes, and more clothes. Then there was everything Harper needed, which had been mostly clothes and toiletries. She'd asked Lindsey to go through her things, which he was happy about, since he didn't want any of the guys pawing through her intimates. Karen had made a list of what she needed as well, which Abbott and Mancini were currently retrieving for her, after being relieved from their post by two contract agents.

Once everything was settled, the only people left in the apartment were Marco, Harper, Karen, and little Mara, who was drinking from the bottle her grandmother was giving her. Harper was organizing Nick's office into a nursery, and Marco had just been in the way, so now he was sitting in a recliner, staring into space and trying to figure out why she was a target.

"Marco?"

Karen's calm voice startled him from his thoughts. "Huh? Something wrong?"

Cradling the baby in her arms, she stood from the couch. "No, nothing's wrong. Would you mind holding her for a few minutes? She's not done with the bottle yet, and I have to take my blood pressure medication. I'm getting a headache."

His eyes grew wide, and he tried to back away, which was impossible due to the recliner being remote controlled, as she leaned over and placed the precious bundle in his arms. For a man who had held dozens of different types of weapons and explosives, he had no idea how to hold a twelve-pound baby. Panic set in, almost as bad as it'd been when he'd been standing on the landmine. "W-wait a minute. I-I don't know a thing about—"

"*Shhh*. You'll do fine," she assured him. "Just hold her head in the crook of your arm and lay her across your lap. Yes, just like that. Hold the bottle upright, so she doesn't get any air. That's it. See, you're a natural. Just try to relax."

Holy shit! He was doing it. He hadn't dropped Mara, and she wasn't screaming her head off at him. Gazing in awe at his daughter, he tried to ease the tension in his shoulders, back, and arms. Everything would be fine as long as neither of them moved. If that happened, he was certain the initial terror he'd felt would return.

His mouth ticked upward as he watched her. The little sucking noises she was making were adorable. Her eyelids lifted, and she stared at him with eyes that matched his own. She was beautiful... just like her mother.

Karen stepped away, pulling him from his trance. "Why the turnaround? Two nights ago you wanted to castrate me."

She smirked. "You're still not out of the woods yet, but Harper convinced me you had no idea Mara existed. However, I'm still a tad pissed you got my daughter pregnant in the first place, but every time I look at my granddaughter, I forgive you a little more."

Leaving him sitting there, feeding the baby, she retreated to the master bedroom. It was a few minutes before Harper emerged from the office and stopped dead in her tracks when she noticed him. "Wow. There's a picture I'd never thought I'd see."

"Yeah, well, join the club." A sudden sensation made him pause. "Um... shit... I mean, I think she just... you know... down there."

Harper threw her head back and laughed. "Don't worry, that's what diapers are for. And it's probably just a few farts. She does that a lot when she eats."

Snorting, he looked at Mara. "Like father, like daughter, huh?"

Grabbing a piece of cloth from a nearby diaper bag, she strode toward him and placed it on his shoulder. "Now that you fed her, you get to learn how to burp her."

"Um... okay. What do I do?" It shouldn't be too hard, right? After all, burping was as natural as farting. He did it all the time.

Harper took the now empty bottle from him. "Put one hand behind her head, the other on her butt, and gently put her on your shoulder with the burp cloth under her." With awkward movements, he followed the instructions, then glanced up to see if he had done it right. "Yup, just like that. Now, rub her back in circles... uh-huh... you can rub a little harder than that until she lets out a loud one."

"Loud one, huh? *Jeez*, she really is my daughter."

After a few minutes of rubbing, sure enough, Mara

let out a healthy belch… along with a splash of formula. But Harper was still standing nearby and helped clean him, the recliner, and the baby before taking her from his arms. "She'll be asleep within a few minutes. I'll just put her in the crib."

"'Kay… um… I'm not sure what Jake and Nick have in the house in terms of food. What do you want to do for dinner? I could run to the store or order take-out."

With the baby on her shoulder, she headed for the hallway. "Actually, Kristen was nice enough to make extra of the chicken parmigiana and linguine she was making for Devon tonight. She said she'd call when it was ready, and you can run over to get it."

"That woman is a saint. I love her chicken parmigiana."

"That's what she said."

As she disappeared from sight, he was about to stand and check the pantry and fridge for drinks when his phone rang. *Ian.* He connected the call. "What's up?"

"Meet me out front. TPD has a suspect from the print." As usual, his boss hung up without further fanfare.

Damn, that was fast. He hadn't been expecting any matches, if they found one, until the morning.

Marco jumped up, grabbed his keys, and checked his lower back and rear pocket for his weapon and wallet. Satisfied he had everything, he hurried to the darkened, temporary nursery. Remembering the baby was falling asleep, he lowered his voice as Harper covered Mara with a pink blanket. "The police have a suspect. I'm heading over there with Ian. Stay inside. Call Cain if you need anything. He'll be posted outside." He'd programmed her phone with the numbers of all the team members, just to be on the safe side.

"Okay." She hesitated, then stepped toward him and put her arms around his waist, pulling him close. "Be careful, please."

Unable to resist, he hugged her back before placing a kiss on the top of her head. "I will. I'll call as soon as I know anything. Save some dinner for me."

Giving him a final squeeze, she let go, and her gaze met his. "Okay."

The urge to plunge his hands into her hair and kiss her senseless was strong, but this wasn't the time or the place. Besides, he didn't have the right to do it—she wasn't his. She'd only been his for a few hours over thirteen months ago and then had been gone when he'd awakened the next morning. He'd planned on calling that day to check on her, but then an urgent mission had come up, and by that afternoon, he'd been on a plane bound for Central America, where he'd remained for an entire month. He could've passed off the gig to one of the other guys, they all would've understood, but Marco had needed the distraction after Nina's death.

After returning from the mission and finding she hadn't left him any voice mail messages, he figured she'd either regretted the sex or wanted nothing to do with him. The morning after their night together, he'd sent her a quick text, telling her he'd be out of the country, but he'd been an ass and left it informal, not bringing up what had happened between them. While it had been one hell of a night, Harper was the type of woman who wouldn't settle for casual, and he didn't want anything more than that. After a few more months passed, he'd just assumed they'd gone back to where they had been before—two acquaintances, joined together because of one common denominator who was now deceased.

Now, forcing himself to leave, he rushed down the stairs and out to the parking lot where Devon, Brody, Tiny, and Boomer were waiting for him. As he turned to scan the area, checking to be sure the guards were all where they were supposed to be, Brody laughed behind him. "Dude! Next time you burp the kid, make sure you have an old shirt on... or a fucking rain poncho."

Grabbing his shirt and peering over his shoulder, he saw what everyone else had started chuckling about. Apparently, Mara hadn't gotten it all on the burping cloth and there was a disgusting formula stain on his back, which smelled even worse than it looked. How the hell had he not noticed it before? "Shit."

Pulling a clean T-shirt from the go-bag in his truck, Brody tossed it to Marco, who quickly changed, throwing the dirty shirt on the hood of his own vehicle. Ian exited the office building with his SUV keys in hand. "Murdock called. They've got the suspect holed up in an apartment over in Dunedin. Bomb squad is on their way and the PD is evacuating the rest of the building. They're worried about booby-traps and aren't taking any chances. Tiny, you hold down the fort. Lock it up tight. McCabe's inside on the cameras. Polo and Dev, you ride with me." He turned to the others and handed Brody a piece of paper and one of the company laptops. "You two follow. Let Boomer drive, and you get me everything you can on the suspect before we get there."

The geek took the stuff and nodded. "Got it."

Loading up, they headed out with Ian's SUV in the lead. As soon as they passed the guardhouse, the gates began to close again. Marco was confident the compound was secure. If anyone tried to gain entry, they'd be met with a hell of a lot of firepower and one very protective K9, who'd proven himself several times in the past.

With the evening traffic, it took close to thirty minutes to reach the address in Dunedin, northwest of Tampa. Ian and Boomer pulled into a supermarket parking lot just outside the blocked off street, and everyone hoofed it to the closest uniformed officer who contacted Murdock for them. The detective hurried over a few minutes later and lifted the "Do Not Cross—Crime Scene" tape for them to duck under.

Ian shook his hand. "Anything yet?"

"Not much. Like I told you, name's Grant Rodgers. The print tech is ninety-five percent certain he's the match to the partial. White male, 28 years old. He's lived here for the past two years. Been in and out of the system since he was fifteen—mostly misdemeanors and one felony for possession and use of a stolen credit card. Served thirteen months in prison for that four years ago. Nothing in his rap-sheet to indicate he's into bombs, but maybe he just got lucky and this was the first we're hearing about it." That was pretty much what Brody had dug up on the suspect on the way to the scene, but the rest of them knew he'd be trying to find out a lot more when he returned to his war-room. Murdock turned and started walking back the way he'd come from, with the team on his heels. "It's the Sheriff Department's call with TPD's bomb squad. They've cleared out the entire apartment complex—sixteen units total—as well as the buildings surrounding it. Rodger's windows are covered, so we don't have eyes on him yet. Phone calls are going unanswered. His car is in the parking lot, and there's music playing in his apartment. Neighbors say he always has the radio on when he's home and turns it off when he goes out."

The detective stopped next to the bomb squad's van and Sgt. Templeton, who nodded at them. "You guys are keeping me busy this week." He gestured toward the building. "Apartment's on the third floor. Third and fourth windows from the left. Mendoza's up there with the Sheriff's entry team. With the radio blasting and covering any noise, they're drilling a hole from the empty apartment next door through to his living room. Then they'll snake in a camera to try to see if there are any booby-traps."

"Heat signatures?" Ian asked, standing with his arms crossed and feet shoulder-width apart.

"None detected. If it looks clear, we'll go up the fire escape and in through the window." Even if the door looked clear from the camera's view, bombers were known to have sophisticated triggers which could be tripped, setting off an explosion designed to maim or kill anyone near the blast. It was less likely the windows on a third-floor unit would be rigged and, using a glass cutter, they could avoid disturbing the wood frame.

All around them, police radios squawked, before the voice of one of the officers inside came over. "Camera's going in."

Everyone held their breaths, waiting silently for the next update. Seconds ticked by.

"Unit 249 to Unit 205, we've got a male D.B. on the living room floor. No signs of triggers or traps. You can take the window."

"Fuck!" Marco put his hands on his hips and fought the urge to hit something… or someone. "D.B." was police speak for a dead body. Chances were Rodgers had been offed by someone, committed suicide, or overdosed, if he was a user. It was highly improbable that a twenty-eight-year-old suspect had died of natural causes just before the police came to bring him in for questioning.

It was another twenty minutes before one of the other members of the bomb squad climbed through a large hole which had been made in the living room window. And another ten minutes passed before Mendoza let his sergeant know that they had opened the apartment's door and all was clear.

"Can you send me a pic of the D.B.?" the supervisor asked over the secure radio channel. They all wanted to see if it matched the mug shot of Rodgers that Brody had on his laptop.

"Yeah. Give me a sec. He's face up. Looks like he was stabbed several times and got his throat slit. My guess is three to four hours ago, but need the ME to confirm. By the way, there's a Frankenstein mask in here, and plans and evidence of the bomb from Clearwater laying right out in the open."

Ian glanced at Marco with a hint of worry. Yeah, they'd found their bomber, but someone had beaten them to him. So now they were back to square one. No suspects and a still unknown motive. "He was probably hired out and then killed, because either the bomb didn't work, or he could lead us to whoever wants Harper dead."

Rage boiled within Marco's veins because he couldn't beat the hell out of the dead guy for information. "Fuck!"

MARCO GLANCED AT HIS WATCH WHILE TRUDGING UP THE stairs to Nick and Jake's apartment. Twelve-forty-eight in the morning. *Jeez.* He'd called Harper earlier to tell her what had happened so she wouldn't worry when she saw the "Breaking News" on TV. As usual, the media would broadcast what they'd scrambled to find out, even if the information wasn't entirely accurate. They tended to act first to scoop other reporters and then backtrack and apologize later, if necessary. He wanted to make sure she knew everyone was all right... well, except the dead bomber.

At the top of the stairs, he placed his hand on the scanner, and when the light turned green, he pushed open the door to the apartment. Hopefully, the two women and baby were asleep by now and would stay that way. Instead of going to his own home, he opted to sleep here on the couch. Too bad the guys hadn't gotten around to adding a spare bed for the third bedroom yet, but that would be fixed by tomorrow night.

Silence and a note on the coffee table greeted him.

M— Hi. Hope you're not too tired. I left a dinner plate in the fridge for you. Just reheat. See you in the morning. H—

He smiled. It felt weird coming home to something like this. Nina was the only person who'd ever left him a note about dinner before now.

He'd just pivoted toward the kitchen when an unfamiliar noise caused him to freeze. Just as it registered in his brain, it got louder. *Shit!* Mara was crying.

Hurrying into the office, he found Harper had installed a nightlight, making it easier for him to see. The cries increased in volume, and he flipped off the baby monitor to keep her from waking the two women sleeping in the master bedroom. Peeking into the crib, he found Mara red-faced with wet eyes, opening her mouth to let out another wail. "*Shhh,*" he crooned. "Hush, sweetheart. No crying now. We don't want to wake your momma or grandma."

She paused mid-cry and stared up at him, obviously unsure what to make of him interrupting her nighttime routine. Her cries began to alternate with softer whimpers as he leaned a bit closer and took a hesitant whiff. "Oh, crap."

He gagged and waved a hand in front of his nose because his statement was meant both figuratively and literally. His first thought was to get Harper, but he decided against it. She needed a good night's sleep after what she'd been through the past few days.

"Okay. I don't suppose you know how to talk me through changing your diaper, do you? Should I call Uncle Brody? No, he'll laugh at me and bust my chops." He snapped his fingers, which drew her attention, then pulled his cell from his pocket. "YouTube. There's got to be a video of this on YouTube, right? Right."

He brought the website up on his smartphone and quickly searched diaper changing. Several videos came up, and he picked one where the baby was wearing pink. Mara was still sniffling but remained focused on the video as Marco held it up so they could both see it. After running through it once, then twice, he looked at her and asked, "So, what do you think? Between you, me, and social media, think we can get you into a clean diaper? I'm game if you are. Let's give it a shot, all right? Hang on a sec."

Sorting through the supplies Harper had set up neatly on the desk, he found a new diaper, baby wipes, and a changing pad. He set it all up on the floor, for lack of any other place to do it in the room—this would also ensure Mara couldn't roll off something and fall. Her cries began to escalate once more just as he turned to get her. "*Shhh*. None of that. I've got you."

She calmed a little as he picked her up and placed her on the floor with the pad under her. As he knelt, a quick thought popped into his head. Grabbing his phone again, he brought up his music playlist and searched for something that would be soothing to her. Choosing "Rhiannon" by Fleetwood Mac, he lowered the volume and set the phone next to Mara's head. Convinced his daughter was satisfied with his choice of music, he returned to the task at hand. With suddenly clumsy fingers, he pulled the tiny zipper of the pink sleeper down her torso and leg, then grimaced. "Whoa, that's one nasty-smelling poop you did, little girl."

After removing the pajamas, he unsnapped the white onesie. Her little legs kicked as he pulled the tabs of the diaper. He immediately tucked his face into his upper arm and gagged for a moment when the strong odor intensified ten-fold. "Whoa! Shit! I mean... holy cow, girl! Ugh!" Despite his surprise, watering eyes, and curling nose at the mess and stench, he somehow managed to keep his voice down. "*Jeez*, your Uncle Brody wasn't freaking kidding. Yucky poo-poo."

He grabbed a few wipes, then wrapped a hand around both her ankles and gently lifted her legs until her butt was off the dirty diaper. Sliding it from under her and to the side, he shook his head. *How the hell could someone so tiny shit this fucking much?*

It took more wipes than he expected, but he finally got her baby-soft skin nice and clean. With one hand still holding her up, he used his other hand and teeth to spread the new diaper wide, then placed it underneath her. Folding it around her hips like the video had shown, his fingers fumbled with the tabs. Meanwhile, Mara smiled and giggled, a few bubbles escaping her tiny lips. "Like that, huh? I don't blame you. All fresh and showroom new. Not that you're going to be showing your tush off to anyone if I have a say about it —which I do. But we'll discuss that when you're a lot older, okay?"

Jeez, if the guys heard me now, they'd be slinging some serious jokes.

It took longer to get her onesie and pajamas back on than it had getting them off since she was now happily thrashing all four limbs, but somehow, he managed it. Throwing the used wipes into the diaper, he rolled it up into a ball. "This is going in the garbage in the kitchen, and then that's going out the front door, little girl, because this stuff is toxic."

"You did that very well."

Harper's voice had him glancing over his shoulder. "Hi. How long have you been there? You could've lent a hand, you know."

"You were pretty much done when I got here. I would've stepped in to help if needed. How'd you learn to do that?" Dressed in a blue silk pajama set, she walked in and bent down to lift Mara as he reached up and put the package of wipes back on the desk.

Standing, he grabbed his phone and held it up for her to see. "YouTube."

Harper grinned, then started chuckling, which had Mara giggling again. "I should have known. Did you just get in?"

"Yeah, and I'm starving."

Carrying the baby, she headed out the door. "Then come on. You can eat while she does too."

Surprisingly, he was looking forward to sharing a meal with his daughter.

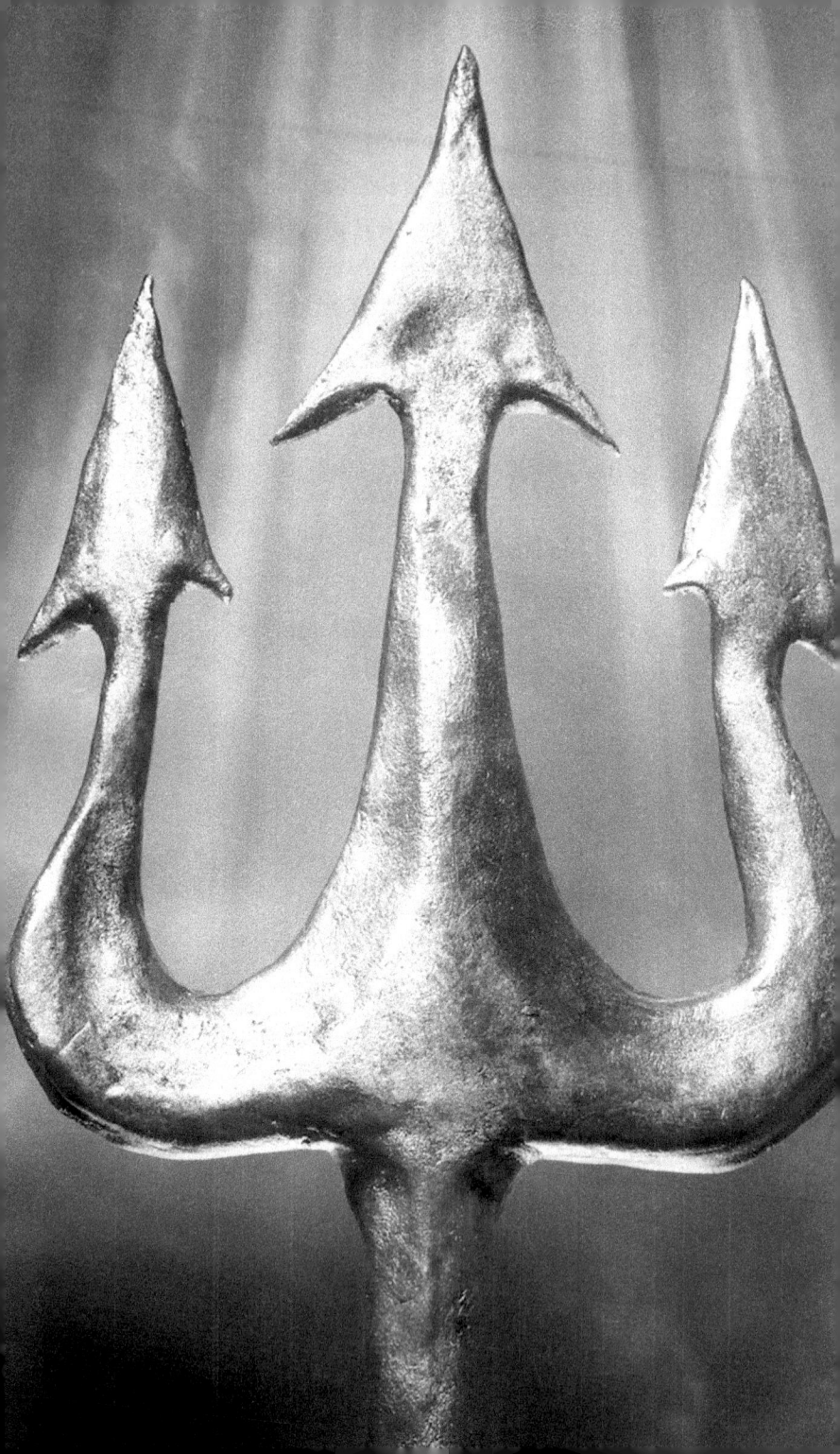

CHAPTER ELEVEN

When a wave of nausea overtook Kristen, she threw the covers off and ran for the bathroom. She'd heard all about morning sickness, but this was her first bout of it as she hugged the porcelain god. In between her retching, she heard Devon walk in behind her. "Pet, what's wrong? Okay, stupid question, you're obviously sick to your stomach."

Straddling her naked hips and thighs, he pulled her hair out of her way and rubbed her back. "Easy, sweetheart."

"Ugh. Tell that to my stomach." She barely managed to get the retort out before her stomach rebelled again. It had been five whole days since she'd found out she was pregnant, and she still hadn't found the right time to tell Devon. Between the club, Trident's caseload, protecting Harper, Mara, and Karen, and having a conniption about her ex-husband's lawsuit, it had been a rough and busy week for him. Besides, she'd been trying to devise a unique way to tell him and finally put a plan together. She would do it this morning, just as soon as her stomach settled.

It was another few minutes before the rolling nausea subsided, and with Devon's help, she stood, washed her face, and brushed her teeth. Her sweet husband wrapped one arm around her waist and held her arm while escorting her back to bed.

"Climb in and let me see if there's any of that ginger ale left in the pantry from when Shelby was going through her chemo. It should help settle your stomach." Shelby Whitman, soon-to-be Christensen, had started as one of her beta readers for her novels and then became a good friend. Thanks to her, Kristen had gone to The Covenant for research before falling in love with one of its owners. Now cancer-free, the blonde pixie was planning her own wedding to her Dom, Parker.

"Can I get you anything else?" He retrieved one of his T-shirts from the dresser, then pulled it over her head, holding open the sleeves so she could put her arms through the holes. She loved it when he was in tender Dom mode.

Relaxing back against her pillow, she gave him a small smile. "There are some saltines in there too. Can you grab some?" Harper had told her to make sure she had some in the house for when the morning sickness started, and she was so glad she'd picked a box up yesterday while grocery shopping.

After pulling the covers over her legs and torso, Devon leaned forward and kissed her forehead. "You bet I can. I'll be right back."

Watching his still-naked backside exit their bedroom, she sighed. Damn, the man had a fine, tight ass.

She opened her nightstand drawer when she was sure he was out in the kitchen. Sitting inside was the small box she'd wrapped last night with leftover *Happy Birthday* paper from his presents last week. Taking it out, she placed it on his side of the bed.

It was a few minutes before he returned and handed her a glass of ginger ale with a bit of ice and set a plate of crackers on her nightstand. While she sipped the soda, he noticed the box next to her. "What's that?"

"Oh, just one of your presents I forgot to give you for your birthday. Open it."

Rolling his eyes, he circled the bed, picked up the package, and climbed in on his side, lying beside her. "You got me more than enough, Pet, and I loved it all— especially the new toys." He waggled his eyebrows at her. "But you didn't have to get me anything else."

She tried to hide her excitement and impatience. "I know. But I saw this and couldn't resist. Open it."

"Couldn't resist, huh?" Sitting up again, he placed a pillow behind his back and leaned against the headboard.

Watching him methodically open the paper, she was ready to take it back from him and rip it off because he was going so slow. Worried her glass of soda would go flying in a minute, she put it next to the plate beside her. After the wrapping was gone, Devon lifted the top of the box and stared at the contents in confusion, just as she'd hoped. "Um, two shotgun shells? What…"

She put her hand on his arm and kept her gaze on his face, wanting to see the moment he got it. "Well, I figure, if it's a boy, you can teach him to shoot… if it's a girl, you can use them to scare away her boyfriends *and* teach *her* to shoot."

"If it's a…" His words came out slow and unsure, but then his eyes flew open wider than she'd ever seen them. "Holy shit! Ho-ly… are you kidding me? You're not kidding me. Please, say you're not kidding me. You're… you're… we're having a… a baby?"

Grinning, she bobbed her head up and down. "Yes, we're having a baby!"

"I'm gonna be a… oh my God, I'm gonna be a dad!" He grabbed the covers and tore them off her body, staring at her abdomen, which was still not showing signs of her pregnancy. Pushing up the T-shirt he'd put her in, he placed a trembling hand on the soft swell she'd never been able to get rid of, no matter how much she tried in yoga class with Angie and Kat. "W-when? How far along are you?"

She covered his hand with her own, using her finger to rub his simple, gold wedding band. "About seven weeks. We'll get a better idea after my first sono-gram next Wednesday."

"So we have about, what… seven and a half months until we meet him or her?" He leaned over and kissed the back of her hand, then moved both his and her hands out of the way before putting his lips on her abdomen. "You just made me the happiest man in the world, Pet. You'll be beautiful carrying our baby and the best mama there ever was or will be." Shifting, he tilted his head upward. "Kiss me, my baby-mama."

"With pleasure, my baby-daddy." She bent down, letting him take possession of her mouth until they were both breathless.

With obvious reluctance, he pulled away. "As much as I want to rock your world right now, I think we should wait until your morning sickness passes. It is morning sickness, right?'

"Yes, I think so. Today is the first day I've had it."

"Then have your ginger ale and crackers while I wrap my brain around this." He ran a hand through his sleep-mussed hair. "Holy shit, we have to call my folks and yours. They're going to be so excited. The first official grandkid on both sides." Kristen was an only child, and none of the Sawyer brothers had started families yet, even though Jenn called Devon's mother and father Grandpa Chuck and Grandma Marie.

Nibbling on a cracker, she retook his hand. "I've been thinking about this since I got the news. If it's a boy, I want to name him John."

Devon stared at her in shock for a moment, then her big, bad Dom's eyes filled, and he began to cry. Horror smacked her right in the face. "Oh my God, Devon. I'm sorry. I just thought—"

He placed his hands on her cheeks and pulled her

toward him, settling his mouth over hers. It was a tender kiss, salted by his tears, and it almost broke her heart. She thought he would like to name the baby after the brother he'd lost many years ago. Devon had been a freshman at college when high-school senior John, a closet alcoholic, had died of alcohol poisoning. Devon had John's initials and dates of birth and death tattooed on his left chest.

He broke their kiss and wiped his wet eyes while still cupping her cheek with his other hand. "*Shhh*, Pet. You didn't do anything wrong—far from it. I'm sorry if you thought differently. I love you and that you want to name the baby John if it's a boy. I couldn't think of a better name. It just hit me all at once."

Sighing in relief, she turned her head to kiss his palm. "My fault. I should have given you a little time to adjust. We don't have to commit to any names yet."

"Nope. If it's a boy, it'll be John Devon Sawyer. But what if it's a girl?"

She was about to answer, but as a wave of nausea hit her again, she slammed her hand over her mouth, leaped from the bed, and made a beeline to the bathroom. Devon was right behind her, pulling her hair back once more as her retching commenced. "That's okay, Pet. We can think of a girl's name later."

SQUATTING IN FRONT OF THE OUTDOOR REFRIGERATOR IN *Ian's Oasis*—as the "backyard" of the compound had been dubbed—Marco slid bottles of beer and soda onto the bottom shelves. Around ten this morning, Kristen and Dev had decided to hold an afternoon barbecue for everyone since the eighty-seven-degree temperature was unseasonably warm for the beginning of February, even for Tampa.

The outdoor kitchen was filling up with enough food to feed the small army they were expecting—both Trident teams and their family and friends, in addition to the extra contract guards still roaming the compound. Harper, Kat, Angie, and Kristen were sorting through grocery bags, putting things in bowls, or leaning over him to store perishables on the upper shelves. Parker, Tiny, and Mitch were stacking some firewood Parker had brought with him for the fire pit for when the expected cooler weather rolled in later in the evening. On the far end of the area Angie had designed for her fiancé, where the koi pond was with its waterfall, sat Karen and Boomer's parents, Rick and Eileen Michaelson. In another sitting area, Jenn, Shelby, and Alyssa Wagner, the Michaelsons' charge, took turns holding and entertaining a giggling Mara. Beau and Parker's dog, Spanky, a huge bullmastiff, were at their feet, watching the tiny new addition to their group of favorite humans. Others would be arriving shortly.

It had been days since Rodgers had been found dead in his apartment. There had been enough evidence at the crime scene to say with certainty that the long-time criminal had been the person who'd planted the bomb at Harper's. Unfortunately, that was all they were able to confirm. Who he'd been working with or for and the motive behind the attacks on Harper were still a mystery. The team had been working with the police, trying to come up with a suspect from the list Harper had given them after going through her files the other day. To Marco's exasperation, though, she was still refusing to provide them with any names from her Friends of Patty cases, which had resulted in a "disappearance." She'd only given them a few names of the women who still lived in the area, with their permission, and their abusive husbands or boyfriends who were behind bars for a long time. He understood her refusal to turn over the other names, even though it was frustrating as hell.

As for how things were going between the two of them, that was just as maddening for him. Being around Mara all the time now had been a bit of an eye-opener for him. He no longer panicked when she needed to be fed, changed, or just held. She was definitely growing on him... and so was her mother. But things between Harper and him seemed to be in some sort of holding pattern. There was no denying the attraction was still there, but their lifestyles were so different. Could he change? He wasn't sure. Did she even want him to change? Again, that was an unknown. After the threat against her was taken care of, maybe he'd sit down and examine if there could be some sort of compromise between them. Until then, he'd continue sleeping on the new bed in Jake and Nick's spare room and taking cold showers.

Finished stocking the fridge, Marco stood and glanced up to see Will Anders, Kristen's cousin, and Kayla and Roxy London joining the group in the backyard. He was surprised when Kayla squealed upon spotting Harper putting some snacks on one of the tables and pulled her into a hug. "Harper! Oh my God, girl! You look amazing. I haven't seen you since we left Heat and joined here. Do you still go there?"

Marco froze. *What the fucking hell? Harper had been to Heat? Oh, no, no, no, and fuck no!* He had to have heard wrong with all the other chatter going on—Heat was the second-most-popular private BDSM club in Tampa, behind The Covenant. *Harper in a fetish club?* He was about to clear out his ear with a finger when he spotted her guilty-as-hell expression as she glanced over her shoulder at him. Turning away again, she hugged Kayla's wife and then excused herself, hurrying back over to where the other women were preparing salads and sides to go with the barbecue, obviously hoping he would ignore what he'd just heard.

Oh, hell, no.

Checking to see that Mara was being taken care of by Jenn and Alyssa, he strode over to the outdoor kitchen and wrapped his hand around Harper's bicep. "May I have a word with you, Harper—in private?"

She paled a little and bit her bottom lip. "Um, I'm helping get the food ready. Maybe later?"

"It may have sounded like a request, but consider it

an order." He purposely dropped his voice an octave, causing Kristen, Kat, and Angie to stop what they were doing and look at him in surprise. It was apparent none of them had heard Kayla's announcement, but they knew his tone well from the club. It was the tone of a Dom who wasn't going to take no for an answer.

For a split second, it appeared Harper would argue with him before she relented and gave him a slight nod. She glanced over her shoulder as he led her toward the parking lot.

"Don't worry," he reassured her through gritted teeth. "Mara is being well taken care of and spoiled rotten. I'd be worried about yourself right now if I were you."

She tugged against his moderate grip, but he refused to let go. "Where are we going?"

"Somewhere where we can talk in private." *And where I can flog your ass...*

Marco didn't say another word as he marched her across the lot, through the inside gate, and then up the stairs to the club. Placing his hand on the security scanner, he waited for the click signaling the door had unlocked, pulled it open, and escorted Harper into the lobby. But he didn't stop there. A few moments later, he had her downstairs in the pit and, finally, came to a standstill next to one of the spanking benches, whirling her around so she was facing him. Her downcast eyes and the fact that she wasn't taking in what should be unfamiliar surroundings, filled with an array of BDSM equipment and implements, told him he wasn't mistaken. Harper was a submissive in the lifestyle. How the hell had he missed that all these years? Sure, they never hung out together unless Nina was with them... *holy shit!* "Please tell me Nina wasn't in the lifestyle."

Startled, her gaze met his stern one. "What? Because she was your sister, she wasn't allowed to enjoy the benefits of a Dom/submissive relationship?"

"No! Yes!" He let go of her upper arm and ran the hand through his hair in frustration. "I mean... yes, she was allowed to do whatever she wanted, but I'll be upset if she hid it from me. She knew I was a Dom and what that meant, but she always told me it wasn't for her."

"Calm down. She wasn't a submissive or in the lifestyle at all."

A flash of relief went through him before he focused on the real issue at hand. Crossing his arms, he frowned. "But you are."

Her gaze dropped to his chest. It had been a statement, not a question, but she responded anyway. "Yes."

"Why didn't you ever say anything to me?"

She didn't answer, and while he would usually let the silence continue until a sub began to squirm and felt compelled to talk, he couldn't wait that long. "Answer me, Harper. Why?"

"Because... damn it!" She threw her hands in the air. "Because I was afraid you would want to play... and then I was afraid you wouldn't want to play. I was attracted to you, but while I wanted a husband, in addition to a Dom, you'd made it clear on several occasions, to both Nina and me, that a wife and kids were out of the question. I was afraid if we played, I…" She turned her head away, and her voice dropped to a whisper. "I was afraid I would fall in love with you, and I couldn't take that risk."

Tears spilled over and ran down her cheeks, and Marco wanted to kick his own ass. How the hell had he been so stupid and blind? It would never have worked between them, but at least he could've nipped her insecurities in the bud. Or maybe he couldn't have.

Fuck! Part of him was thrilled at this revelation, while the other part was scared shitless. Was it because of their past, and not just their mutual attraction, that the urge to top her was so strong? To be her one and only? Was it because of the permanent connection they now had to each other in the form of a child? A child who was growing on him every time he came in contact with her. Maybe this could work. Perhaps he could do the right thing—and reap the benefits of it— without feeling trapped in a relationship he never expected to be in. But she'd already turned down his offer to get married and made it clear that she would only marry for love. Did he love her? Shit, he wasn't sure. He cared for her, yes, but what the hell did he know about love? Of course, he'd loved his sister, but that wasn't the same. And what about what Harper was feeling? She hadn't said she was in love with him, only that she was afraid she *could* fall in love with him.

"Maybe we should give this a shot?"

Returning her gaze to his, her brow furrowed in confusion. "Give what a shot? What the hell are you talking about?"

"You and I. Maybe I was wrong. Maybe there's something between us besides the sexual attraction. I honestly don't know, Harper, but the more time I spend with you—and with Mara—the less I want to walk away after we find out what's going on and put an end to the threat. I'm... I'm just scared, I guess." *What the hell? Where the fuck had that come from?*

She placed her hand on his forearm, her eyes filled with concern and bewilderment. "Scared of what? Me? Mara?"

Desperate to touch her, to get closer to her, he cupped her chin with both hands and silently urged her to take a step forward. "I'm scared I don't know what the fuck I'm doing. I'm scared because I have no idea how to be a father... or a husband. I have no role models. How do you know I won't fuck this up? I'm terrified I'm going to do something wrong... something that would harm Mara or you. Not physically... thank God that wasn't something Nina and I had to deal with growing up. Only neglect. But what if I'm such a horrible father that Mara grows to hate me?"

"Marco..." She closed and opened her mouth again, taking a moment to gather her thoughts. "What do you think makes a good father?"

"What do you mean?"

"I mean, if you could conjure up the ideal father you would've loved to have had growing up, what would he have been like? I'm sure you had dreams of one before you became jaded."

Needing a minute to think about it, he took her hand and stepped over to a wingback chair in a nearby conversation and after-care area. Sitting, he pulled her down on his lap, encircling her hips with his arms. Communication was a huge part of the lifestyle he'd participated in for years, but usually, he was on the listening end. Many subs came to him for advice, comfort, or a sympathetic ear. He didn't know exactly why they were drawn to him, but over the years, he found he enjoyed being needed, and he'd become good at being a Dom the subs could trust with their troubles and trepidations.

But this time, the shoe was on the other foot, and the ordinarily confident Dom needed to trust someone else with his fears. If he were honest with himself, he'd admit seeing his teammates find their significant others had him wondering what it would be like to have someone permanent in his life. Someone to grow old with. Someone to love and who loved him back.

He had to try to open up and trust someone with his heart. Well, not just someone. He didn't want just any woman—he wanted Harper. And not just physically—although there was no denying he wanted to be inside her as often as possible—but he was getting used to her being around all the time again. Like when the two of them had devoted all their spare time to caring for Nina. He suddenly realized the silence nearly driving him crazy the nights he'd been home alone those first few weeks after returning from his mission wasn't only because Nina was suddenly gone, but Harper had been gone too. *Damn, Nina must be laughing her ass off in the afterlife right now.*

Clearing his throat, he adjusted her on his lap to give his growing erection some room. He couldn't help it—the feel of her lush bottom, so close to his cock, was making it impossible to ignore how much he wanted to bend her over a spanking bench and take her from behind. He pushed the thought from his mind and concentrated on answering her question. "I don't know. I guess a father who was always there when I needed him. You know, took me to ballgames, played catch on a Saturday morning, taught me how to fish... how to be a man. Someone who taught me what it was like to be loved—someone I could admire." He paused and swallowed the sudden lump threatening to block his next words. "Someone who took the burden of me having to grow up so quickly in order to take care of Nina."

"Oh, Marco." Harper reached up and caressed his cheek as he leaned into her touch. "I think Mara would love to have a father to take her to ballgames, play catch, and teach her to fish. She also needs a man to show her how a woman is supposed to be treated so she knows what to look for in the men she'll date someday. Someone she can look up to and respect because he's a good man. He doesn't have to be perfect because that's unrealistic—nobody's perfect. As long as she knows she can go to him when she needs comfort or help with a problem… or a burden… then I think she'll have a damn good father."

It hit Marco dead in the face. Carter had been right. Whatever made him a good Dom, who the subs came to in their time of need, could be channeled into parenthood. Nothing would change the fact he was now a *father*, but honestly, he already had the skills to be a *dad* like the one he'd wished for as a child. Realistically, no one was prepared for raising a child—it was something you learned as you went. Trial and error. Could he do this? Could he seriously be the primary male figure in his daughter's life? Images of Mara and him experiencing the milestones of her life—big and small—flooded his mind. Her first steps. The first day of school. Teaching her to ride a bicycle, fish, and anything else she was interested in. Helping with her homework. Showing her how to defend herself against the creeps in this world. Watching as some snot-nosed kid took her to the prom after Marco warned him what would happen if the boy didn't treat her right. Her wedding day.

He didn't realize tears had begun to roll down his cheek until Harper brushed them away with her thumb. "I want to…" Damn, there was that lump in his throat again. "I want to try. No… not try. I want to be Mara's father. In every sense of the word. I'm sure I'll fuck up along the way, but I hope it won't be often." He cupped her chin. "But I want the package deal, Harper."

Her eyes narrowed. "Package deal?"

"You, Mara, and me. A family. I want it all."

Before she could say no, he pulled her face toward his and took possession of her mouth. Now that he was in for the long haul, it was time to convince her he wouldn't settle for less than everything he never knew he wanted.

CHAPTER TWELVE

Harper's eyes fluttered shut, and every thought of why this was a lousy idea flew from her brain as their lips touched. As much as she had dreaded this moment since Marco had reentered her life, she had dreamt of it too—for so much longer. And now her reasons for keeping him at arm's length seemed to have disappeared. He was willing to try to see where this went between them. The key to the locked armor she'd wrapped around her heart to protect it from him slid into place. Now, it was only a matter of time before she knew if she could let him turn the key and free her. Everything she knew about the man said she could trust him with her mind, body, and soul, but only if Marco knew it himself. Once he realized he was the good man his friends and she knew he was, it would be possible for him to fall in love and let her fall in return.

His hand snaked up into her hair, tightening and pulling the strands just to the edge of being painful.

She gasped against Marco's mouth, and he took full advantage of it, plunging his tongue between her opened lips. He tilted her head to the side to give himself better access to taste, tease, and torment her with everything he had. A moan from deep inside her escaped when his other hand found her breast and massaged it through her thin T-shirt. A thought popped into her brain—she wished she'd put on a sexier bra today. After giving birth, her breasts remained fuller than their original size, so she'd had to purchase new bras to accommodate their girth, and since she hadn't been out to impress anyone, she'd picked up only drab, practical ones. At least she wasn't wearing one of the nursing bras she'd used at first. Then again, easy access at this point wouldn't be a bad thing.

Shifting, she brought her legs up to straddle him, grinding her pelvis against his erection and giving him access to both breasts. He didn't disappoint, grabbing her shirt and pulling it over her head. She hadn't needed to worry about the bra since he never even saw it as he popped the catch and dragged the garment off her body. Tugging on her hair, he left her mouth, trailing kisses and nibbles down her jaw, neck, shoulders, and chest. Cupping her left breast, he lifted it as his mouth closed around her flesh, and she cried out at the electricity that shot through her entire body. The moist, wet heat of his tongue on her nipple was replaced with cool air as Marco blew on it, causing the center to extend toward him. He moved to the other nipple and gave it the same treatment.

"Beautiful," he whispered, sounding almost in awe. "You don't know how much I want to clamp your nipples right now. But these beauties deserve ones with jewels on them."

He closed his teeth around one of the taut peaks and sucked. She couldn't control her response if she wanted to. As she cried out again, her hands dove into his hair and held his head in place. She knew what she was doing was wrong—topping from the bottom or trying to control the scene playing out—but they hadn't taken the step of negotiations yet. She hoped he would forgive her indiscretion… or maybe it would be better if he didn't. She was certain any punishment Master Marco doled out to his submissives would eventually result in something that would repeatedly drive her over the brink of insanity.

His hands went around to her back and caressed the soft skin he found there. Releasing her nipple, he pulled his head back, forcing her to ease her grip so he could look up at her with eyes heavy with desire. "How long, baby? How long have you been in the lifestyle?"

Trying to catch her breath, she twirled his soft black hair with her fingers. "Since college."

"Tell me more," he ordered as he kissed her collar-bone. "How'd you start?"

"Our second year, one of our housemates took Nina and me to a munch, and I felt like I found a home, you know?" Oh, yeah, he knew. Munches were get-togethers for people interested in the lifestyle. It gave them an opportunity to talk to experienced Doms and subs without diving headfirst into play. He often saw that "found-a-home" look in newbies' eyes when they realized they were more normal than they'd thought. "Nina said it wasn't for her, but she supported my need to learn more about it. I think it was our senior year when you told her you were a Dom. Of course, she told me since we told each other everything."

His thumbs came to her front and brushed against her ribs. "And yet, she didn't tell me about you, which, in hindsight, I would have reamed her if she had. Privacy and all that. So, was any Dom lucky enough to catch your eye for a long period of time? Any relationships?"

Nodding, she tried to focus on answering him and not on what he was doing to her flesh. "A few. I usually dated a Dom before I played with him. My longest relationship was two years, but in the end, we both realized forever wasn't meant to be. We just grew apart, and soon, play was the only thing we really had in common. I don't have to ask you the same question since Nina knew you never had a long relationship with anyone—sub or not."

"The longest one was about five months, and that was years ago. I never introduced the woman to Nina. I knew it wasn't forever, so why bother to get either of their hopes up?" He shrugged, and she wondered why he suddenly wanted to talk instead of putting his mouth to better use... or at least, a more pleasurable use. His eyes met hers. "I want you, Harper." His hips flexed toward her, showing her just *how much* he wanted her. "There's no denying that. But last time, we put the proverbial cart before the horse. So, this time, I want to take you out... on a date before I take you to my bed. Can we do that? I've never courted a woman before, and it feels wrong not to this time. I can't believe I'm saying this with you half-naked in my lap, but I'm asking you to get dressed. I'm sure Jenn would love to help your mother babysit, and they'll be perfectly safe here with the team. I want to take you out to dinner tonight and romance you..." He raised his brow and chuckled. "And then I want to pick up where we're leaving off... *after* you've completed a limit list, so I know what toys to bring along."

She smiled at his teasing. Clearly, this was important to him. As much as she wanted to jump his bones at the moment, she gave in to his request. "I'd be honored to go on a date with you, but do you think it's safe?"

"It should be, but I'll have two of the Omega team tail us until we get back to my house. We'll be perfectly safe there with the geek's security system installed. Well, I'll be perfectly safe... you, however, will be at my mercy."

Heaven help her! And now he was going to leave her like this... wanting... needing. Maybe a little nudge...

Shifting her hips one more time, she moaned when her clit rubbed against the hard bulge in his jeans.

Clutching her ass, he stilled her movements. "You're killing me here, sweetheart. When was the last time you had an orgasm?"

"Before the baby was born." Even she could hear the yearning in her voice. "About a month before."

"Seriously? You haven't gotten off in over six months?"

His wide eyes and the incredulous statement made her giggle. "Um... yeah. Dealing with an infant while working full time tends to be a tad tiring."

"Shit. Well, let's see what we can do about that." He turned her body until she was sitting sideways on his lap again. Tugging on the string at the top of her stylish sweatpants, he undid the knot and then slid his hand under the waistband faster than his intent registered in her mind.

"Wh-what're you doing? Oh God!"

He found her pussy soaking wet. Using two fingers, he stroked her clit and swollen lips, causing her to gasp and moan. "Like that, huh? Just because I want to hold off fucking you for a few hours doesn't mean I can't give you a little taste of what's to come. Damn, you're on fire down there, and no matter how wet you get, it won't be enough to put that fire out until I make you come."

Curling the tips of his fingers, he breached the entrance to her core. She spread her legs wider to give him more room as his mouth latched on to the tit closest to him. "Oh, fuck, Marco! Yes!"

A pop sounded when he stopped sucking and

looked up at her. "This is going to be a quickie, baby. Just enough to take the edge off but not completely satisfy you. That we'll take care of later."

"Anything. Oh, please, anything."

His fingers plunged deep, then withdrew and plunged in once more. Over and over. Faster and faster. Then he held them inside her and searched... searched for the hidden spot which would send her flying. She panted for air as her body soared higher and higher. He'd been right. This was going to be a quickie —she was right there... just a little—

"*Ahhhhhhh.* Oh... oh shit... *ahhhh...* ssssshhhhhhit...*"

"That's it. Ride it, baby."

He prolonged the orgasmic waves as long as he could with the two fingers rubbing her G-spot and his thumb strumming her clit. Flashes of light appeared before her closed eyes until she had nothing more to give him and began to float back down to earth. His mouth nuzzled her neck, and all she wanted to do was fall asleep in his arms, then wake up and do it again.

"Thank you... Sir."

WHEN THEY RETURNED TO THE BARBECUE, MARCO noted a few more people had arrived. Mistress China, a.k.a. Charlotte Roth, was chatting with Colleen and her Dom/fiancé, Reggie Helm. The Omega team members, who weren't currently on guard duty, were also scattered about. The enormous flat-screen TV on the wall had been switched over to Skype and showed Jake and Nick sitting on the couch in their living room in San Diego. Jenn was standing in front of the camera attached to Brody's laptop, holding Mara for them to see, with Alyssa blowing softly in the baby's face to make her giggle.

Devon's face lit up when he saw Marco and Harper. "Great, you're back. Now, we can get down to business. Everyone gather round." He pulled Kristen to his side as Alyssa picked up the camera and turned it so the two men in California could see Nick's second oldest brother. "I'm glad almost everyone was able to make it today. Kristen and I decided to take advantage of the nice weather and slow day. It's great to have such a wonderful group of family, co-workers, and friends— Harper, Karen, and baby Mara, that includes you too. If someone had told me two weeks ago that Polo would be the first one of us with a kid, I would have laughed my ass off. But as it turns out, we couldn't be happier for him. Aaaaand… it looks like I'm going to be needing pointers from him because my beautiful wife is carrying my future son or daughter."

Delighted gasps and squeals filled the air, followed by shouts of congratulations, whistles, and clapping. The women rushed to hug Kristen while Devon took some fist bumps and back-slapping. After the excitement died down a little, Devon put his arm around Ian's shoulders and looked up at the big screen where Nick and Jake had huge grins on their faces. Alyssa moved to get all four of them in the camera range. Devon held up a glass of soda. "Kristen made a few suggestions, and I wholeheartedly agree with them. First, if it's a boy, his name will be John Devon Sawyer." A chorus of "*aww*" met his statement from those who knew about the deceased Sawyer brother. "And Ian and Angie, we want you to be the baby's godparents."

"Yes!"

Everyone laughed as Angie's hands flew into the air, and she did a little happy dance. Ian's smile couldn't have gotten any bigger. "As my fiancée has already indicated, we'd be honored, brother. Congratulations. Shit! Did you tell Mom and Pop yet?"

"We called all the soon-to-be grandparents this morning," Kristen answered, her arm wrapped around her husband's waist. "With everyone here, the only other people we still want to tell are my editor, Jillian, who I'll call tomorrow, and Carter, but Devon left a message for him to call when he can." The spy had a system where messages were left at a phone number very few people knew, and he checked them when he could safely do so. "We'll also tell everyone else at the club tomorrow night."

Standing next to Harper, Marco sighed, then whispered in her ear. "This is going to alter our plans, sweetheart. We can't leave the party after that announcement, and I'll also be expected to be at the club tomorrow night."

She leaned into him, and the honeysuckle shampoo she'd used tickled his nose. "Don't worry. I'll think of something. I really don't care about the dinner... just the dessert."

His eyebrows shot up as he turned to face her. Keeping his voice low so only she could hear him, he chided, "Oh, woman, how you tempt me. But I'm serious. I want at least one date with you before we wind up in bed together again."

"Fine," she replied with an exaggerated huff. "How about lunch tomorrow? Then we'll come back and go to the club later on." A blush came over her face. "Oh, wait... I mean, that is if you want me at the club."

Growling, he put his hands on her waist as he stared at the bottom lip she started nibbling on. "Sweetheart, I want you in the club, my bed, the shower... hell, I'd take you right here if it were just those of us in the lifestyle. Lunch tomorrow and then the club in the evening is fine, but we won't be able to play *in* the club until you've been fully vetted and cleared. The policy applies to everyone. Even Kristen, Angie, and Kat had to wait to be cleared. But as you said a moment ago, don't worry... I'll think of something." And he would because the wheels of creativity were already spinning with his options. Something else came to mind as well. "Tell your mom we'll take Mara with us to lunch so she can have a few hours to herself. She can relax here, or if she wants a change of scenery, maybe visit some friends. I'll arrange an escort for her with Dev."

Harper grinned, clearly pleased he wanted to include the baby in at least part of their plans. "I'd think she'd like that—she's going a little stir crazy, just like everyone else. One of her friends had hip replacement surgery the other day, and I know she'd like to go visit her at the hospital."

"Done. I'll talk to Dev later about adding it to the schedule." He took her hand and led her to where Ian was opening a few bottles of champagne, which Kristen had hidden earlier in a nearby cooler. "Come on. Let's get something to drink and eat. We've got a lot of celebrating to do."

"God damn it! Are they ever going to leave that fucking compound? And why didn't you take care of the bitch the other day when she was at her office?"

Lairson was getting fed up with being yelled at. This was supposed to have been an easy gig, but that was before those military assholes got involved. "How the fuck was I supposed to do that with all those goons watching over her? It'd be fucking suicide." He was still upset that Grant Rodgers had been killed. Not that he gave two shits about the jackass, but he was afraid he might be next, despite reassurances that it wouldn't happen.

After hearing about it on the news the other night, he'd picked up the throwaway phone he'd been using for this cluster fuck and hit the speed dial number he'd programmed in. The explanation he'd been given was that Rodgers was a loose end who would've blabbed when the cops came looking for him. And it was apparent the jackass had screwed up somehow because why else would the bomb squad and half the cops in Pinellas County have been knocking on his door?

"I don't want excuses. I want results. If you can't get close to her, then use your fucking head and get her to come to you. And do it soon, or I might start thinking you're a loose end and find someone else who can get it done."

The caller disconnected, and Lairson was tempted to throw the phone across the room. "Fuck!" There was no way he was getting out of this alive unless he got the job done, left Tampa for parts unknown, or took out the person who hired him. "Fuck!"

CHAPTER THIRTEEN

P ulling into a parking space in front of Donovan's Pub, Marco killed the engine, as their escort did the same in the space behind him. He'd picked this place for several reasons—in addition to knowing the owner and the fact that the team spent a lot of down-time here. One—the food was excellent, and the atmosphere was relaxed and comfortable. Two—when Trident first opened its business, Ian and Devon created several escape-and-evade routes in case anyone ran into trouble like Angie and Brody had last year. The brothers paid to have the inside door to the restaurant's office and the one that led to the back alley reinforced with bulletproof materials. The locks were heavy-duty, and the doors couldn't be kicked in easily. In fact, it would probably take the impact of a dump truck to break them down. A weapons safe was installed next to the business's safe, and it had every-thing the team would need in a crisis. Like the system at the compound, the safe could only be opened by a hand scanner. Mike had been trained to help if needed, although his and his staff's safety was his priority if something happened.

Before opening his door, Marco glanced at Harper. "Stay there until I come around for you."

While he was being very cautious with their surroundings, he knew she'd been excited to get out of the compound for a while, and the change of scenery would do them good. It was one thing to keep Harper and Mara safe but another to stop enjoying life because of some maniac. He wouldn't have even considered this excursion without his backup being in place.

The usual Sunday traffic and shoppers were out and about, but nothing seemed out of the ordinary. Foster and McCabe confirmed they agreed to his silent assessment with quick nods of their heads. He'd sent the two men over here this morning with Brody when only Mike, his chef, and sous chef were inside getting ready for the day. The geek had programmed their palm prints for the safe, and he showed them around so they were aware of the setup.

Marco opened Harper's door and held her hand as she climbed down. He then opened the rear door and pushed the release buttons to unlock Mara's car seat before lifting the sleeping infant out of the vehicle. The kid had passed out cold as soon as they'd hit the highway.

Retaking Harper's hand, he led her to the entrance of Donovan's with their two guards—one on point, the other on their six. Foster posted himself at a small table reserved for him at the front of the restaurant while McCabe strode to his assigned seating at the rear. The men had the entire bar and dining area within their sight and would quietly monitor the patrons coming and going.

Taking a booth near the back so the office was only a short distance away, Marco set the baby seat on the bench and stepped aside to let Harper sit beside their daughter. Just as he took his own seat, Jenn came rushing over, having spotted them as she came from the kitchen after dropping off an order. "Hi, Harper. Hi, Uncle Marco. *Aww*, you made my day bringing Mara in, but I wish she was awake. Any time you need a babysitter, look no further. I'll even do it for free."

Harper grinned as she removed the sleeping baby's blanket, showing off the cute pink-and-purple outfit she'd dressed her in. "You're on. As much as I love spending time with her, I'd be crazy not to take anyone's offer to babysit. But I insist on paying you if you do it. And don't worry, she'll be waking up again soon, I'm sure."

Placing his cell phone on the table, Marco glanced from the baby to Jenn. "Do you believe I remember when you were that tiny, Baby-girl? Back then, the entire team was terrified to hold you—not just me."

"It's hard to believe I was that small." She smiled at him. "And you were great holding her last night—you'll be an awesome dad. Trust me on this because you're an awesome uncle." He winked at her in appreciation as she began to step away from the table. "Let me grab you some menus and the specials."

The young woman hurried off, returned with two leather folders moments later, and then took their drink orders. While Harper perused the menu, Marco, knowing the choices by heart, only glanced at the specials before folding his arms on the table and watching her. She must have sensed his stare because her gaze met his. "What's the matter?"

He shook his head. "Nothing. I'm just remembering the last time we were here together—"

"Nina's funeral."

"Uh-huh. It's just amazing how much has changed since then." He jutted his chin toward the baby. "And not just the new addition. It's weird, but when Nina passed away, Kristen and Devon had only been dating a short time, which had already blown everyone's mind since Devil Dog never dated. Then Angie came along and, *boom*, there goes Ian. Kat and Boomer were next, followed by Jake and Nick, who blew everyone's mind again. No one saw that coming, including them. And I was happy for them. All of them. But it wasn't for me. I figured Brody was next, and I'd remain the team's consummate bachelor."

She closed the menu and leaned back against the leather padding. "And now?"

"I think Nina is laughing her ass off at me. Seriously. I had a dream last night about something that happened years ago. We were kids—I was maybe fifteen or sixteen. I'd come home from school, and our grandmother had gone to the casino again or some-thing. Nina had been taking a home-ec class and had learned to make meatloaf. Or thought she did. That afternoon, she'd taken her babysitting money and picked up the ingredients at the store to surprise me. It'd been years since we'd had a meal that wasn't frozen, out of a box, or fast food. I asked her what she was up to, and she said she wanted to be able to cook for her family someday. She wanted to get married and have kids. I thought she was crazy and asked why since our home life had been such crap." He paused, and then the corner of his mouth ticked upward. "You know what she told me?"

"No. What?"

He snorted and shook his head at the memory. "She said everyone was entitled to their own happily-ever-after, but it was up to us to want it and demand it. If we wanted it badly enough, we could look beyond our past and embrace our future."

"Nina said that? At what, thirteen? That's pretty deep. But, actually, I can hear her saying something like that. Despite what you two went through, that woman had the sunniest disposition I've ever encoun-tered. And I think it was because of you. She thought you walked on water." He took a deep breath, but she held up a hand to stop him from interrupting her. "Don't think she didn't know you were human and made mistakes like everyone else, but you put her first no matter what, Marco, even from a young age. She once told me she wanted a son someday so you could be his idol. She said every boy deserved an uncle like you to look up to." She paused, and when he remained silent while absorbing everything she'd told him, she asked, "What ever happened with the meatloaf? You said she *thought* she'd learned how to make it."

A chuckle escaped him as he leaned back in the booth, his face lighting up with amusement. "Oh, God, it was awful. I don't know what she put in it, but I didn't want to disappoint her, so I said it was good and tried to swallow it without tasting it. She finally took one bite and spit it out all over the place. It was the first time in ages the two of us laughed until our stomachs hurt. We threw out the meatloaf, or whatever the hell it was, and I used the money from my part-time job to take her out for burgers."

Harper smiled and pointed at him. "And *that's* why she adored you…"

Whatever she was about to say next was interrupted when Jenn returned for their food order. The rest of their lunch was spent chatting about a variety of things. Marco realized that as close as he was to Nina and as close as Nina was to Harper, there was so much about the woman sitting across from him he never knew. It really did feel like a first date, getting to know each other in a way they never had before. The more they talked, the more he recognized they were compatible in more than just sexual attraction. This was a woman who would challenge him every day yet submit to him in the bedroom. She would be his equal as well as his submissive. Well, technically, she wasn't his... yet. But he was hoping to change that real soon.

She swallowed the last of her sandwich, and the movement in her throat brought his gaze to her bare neck. He didn't have any collars in his toy bag except a simple black leather band, which had been worn by very few women and for only the length of a temporary contract. And that wouldn't do—not for Harper. He wanted to give her one that no one else had ever worn. Tonight, when they went to the club, he'd take her into the fetish store on the second floor. There, he could purchase one she could wear in the club for now. But if things worked out for them how he hoped they would, he'd have to check out the jeweler where his teammates had gotten permanent collars for their subs. *Huh.* It was amazing how his life had changed in just one week.

After paying Jenn for their lunch, he stood while Harper bundled the baby back up. The temperatures had dropped back to normal for this time of year. Out of the corner of his eye, he noticed someone approaching, and after seeing who it was, he inwardly sighed and gave McCabe a subtle signal that everything was fine. He pasted on a thin, polite smile for the newcomer. "Hi, Paula. How are you?"

The former Trident secretary beamed as she stopped in front of him. "Hi, Marco. I didn't expect to see you here. I'm good. Just meeting some friends for lunch, but it looks like I'm the first one here." She turned toward Harper. "Hi. I'm sorry. I remember you were a friend of Marco's sister, but I can't recall your name."

Harper stood and held out her hand, which Paula shook. "Hi. It's Harper."

Recognition dawned on the shorter woman's face. "Harper. That's it. And who's this?" She pointed to the car seat, which Harper reached over to pick up. The baby was now wide awake and would probably want a bottle as soon as they returned to the compound.

Growing more accustomed to calling her his child, Marco chose to answer. "This is our daughter, Mara."

Paula's eyes opened wide in shock. "*Your* daughter? Oh my gosh. Congratulations, but I didn't know you were a couple, and I thought you didn't want children, Marco."

It was obvious the former secretary had been more meddlesome than he remembered. He recalled a few times she'd overheard personal conversations at the office and interrupted with her own opinions, which hadn't been asked for. "Yeah, well, things change, don't they? Sometimes life gives you what you never knew you wanted."

The woman laughed. "Isn't that the truth? Well, it was nice seeing you. Tell everyone I said hello."

She stepped out of the way to let them pass, and Marco took the baby from Harper. "I will. And it was nice seeing you too."

As they walked to the car with McCabe and Foster flanking them, Marco couldn't help but think that their first date had been really special. Now, he couldn't wait for their second date this evening at the club.

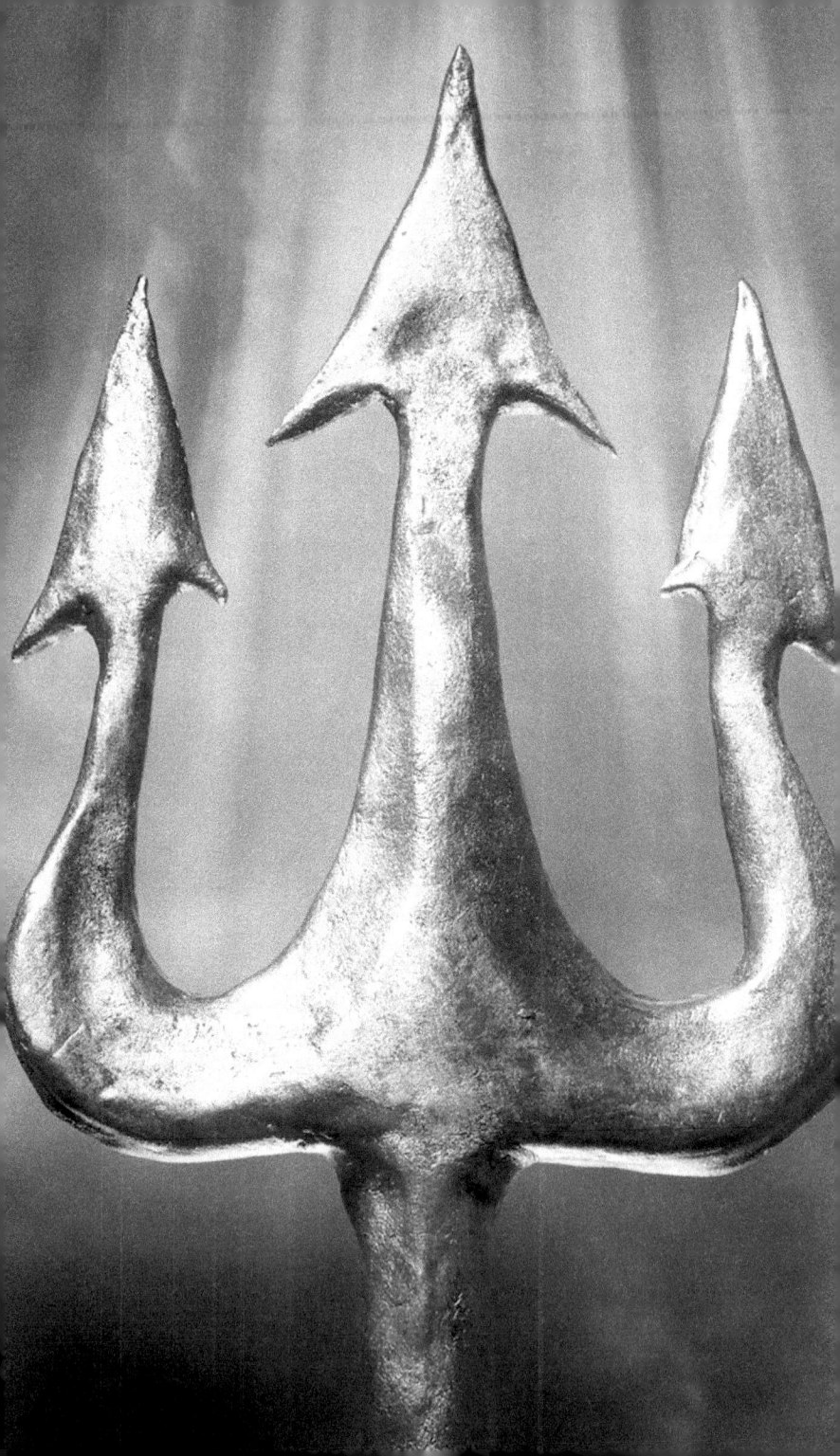

CHAPTER FOURTEEN

Standing outside the women's lounge entrance, Marco waited impatiently for Harper to change into appropriate club wear. They stopped by her house earlier to check on things and let her pack a duffel bag. She couldn't exactly get dressed in something skimpy back in the apartment with her mother there, so she'd put on a black skirt, a comfortable top, and a pair of killer high-heeled shoes. He still had no idea what she was changing into, but knowing Harper, he was sure she'd rock whatever she put on.

As for him, it hadn't taken him long to swap his jeans for a pair of black club leathers to go with his black boots. He'd kept his shirt simple, opting for a heather-gray T-shirt, which showed off his muscular physique. Cassie, one of the submissive waitresses, walked by, and he grabbed two plastic bottles of water from her tray. She would add them to his monthly tab when she went back to the bar and the computer they had there. In addition to keeping track of members' bar tabs, the system ensured that no one who'd consumed more than two alcoholic drinks entered the play area downstairs. It also alerted if a member had missed a six-month medical clearance needed to maintain their privileges. Security was posted at the grand staircase leading down into the pit, and everyone had to present their membership card so it could be swiped and approved.

"Hi, Master Marco." He spun around as Shelby walked through the door, which led to the stairs down to the lounges. "Harper will be up in a minute."

"Hey, Shelby. Thanks." He glanced around before turning back to her. After temporarily losing her hair during two battles with cancer, which she'd beaten both times, the little pixie was now known to wear different colored wigs to go with her equally colorful outfits. Tonight's hue was bright orange, with white accents on her bra and short skirt, which made her look like a delicious Creamsicle. "Where's Parker?"

"He'll be here in a bit. There was a problem on one of his job sites, and he dropped me off so I could chat with the subs for a bit. This is my first time here without him since we signed our contract, so it feels odd."

Marco smiled at the woman he'd played with often in the past, sometimes in a ménage with Brody. He was thrilled she'd fallen in love after resisting it for so long. Shelby's bubbly personality had made her a club favorite and a social butterfly. However, Master Parker had finally lassoed her in and not only put a beautiful, multi-gem collar around her neck, but the Dom had also put a matching engagement ring on her finger. "I'm sure you'll get over it two minutes into the gossip, so don't let me stand in the way of you catching up on it."

She gave him a girly wave of her fingers before heading to the bar where a few of her girlfriends were gathered. As Marco glanced at his watch, the door leading to the locker rooms opened again, and out stepped Harper. His mouth went dry, and for a split second, he thought his heart stopped. But then it started pumping double time, sending blood to his cock, which chose that moment to grow hard as granite. *Holy shit,* the woman was the definition of sin.

He dropped his gaze to the stilettos he'd insisted she keep on instead of going barefoot like some of the submissives. Slowly, he followed the upward line of her long legs encased in sheer, black, thigh-high stockings attached to a garter belt. A skimpy bikini bottom, which he prayed was a thong, covered what he knew was a waxed bare pussy—at least, he hoped it still was after all this time. Her trim waist was snug in a black corset laced down the front. The cups of the garment pushed her lush breasts together and up into two perfect orbs, which he was literally drooling over. Some women were lucky to have their bodies quickly bounce back almost to where they'd been before getting pregnant, and Harper was one of them. However, he could tell her hips were wider than they had been, her breasts were fuller, and she still had a tiny baby pooch in her abdomen. Knowing it was all the result of his child she'd carried tugged at his heart and made her even more beautiful in his eyes. She'd pulled her hair up into some sort of twist but left a few strands falling over her right temple, giving her an air of mystique.

His eyes finally reached her face and found her gaze was submissively focused on his feet. Marco took a step forward and used all his strength not to haul her up against his body. "Look at me." He waited until her eyes met his. "You're gorgeous and my fantasy woman come true. Every other woman will always pale in comparison to you." Holding out his hand, he was pleased when she didn't hesitate to take it, and he brought her hand to his lips to kiss her knuckles. "To have you offer me your submission humbles me. Thank you."

"You're welcome, Sir."

His nostrils flared at that one word—*Sir*—and hard-core desire flashed through him, but he swallowed his impatience. He'd promised her an evening away from the baby, her mother, her job, and the threat against her, and it was a promise he intended to keep, even though he was horny as hell after seeing her outfit. "Are you ready? Do you want to have a glass of wine first or walk around in the pit for a while? I know you didn't get much of a chance to see the place yesterday afternoon."

Harper gave him a sexy grin. "I think I'd like a glass of wine. I don't get to have one often nowadays."

Tucking her hand into the crook of his arm, he led her over to the bar. "A glass of wine it is then." When the bartender approached, Marco introduced the two. "Master Dennis, this is my submissive, Harper Williams. Harper, Master Dennis."

The stocky man nodded at her. "Harper, it's a pleasure to meet you. Welcome to our club, and I hear congratulations are in order for both of you."

She took the stool, which Marco had gestured for her to sit on, briefly showing him her back. He was stunned to see a butterfly tattoo on her left shoulder blade with "BFF~Nina~RIP" written in scrolled lettering underneath it. Her lyrical voice brought him back to the conversation. "Thank you, Sir. And it's a pleasure to meet you too."

After ordering a wine for Harper and a beer for himself, Marco stepped inside her personal space, leaned forward, and put his mouth to her ear. His voice was low and seductive. "I was hoping that was a thong, but even though it's a bikini, you still rock it like a Victoria's Secret model." He nuzzled her neck. "I read your limit list earlier, and we're very compatible, though I had little doubt about it. Just thought you'd like to know."

A shiver passed through her, and he eased away, pleased to see the desire in her eyes. She reached for the wine glass, which had been set in front of her, and took a sip. "Have you decided on a scene, Sir... and where it will take place since we can't play here."

"Oh, yes, my little butterfly. But you'll have to wait to find out."

A spark of recognition appeared on her face at his endearment. "You saw my tattoo."

He nodded and then pushed up the left sleeve of his shirt to reveal his own tattoo, twisting his torso slightly so she could get the full effect. After much deliberation of what he wanted to get in his sister's memory, he'd asked the artist to design one especially for him. It was a raven-haired, haloed angel with colorful butterfly wings instead of traditional white, and "Nina" was written in a similar style as Harper had used on hers. "Great minds think alike."

Giggling, Harper traced his tattoo with her fingers. "It's beautiful. She would have loved it."

Damn, just the touch of her hand on his arm had his libido shooting through the roof again. The woman would be the death of him, or, at least, give him another case of serious blue balls, like he'd had numerous times since she'd come back into his life. Hopefully, he would fall asleep tonight, completely sated, as would she. Shifting his hips, he tried to adjust himself furtively.

Their conversation was interrupted as the music volume was lowered dramatically, and they heard Devon bellow above the crowd gathered in the pit, trying to quiet everyone. Joining others in the balcony gathered along the railing, they looked down to see the co-owner and his wife standing on the round stage in the center of the room. Behind them was a St. Andrew's cross, which was seldom used except for special scenes. The stage itself tended to be where commitment ceremonies and demonstrations were held. Devon raised his hands. "Can I have everyone's attention, please?"

A few sharp whistles sounded from several Doms, causing the loud chatter of the crowd to drop to mere murmurs. Members, some in the middle of scenes, paused and turned their attention to the couple. Devon held up a plastic champagne glass, which Marco knew was filled with soda and not booze since the man didn't drink alcohol. "I have an announcement to make. For those of you who haven't heard yet, my beautiful wife will make me a father in about seven months. And we couldn't be any happier."

Clapping ensued, along with cheers of congratulations and a few *mazel tovs* before the wolf-whistles followed as Devon grabbed Kristen around the waist and kissed her senselessly. Even though there had been a similar celebration on a smaller scale the day before, Marco's gut twisted a little. He'd missed out on this with Harper and Mara—making a huge announcement to their friends. Hell, he'd almost missed out on realizing he wanted to be a father to Mara. If only he could figure out who had fucked with the phones and sent that letter to Harper fifteen months ago, preventing him from knowing she was pregnant.

Holy shit! A sudden thought occurred to him, and he

couldn't believe he'd forgotten about an incident that had occurred a week before Harper was assaulted. At the time, it hadn't meant a thing to him, but now... now he wasn't sure. His eyes scanned the crowd below and then the one on the balcony. Ian was downstairs with Angie, but Brody, Boomer, and Kat walked toward Harper and him on the second floor. Boomer's shirt and pants were similar to Marco's, while Brody wore his usual jeans and cowboy boots, topped off with a leather vest. Kat had donned an emerald green teddy with matching bikini underwear, and like many of the submissives, she was barefoot.

Before any of the trio could greet them, he pointed at the geek. "We're missing something. Something I hadn't thought of until now. Unfortunately, it doesn't solve the puzzle."

Brody's eyes narrowed in confusion. "What the hell are you talking about?"

The others were just as lost as he paced before them, trying to gather his thoughts. "We got side-tracked with Harper's assault and then the damn bomb. We weren't sure if the person who fucked with our phones and sent Harper that letter, supposedly from me, had anything to do with the assault and bomb, right? There was nothing to connect them, but what if there is?"

"I'm still lost. What difference does it make?"

He stopped in front of his teammates, hoping they would follow his jumbled line of thinking. "There weren't any attempts on her life until recently. The phones and the letter happened over a year ago. Someone didn't want me to know Harper was pregnant with my child. Someone who knew Mara *was* my child. That list has to be damn small because I didn't even know. Someone made sure I wouldn't find out, then nothing else happens... absolutely nothing, until *after* Mara is born." He ran a frustrated hand through his hair. "I forgot all about this, but at the time, I just thought it was a prank or someone had the wrong address, and I ignored it. About a week before Harper's assault, I came out of my house one morning, and there was a rose tucked under the windshield wiper with a note. There was only one word on it—*Soon.*"

The four stared at him, but Boomer eventually broke the silence. "You mean Harper's stalker is really your stalker?"

"I don't fucking know—a stalker or someone bent on revenge. But if it is all connected, someone waited until after Mara was born to try to kill Harper. Me stepping on the bomb was pure coincidence, and if Harper had stepped on it instead... God, I hate that thought." He reached for her hand and pulled her to his side, needing to keep her close. "If Harper had been killed, what were the killer's intentions about Mara? I get the feeling that someone wants Harper dead, but Mara and I alive. Or am I crazy and making this shit up as I go along? Maybe the phones, the rose, and the attempts on her life have nothing to do with each other. Fuck, I have no idea, and it's driving me fucking nuts."

He could almost see the wheels spinning in Brody's and Boomer's minds as they tried to piece everything together. Hopefully, one of them would figure out the final piece to this puzzle... and fast.

Brody crossed his arms and leaned against the railing. "Okay, so there's a really long list of people who have a grudge against you... and any one of us as well. It comes with the territory. We have a few scenarios here. One—all these things happening are just a coincidence, and as we've established many times, none of us believe in coincidences. So that's out. Two—someone is after Harper, and it's because they have a grudge against her for some reason—whether it's because of Friends of Patty, one of her court cases, or some other fucked up reason. Three—this is about Polo, and then we have to start compiling that long list, *but*... if we figure out who the hell knew Harper was pregnant, then we can eliminate ninety-nine percent of it." He looked back and forth at Boomer and Marco. "Did I miss anything?"

Both men shook their heads. While they had come up with two out of three viable scenarios, they were still no closer to finding out the who, how, and why. *Fuck.*

Slapping his best friend on the back, Brody told him, "Look. Tomorrow, we'll start fresh. For now, enjoy the evening and this gorgeous woman. And if you're smart, you'll walk her over to the shop and get a collar around her neck because a bunch of sharks are giving her the eye."

Glancing over at the bar, Marco saw that, sure enough, the single Doms had detected fresh blood, and he snorted. "Fuck. I meant to do that earlier but got sidetracked." He looked Harper up and down in appreciation, then smirked. "And distracted. Yeah, a collar is definitely something we'll pick out right now. Come, my little butterfly. I need to stake my claim. Otherwise, there's going to be a brawl."

He led her to the club store with his arm around her waist. It wasn't huge, but there was enough space for a decent selection of fetish wear, BDSM toys, and lifestyle jewelry, including collars. Behind the counter was an attractive submissive who bore a striking resemblance to singer/actress Jennifer Hudson, but she swore there was no relation between them. However, there had been numerous occasions when she'd been mistaken for the famous woman and joked that people got over their confusion the second she opened her mouth to sing. Carrying a tune was not something she was blessed with, apparently.

Marco stopped in front of the display case of collars. "Good evening, Sasha. This is Harper."

The pretty woman was dressed in the uniform of the female staff members—a black skirt and bra, with a red and gold bow tie. Most of the wait staff and store employees worked full or part-time toward their membership fees, and Sasha was one of them. She smiled. "Good evening, Master Marco. Hi, Harper, it's nice to meet you. What can I help you with tonight, Sir?"

SAMANTHA COLE

He chuckled. "If I don't put a collar on my submissive, I'll be beating in a lot of heads before the night is through."

"Well, we can't have that happening, now can we? Did you have something in mind?"

Glancing at Harper, he shook his head. "Not really. Something nice, but temporary." Harper's astonished gaze would have knocked him on his ass had he not been expecting it. Her eyes were blazing, and he could almost feel the heat. He grinned at her. "I'm teasing, Butterfly—I like that nickname for you, by the way. We just need something temporary until I can have one designed for you. If that's all right with you."

Her shoulders and jaw relaxed slightly. As Sasha pulled out two trays of assorted collars, Harper nodded at him. "That would be fine, Sir."

Shit. Her matter-of-fact tone told him this wasn't something to tease her about. He cupped her cheek. "Hey, I'm sorry. Bad time for a joke. I'm new to this couple and dating thing, so I'm sure it's not the last time I'll say something stupid. Forgive me?"

She took a deep breath, then gave him a small smile. "Of course. And I know this is new for you, but I've had over a year where I thought you had rejected Mara and me, so it will take time for me to get past that."

"Understood." He leaned in for a quick kiss. "Now, let's enjoy ourselves, shall we?" They turned to face the submissive, waiting patiently behind the counter. "Okay, Sasha. Show us what you've got."

Ten minutes later, Harper sported a black leather

and rhinestone collar, which told all the other Doms she was spoken for. Marco took her for a tour of the pit since he no longer had to worry about anyone approaching his sub. She'd been in the lifestyle and clubs like this for a long time, so her responses to what she saw weren't the same as someone new going through culture shock. Instead, as she watched a scene, he watched *her*, looking for the subtle changes in her body when she saw something that turned her on. A hitch of her breath. A flush to her cheeks and chest. An increase in the pulse rate of her carotid artery. The slight shift of her hips. The clenching of her thighs. And the fire in her eyes as her arousal grew. He noted everything, storing the information for recall later when they were playing.

One of the scenes she responded positively to was a ménage—two male Doms and their female submissive. With any other sub, this would have led to asking Brody to join them before the night was through, but Marco knew he had to give the idea more thought before that happened. First off, he wanted her all to himself for now. And secondly, it was something he and Harper would have to discuss at length. He knew a ménage was on her green limit list, meaning it was something she had tried and was interested in experiencing again. However, he would have to find out if she'd be willing to let Brody be the one to join them, knowing she was going to be seeing a lot of the geek afterward. He also had to examine his own feelings about his best friend being their third in a scene. With any other sub, it wouldn't be a problem at all, but Harper was far from being just another sub. In addition to the ménage, there were several items on her yellow "haven't-tried-but-want-to-try" list, which they would have to discuss and possibly explore, but he'd save them for another time.

He walked them around for a bit, introducing her to other members. Some of them recognized her from the other club, Heat, and it irritated him to think of her playing with another Dom. But he had no right to complain about it since it was no different than her dating other men prior to him. The one thing he was overjoyed about this evening was the way she stayed tucked into his side yet didn't come across as being clingy. She was her own woman and could handle herself conversing with new acquaintances but still respected him and the lifestyle rules. If their attentions were divided while in a group, he noticed her gaze darted to him as if reassuring herself he was still with her, but she had nothing to worry about—with her was where he wanted to be. It pleased him that she was becoming as attached to him as he was to her. They could do this... this thing between them. He was sure of it. But did he have it in him to fall in love with her? How did one know they were in love as opposed to just caring for someone? Was there some epiphany he would have someday, where... *boom*... he knew he was in love and couldn't live without her? *Jeez*, he couldn't ask the guys—they'd laugh their asses off at him. Again, something to think about at another time.

He glanced at his watch after another trip around the cavernous play floor. Two hours was more than enough time to have made an appearance and chat with friends. It was time for the second half of the evening to commence, and he was more than ready for it. *Let the games begin.*

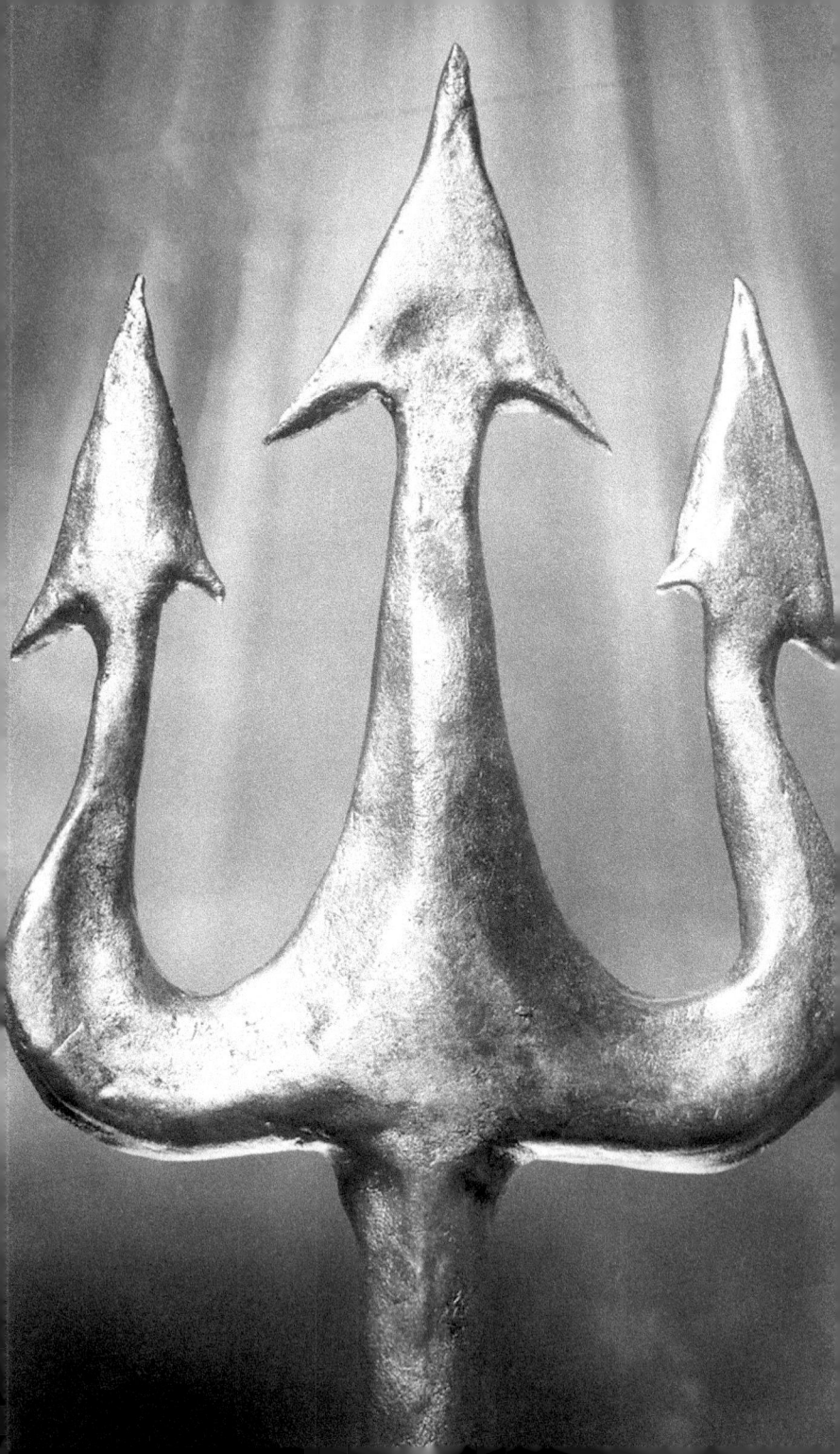

CHAPTER FIFTEEN

Harper followed Marco across the parking lot and waited as he placed his hand on the scanner to open the compound's inner gate. He'd told her to put her skirt and shirt back on over her club wear, then meet him in the lobby. Returning to the locker room, she'd obeyed his instructions, curious to know what he had planned since he refused to give her any hints earlier. Now, she couldn't resist asking, "Where are we going?"

Instead of answering her, he gave her a sexy, evil grin, then gestured for her to proceed him through the gate. Several armed men patrolled the perimeter fencing, and aside from a glance, they ignored the couple. Marco took her hand as the gate closed behind them, leading her toward the third building in the row of converted warehouses. It was the only building she hadn't been in yet, but she'd been told it housed the gym, training rooms, and storage. Was he planning on some sexual gymnastics? The thought made her giggle, and he raised an eyebrow at her. "Something funny?"

She shook her head as he unlocked the door with another palm scan. "Not really. Just imagining a few scenarios based on what I was told about this building. Mainly the gym."

When they entered, he flipped on one light switch, partially illuminating a workout room that would rival any high-end commercial gym. There were racks of weights, nautilus machines, a boxing ring, and every piece of aerobic exercise equipment she'd ever heard of —treadmills, cycles, stair climbers, ellipticals, and more. But Marco obviously had another destination in mind since he bypassed all of it. Guiding her down a hallway that ran through the second half of the building, he slowed at an ordinary-looking door, turned the knob, and entered the room with her in tow. Confused, she glanced around as he strode over to a shelving unit. "What are we doing in a storage room?"

He opened what looked like a standard metal junction box and placed his hand on another scanner. The shelving and wall swung open, to her amazement, revealing a hidden entrance. "What the..."

He reached in and flipped a switch, bringing the lights on. "Come on in, and watch your step. This is our panic room, so to speak. The compound used to be owned by a drug cartel. The government seized it, and Ian bought the place for a song at an auction. Jake found this underground bunker when we were taking inventory of the place. We fixed it up for our needs and added to it. Egghead's got a duplicate war-room down here, where he can run everything from if needed. Once a month, we strip and clean all the weapons in the locker and rotate out cases of water and MREs as they approach their expiration dates."

Harper was shocked at the size of the place as she descended the stairs and found herself in a vast room. There was a computer terminal and security set up similar to the one in Brody's office, bunk beds, lockers, tables, chairs, shelves with supplies, and anything else they needed to hunker down if the compound came under attack. From the looks of it, over two dozen people could stay down there. "What happens if someone finds the entrance?"

Pulling out the chair from the computer desk, he pointed to a door on the far side of the room. "That's sort of a porta-potty bathroom since the plumbing wasn't run down here, and through there is an escape route that takes you out into the woods to the west of the compound."

He punched two buttons on the computer console, and the bright, white lights dimmed and changed to a soft red, giving the room a sensual feel. She assumed it was to allow anyone in the bunks to get some sleep while letting others still see. Sitting in the chair, Marco crooked his finger, silently calling her to him. When she stopped before him, he held out his hand and waited for her to take it. "I have to ask... to be sure. Is this what you want tonight? To submit to me? To obey my orders?"

Without hesitation, she replied, "Yes, Sir."

"What's your safeword, Butterfly?"

At Heat, they didn't have a universal safeword as they did at The Covenant, so each submissive chose their own word. "It's cauliflower, Sir."

He snorted. "I take it you don't like cauliflower."

"No, I don't. And there's no chance I'd accidentally say it during a scene."

Rubbing his thumb over her wrist, he nodded. "Okay. Cauliflower it is. But I will also honor the word 'red' since it's used by everyone here. If you say either word, I will immediately stop the scene, and we'll talk about what went wrong. 'No' and 'stop' will not be heeded. Understand?"

Having played in the lifestyle for years, Harper knew all this was the sign of a good Dominant making sure his submissive fully comprehended what was about to happen, but she still wished he'd hurry things along. She was horny as hell between being so close to him all night, observing some hot scenes, and the fact that it had been over a year since she'd had sex. "I understand, Sir. Red and cauliflower are my safewords. No and stop will mean nothing."

`"Good girl. Take off your skirt, blouse, and shoes, then present for me."

Disrobing once more until only her corset, stockings, garter, and underwear remained, she placed her discarded clothes on the desk next to him. Then, using his hand for support, Harper lowered herself to her knees and sat back on her heels. With her head bent forward, eyes downcast, she placed her hands, palms up, on her thighs, then took a deep breath and slowly let it out.

This was it—what she'd been dreaming about for years. To completely submit to Marco DeAngelis. Yes, she had the power to stop him at any time by using her safeword, but she highly doubted it would be needed. He had been tender and caring with his sister through her entire battle with cancer, and Harper knew he would be the same thoughtful man during sexual play. She knew he would never hurt her... but that didn't mean he wouldn't use a bite of pain to give her the pleasure she desired. Oh, no. She fully expected him to make her body sing the way it had during their one night together, even though he'd kept his dominant side in check back then.

Impatiently, she waited. When he shifted and opened a desk drawer, she fought the urge to see what he was up to. It really didn't matter since she was sure she would know soon enough. And Marco didn't disappoint. Dropping whatever he'd retrieved on the desk, he leaned forward and tucked his fingers under the cups of her corset, pushing them down under her breasts. She held her breath to keep from begging him to play with them.

"Beautiful. I told you yesterday that those nipples deserved to be decorated, so that's what I'm going to do, sweetheart." His voice had dropped to a sexy rumble, and she felt every word penetrate her body and settle between her legs. She was already wet for him, and they had barely started. His thumbs brushed over her nipples, and they immediately responded, puckering and tightening. He pulled and tugged them with his fingers until they were distended enough for what he wanted to do to them.

Marco picked up what she now knew were nipple clamps. Squeezing the rubberized clasp of one of them, he instructed, "Take a deep breath."

When she did, he clipped it on her right nipple, and the pain pushed a groan from her mouth. It had been a long time since she'd been clamped, and even though Mara had been breastfed for the first few weeks after her birth, it was nothing compared to what she felt now. Marco tugged on her left nipple and quickly attached the second clamp. The pain was already morphing into pleasure for her. Damn, how she'd missed this. In the hands of an experienced Dom, a submissive like Harper was in heaven. She didn't know why she craved the pain—all she knew was she did. Her body and mind were just wired that way.

Marco held the ends of the attached strings in his palm so she could see them. Finely polished stones were spaced evenly along the three-inch lengths, providing enough weight so the clamps tugged downward. Each time she moved even a fraction of an inch, the stones swayed, shooting electricity through her nipples into the rest of her body. "Someday, these will be gems because you deserve them. But for now, these will do. Stand for me, Butterfly."

She did as she was told, and he pointed to a leather

recliner he must have placed in the middle of the room earlier. "Bring me the two items sitting on the right side of the chair."

Pivoting on the ball of her foot, she carefully walked over to the chair. Each step caused the clamps to pull down under their attached weight, and by the time she reached her destination, her clit was throbbing in time with her the aching in her breasts. On the chair, she found three items. On the right side was what she was supposed to bring him—a new, pink anal plug and a tube of lubricant. On the left side was a matching vibrator. Oh God, he was going to drive her insane before he fucked her—she just knew it. Then again, the man was a Dom, so she really shouldn't have expected anything less.

Picking up the plug and lube, she turned around and found he'd shucked off his boots and removed his T-shirt. How had she forgotten how gorgeous his body was? Sculpted like an artist had designed him using a Greek or Roman god as their guide. He had a smattering of dark hair on his tanned chest, which thinned into a line going straight down his torso, disappearing into his black leathers. The bulge behind the laced fly was unmistakable and made her mouth water. She'd sucked him off the last time they'd been together, during a middle-of-the-night shower to clean the sweat and sex from their bodies. And now, she couldn't wait to do it again. Well-hung was an understatement when it came to Marco.

After returning to him, she placed the items in his

outstretched hand and awaited his next orders. She needed this—someone else to take control so she could just relax, shut her brain down, and feel. That was one of the first things she'd noticed about playing in the lifestyle. When she handed over control of the scene to a Dom, she didn't worry about anything. The questions every woman tends to ask herself during intimacy no longer came to mind. How do I look? How do I sound? Does he think about someone else while he's with me? Does he like what I'm doing? Should I do it differently? And so many others. Instead, her mind went blank to everything but pain and the pleasure it produced. There was no stress of her college and law classes, passing the bar, court cases, watching her best friend die, being a single mother... nothing.

He undid the clasps of the garter from the top of her thigh-highs. "Turn around." When she did as ordered, he unsnapped the back ones and then grabbed the sides of her bikini underwear and the garter belt, sliding them down her legs until she was able to step out of them. Biting her lip, she fought the urge to brush away her stretch marks as if she could make them disappear. She didn't hate them since they were the battle scars of carrying her daughter, but that didn't mean she still wasn't self-conscious about them. However, if she did give Marco any indication they bothered her, she was sure he would make her regret it. Many of the Doms she'd known in the past didn't like their submissives putting themselves down for any reason, and she doubted he was any different.

"Bend over and grab your ankles." After she was in position, he caressed her ass with his palm, then stroked the moist, sensitive area between her legs before continuing, "Very nice. You still keep yourself bare. I fucking love that." Jeez, the man was practically purring like a male lion sensing his mate was in heat. "When was the last time you were plugged?"

He knew she was experienced in anal play since she'd checked it off in the green column of her limit list. "About two years, Sir."

"My assumption was right then. I chose a smaller plug so we can build your tolerance back up again. Although, I have a larger one in the drawer just in case."

His hand left her ass, and she was caught off guard when cool, thick liquid landed at the base of her spine and drizzled down the crack between her cheeks. Involuntarily, she tensed and was reprimanded with a quick smack to the sit-spot at the top of her right thigh, which elicited a squeak from her lips.

"Relax, Butterfly. You know this goes easier if you relax."

Forcing her body to ease, she answered, "Yes, Sir."

Clutching one hip to hold her steady, he used his other hand to spread the lubricant around her back hole with the hard silicone plug. Instinct had her wanting to tense again, and she fought the response. The slight pressure he was using was already lighting up the nerves of her rectum, and she moaned in antici-pation of the pleasure she knew was coming. He paused at the entrance. "Bear down, sweetheart, and let it happen."

She did as commanded at the same time he pressed the plug into her anus. There was a moment's hesitation before the toy breached her sphincter and then slid home, causing her to gasp loudly.

"Beautiful." Marco tapped the flared end of the plug protruding from her body, and the vibrations shot through her ass, combined with the pain/pleasure in her nipples, then went straight to her pussy, causing her wetness to grow. Her thighs clenched as her clit throbbed. Her breathing increased. Holy shit, it was going to be hard to hold off her orgasm if she was this close already, but she had to. Her Dom would surely punish her for coming without permission.

Her Dom. Wow. Never in her life had those words meant so much to her. Marco DeAngelis was her Dom, and she would do everything she could tonight to please him and make their play perfect. After all, the first scene between a Dom and a sub could be the equivalent of many firsts for a couple. A first look. A first date. A first kiss. Or the first time they'd made love. Well, they had already experienced the first three, but she was under no illusion that the night Mara was conceived could be considered "making love." It had been a comfort fuck... actually, several comfort fucks... but nothing more. While tonight would be far more than a comfort fuck, it still couldn't be called making love. They still had a lot of things they had to work out between them, but, for now... at this moment... she was his submissive. And she was looking forward to whatever he had planned for her.

"Stand back up and sit in the recliner, sweetheart."

This time, her pace was even slower. Not only did the strings and stones of the nipple clamps swing with every step, but she also had to clench her ass cheeks to make sure she didn't lose the plug. When she finally reached the chair, she picked up the vibrator, then turned and slowly lowered herself to the seat.

From across the room, Marco instructed, "Sit back. Push on the arms so the back reclines a bit, but leave the footrest down. It'll just be in my way later. Good girl. Now, spread your legs as far as possible while still being comfortable. Put one hand above your head and relax."

Relax? Was he serious? Her body was humming, and he wanted her to relax? Like that was going to happen. Not.

"Turn on the vibe and hold it between your legs so it's stimulating both your clit and pussy. You know the routine. You do nothing unless I tell you to, including coming."

The man was going to be the death of her tonight. She flipped the switch and brought the slim, artificial phallus to her core. Even though she was expecting the new sensation, combined with the stimulus to her tits and ass, her hips bucked the moment she touched her already sensitive clit. "*Ahhh*. Shit!"

"Easy, baby. Relax."

Damn, she was ready to tell him to take that word and shove it.

"Now. Tell me. Have you dreamt about me... about us together? Because I sure as hell have. You've starred in many of my fantasy dreams over the years." Her gaze flashed to his at that revelation. "Oh, yes. I've had many, many dreams about you long before you ever rocked my world. Asleep and awake. One of my favorites was when I was in the shower, and you were on your knees, giving me a blow job. But I confess, my dreams came nowhere close to reality, sweetheart. I jacked off to that memory many times since then. So tell me, did you dream of me? I want an honest answer, Harper. Not what you think I want to hear. It's okay if the answer is no, but I think it's yes based on that expression on your face. Either that or you're about to explode."

She could just imagine what expression he saw on her face because as soon as he started talking about dreams and fantasies, her favorite ones of him popped into her head... and there were many of them. "Yes to both, Sir." His eyes narrowed in confusion, so she added, "I mean, yes to dreaming of you and yes to the fact that I'm about to explode."

He smirked. *The bastard.* Standing, he unlaced his fly but remained over by the desk. Her eyes dropped to watch his hands work, but he admonished, "Uh-uh, Butterfly. Eyes on mine. Good girl. Now, I want you to make small circles over your clit and pussy with the vibe and tell me your favorite fantasy of me."

"What? Y-you want me to... to..." *Oh, shit.* He wasn't serious, was he?

"Yes, I do. I want to hear what I did to you in those dreams of yours... and what you did to me. And I don't see your hand moving at all. I'd rather our first scene didn't include a punishment, but that doesn't mean I'll let you get away with anything."

Shit.

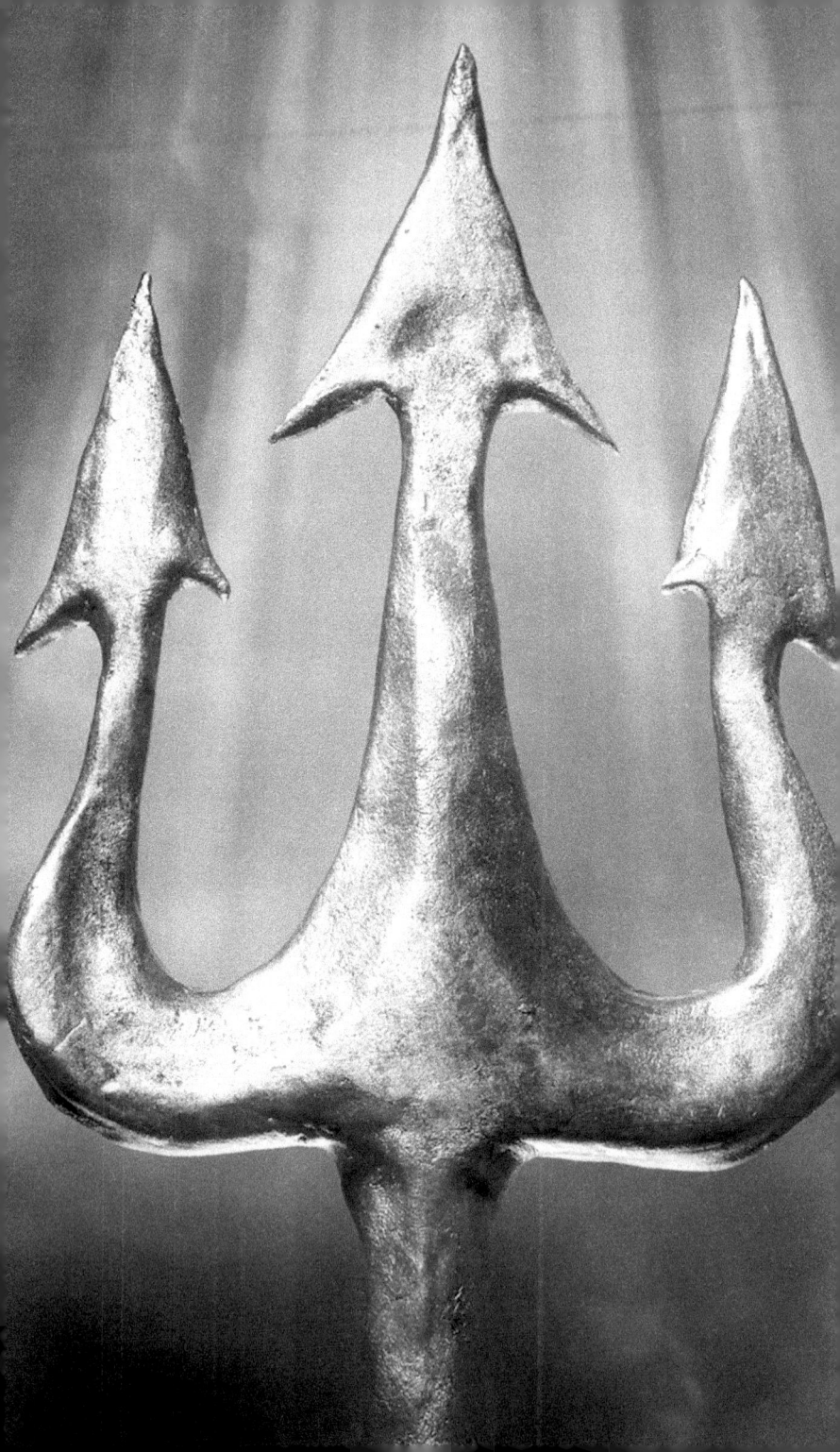

CHAPTER SIXTEEN

Marco chuckled as he sat again, then leaned back and settled in for the upcoming entertainment. This was going to be fun... and hot. He hadn't removed his leathers but loosened the laces to give his hard cock some breathing room. She was going to be the death of him tonight if he wasn't careful. She looked so fucking beautiful wearing only her stockings and corset. Her breasts were incredible, to begin with, but clamped, they were stunning. He watched as she began to rub the vibe over her exposed pussy lips and clit. Even with the distance between them and the low lighting, he could see how wet she was. "I'm waiting, Harper. And you'll find I'm a very impatient man when a submissive makes me wait for what I want."

She swallowed hard and squirmed a little. "Um. I, um... well, there are so many different ones I've had that I'm not sure which is my favorite."

He loved how off-kilter she seemed. This was obviously something she'd never done before. Well, neither had he, but Devon had told his teammates how hot things got when Kristen read him the sex scenes she'd written. But Harper wasn't the author of any steamy romance novels, and he didn't want her reading someone else's fantasies to him—he wanted to hear hers. "*Hmmm.* Then pick one, and we'll save the others for another time."

"Okay. Um. I'm not exactly sure how I'm supposed to do this." She licked her lips, and he bit back a groan as he remembered them wrapped around his cock. "I mean, I don't know how to start."

"All right. Let's try this. Close your eyes. Keep that vibe moving, and I'll start by asking a few questions. Then you can tell me what I'm doing to you in your mind like you're giving me a play-by-play of a movie you're watching." He could see the moment she relaxed a little after shutting her eyes. "Ready?"

"Yes, Sir."

He reached into his leathers and adjusted himself. "Good girl. Okay. First question—where are we?"

"Um… on a deserted island in the Caribbean."

"Nice. Did we go there on purpose, or are we shipwrecked?"

"*Hmmm.* I like the thought of being shipwrecked. It sounds barbaric."

He smirked and stood to remove his pants. Might as well, since he would be fucking her senseless soon. "Barbaric, huh? Okay. What are we wearing?"

"We were on a dinner cruise and fell overboard, so I'm in a little black dress, and you're wearing a white dress shirt and pants, but we take them off because they're soaked. Now I'm in a bra and thong." She smiled, but her eyes remained closed. "You're going commando."

"Figures," he murmured, sitting down again, now completely naked. He leaned back in the executive desk chair, wrapping a fist around his shaft and, with his other hand, retrieving a few condoms he'd stashed in the drawer with other items. "Go on."

"We thought the island was deserted, but it's not." Her voice had gotten raspier... sexier... lustier. "You make a fire, and instead of attracting a rescue, natives find us. They're mad we invaded their island and take us back to their camp at spear-point. The only way they'll let us go is if we make a sacrifice to their god."

Chuckling, he dragged his fist up and down his dick, slow and steady, feeling the rough calluses against smooth flesh. Devil Dog hadn't been kidding—story time was fucking incredible, and they had just gotten started. "What kind of sacrifice?"

"We have to have sex on their altar, in front of everyone. *Mmmm.* But before that happens, I have to lay on the altar and be prepared by them."

"I like this." And so did she. Her breathing had increased even more, and her hand was moving faster. Groans escaped her as her legs and hips fidgeted in the chair. "Keep going. How do they prepare you?"

"Th-they all have to touch me. Four or five at a

219

time. And all over. My breasts. My ass. My pussy. Legs, arms, everywhere."

"Just the men, or are the women involved, too?"

"Both. Oh, God. Um… a dozen hands are touching me, all at once. Stroking me. They move me, so my head falls over the altar's edge. You're standing there, and they tell you to put your hard cock in my mouth and fuck it."

"Shit, that's fucking hot." Deciding to get into the fantasy, he got to his feet and walked toward her, rolling on a condom along the way. "Keep going, baby. Start moving that vibe faster."

"I'm sucking you off. My pussy is throbbing as someone fucks it with their fingers. More fingers are fucking my ass. Two mouths are sucking my breasts." Her one-handed grip on the recliner above her head tightened. "There's no part of my body that someone isn't touching. I don't… I don't know where I stop and everyone else begins. Oh, fuck me, please!"

Marco dropped to the floor and knelt between her legs. He licked her inner thighs, and she jolted and gasped, obviously not expecting it. Her groans increased as he trailed one hand up her torso and found the clamp strings, tugging them lightly. She was close, but he wanted to be the one to send her over. Taking the vibe from her pussy, he replaced it with his mouth, then alternated between licking her folds and flicking her clit with his tongue. Fuck, she was delicious. "Come for me, Butterfly."

He impaled her with his stiffened tongue, and she

shattered. Screaming, she came in his mouth and rode wave after wave of the intense orgasm to completion. But he didn't give her a chance to recover. Jerking her hips, he brought her to the edge of the chair and lined his cock up with her slit. She gazed at him through heavy eyelids. With one thrust of his hips, he entered her and saw stars as her wet heat surrounded him. "Fuck! Baby, you feel incredible. So damn hot."

He slowly withdrew and then slammed back into her. Again. And again. On the next pass, when his pelvis struck her clit, she went over the edge for the second time. His eyes rolled back in his head as her channel spasmed around him, and her cries of release reached his ears. Increasing his pace, he fucked her... harder, faster. If he died right now, it would be with a smile and a look of ecstasy on his face. A bolt of electricity shot from his spine to his heavy balls. One more thrust, and he held himself deep within her, shouting as he shot his cum in multiple streams into the latex barrier. When his orgasm finally began to recede, he dropped his head on her chest. They both heaved for oxygen. "I... holy shit... damn, woman. I think... that was even better... than the first time we were together."

She giggled and ran her fingers through his sweat-dampened hair. "Could be. But I think... we might... have to do it again in a little while... just to be sure."

PAULA LEIGHTON'S ANGER GREW AS SHE DROVE PAST Marco's house for a third time in the past hour. She glanced at the dashboard clock. Almost midnight. Where the fuck was he? It had been over a week since she'd seen his truck in the driveway, and he wasn't at Harper's house either. He must be staying at the compound with all the others. *Fuck!*

She'd taken a chance earlier in the day when she'd spotted the familiar vehicle outside Donovan's and entered the restaurant to catch a glimpse of the man she'd fallen in love with a year and a half ago. Her affection hadn't been returned, but never one to back down from a challenge, she'd begun to find out everything she could about him, hoping she could one day change his mind. But then that bitch had to get pregnant with his baby, and it had put a damper on Paula's plans.

Having been Trident Security's secretary for a few months, she'd been able to snoop around a lot when the men had been out of the office. Unfortunately, she'd gotten caught by that asshole, Evans, one day when she didn't expect him to return so soon, and he'd found her in his "restricted" war-room, as it was called. She'd been fired that afternoon, but by that point, she'd had access to much information, even though they'd obviously thought she hadn't been smart enough to figure some things out on her own. She knew everyone's phone number and their provider's account number since she received the monthly bills in the office mail. Finding all their home addresses on the payroll sheets had also been a piece of cake. Then she had gotten samples of Marco's handwriting and found a forger who'd been able to draft a letter to the whore, basically telling her to go fuck herself along with her unborn brat.

It had been pure coincidence finding out Harper was pregnant two weeks before Paula had been fired. They had the same GYN, who was also one of The Covenant's contract doctors for medical exams. Oh, yeah. She knew all about the sex club her former bosses had tried to keep her from finding out about. But it wasn't her thing—people fucking each other in public... such whores. When Marco became hers, she would insist they only had sex in private.

Paula had been in the waiting room for a routine physical when the other woman and a doctor walked out of the examining room. Harper had clearly still been in shock from getting the news and didn't glance in Paula's direction. It had taken Paula a moment to figure out the woman's stunned expression. While the new-mommy-to-be stood next to the front desk, the doctor told the receptionist to schedule an ultrasound and order prenatal vitamins from Harper's pharmacy. She then placed her hand on Harper's arm and offered support for when she told Marco he would be a father.

Paula had seen red at the mention of Marco, and her original thought had been to kill the bitch right then and there. But then, another idea had formed. She would bide her time and wait for the baby to be born, then eliminate the competition. Once Harper was out of the way, Paula, Marco, and the baby could be one big happy family.

Now, pissed off, she vowed to stick a fork in Lairson's ass to get him to finish what she'd hired him to do and steered the vehicle toward home. Well, it wasn't exactly her home. After getting fired from Trident, she'd used the measly severance pay they had tossed her way to live on while she searched for the perfect job opportunity. She'd found it three months later on Craigslist. An elderly recluse of a man with the beginnings of dementia had advertised looking for a cook/housekeeper/companion. Paula had dressed nice and turned on the charm, all but guaranteeing her the job. It didn't take long to figure out the man had no family or good friends who would notice if he went missing. The house was in a quiet neighborhood where most people kept to themselves and ignored those living around them. She'd slowly gained access to all the man's bank accounts and powers of attorney. Once she had everything she needed, she took advantage of his failing health and suffocated him with a pillow as he slept in his bed. The next day, she'd had a full-size freezer delivered and placed in the garage so she could stuff his body in it and avoid stinking up the house with decaying flesh.

Happily using the old man's money, car, and house, she didn't have to worry about having to work or deal with the nosy neighbors she'd had in her apartment complex anymore. She could devote all her time to planning her new life as Mrs. Marco DeAngelis.

CHAPTER SEVENTEEN

Marco was glad Harper's case had been adjourned for another day. It meant he could get her back to the safety of the compound while they continued to try to figure out who was after her and why. Things had been quiet since the day at the bomber's apartment, but he was worried a clock was ticking down and they'd soon be facing another attempt to kill Harper.

Cain Foster was walking in front of them out of the Hillsborough County courthouse in downtown Tampa and descending the steps to the parking lot across the street. Tristan McCabe had their six from about four paces behind. All three men, dressed in suits for court, had their heads on automatic swivel, scanning the area for any threat. Somehow, they timed it right with the walk-on-red signal and made it to their vehicles with nary a pause. After ensuring Harper was secure in Marco's truck, the two other men jumped into one of

Trident's SUVs and got ready to follow. They hadn't been worried about anyone tampering with either vehicle since, back in his war-room, Brody had hacked into the video feed of the courts' security system. Someone from the teams had been watching both vehicles the entire time court was in session to make sure no one had approached them.

After starting the truck, Marco eased out of the space, and once he was sure the others were right behind him, he exited the parking lot. While the Monday traffic was moderate, it wasn't close to what it would be in another hour or two when most commuters would leave their offices for the day. Stopping at a red light, he glanced at Harper, trying to keep his gaze off her long legs. The skirt of her gray suit had risen a little higher above her knee than it had been in court, due to her climbing up into his truck. Damn, he wanted those legs wrapped around his waist again—just as they had been the second time he took her last night before they'd reluctantly returned to the apartment to sleep in separate rooms. Out of respect for her mother, Harper wanted to tell her she would be sleeping in his bed from now on before actually doing it.

Loosening his tie, he yanked it over his head, then undid the top button of his dress shirt. Beside him, she sighed, and he took a quick peek at her before accelerating when the light turned green again. "Are you okay?"

"Yeah." The shake of her head was in contrast to the

one word. "It just pisses me off that some of these dirt-bags can manipulate the system and drag these cases out. My client's husband refused to let her work, kept full control over her money, abused her, and cheated on her. Then, when she finally dared to say she'd had enough, he hired a lawyer who was only in it for the billable hours. They file motion after motion, keeping my client in limbo. I freaking wish Florida was a community property state—assets acquired during a marriage get split 50/50. End of story. None of this bullshit."

Marco chuckled at her last sentence.

"What's so funny?"

"You just cursed, and the first thought that popped into my brain was you owe a dollar to the swear jar. I think there's more money in there from you than me." Both of them were trying to curb their language, so by the time Mara talked, she hopefully wouldn't pick up any bad habits. He couldn't stop the quick grin that spread across his face at Harper's scowl. "Sorry. Look, I know you were being serious, and I agree with you. I think a lot of times, the person who needs and deserves a good portion of the assets isn't the one who gets it. At least not in this state."

She was about to say something more when his phone's ringtone cut her off. Hitting the Blue Tooth feature on the steering wheel, he connected the call from McCabe a few cars behind them. "What?"

"Think we've got company. Blue Impala, two cars back from you and right in front of us. Male driver appears to be alone unless someone is ducked down." Marco glanced in the rearview mirror and spotted the vehicle. In a standard protection detail, Foster would have been right on his ass, but in this case, the two men had stayed back a little, hoping for this exact scenario to happen. With any luck, this was Harper's stalker. "He's been following since we left the courthouse, and it looks like he's waiting for an opening in traffic to make a move. Not sure if he's just in a hurry and happens to be going the same way or if you're his target. What do you want us to do?"

They had merged onto a highway with three lanes going eastbound. "Give him some room, but not too much. Let's see what he does. In the meantime, get the license plate to Egghead."

"Done already. I've got him on my phone and you on Foster's."

"Good. Then stay on the line with both of us." After a few minutes, he started thinking they were wrong about the vehicle when it made a sudden lane change to the right and accelerated quickly. Marco scanned what was ahead and to the side of him, taking it all in and making a fast lane change to the left, just as the Impala caught up to them. Behind them, Foster tried to get between the two vehicles, but traffic wasn't making it easy for him.

"Oh, my God!"

Trying to keep one eye on the road and the other on the Impala, Marco resisted the urge to look at Harper, who was staring out her window at the other driver. "What?"

"It's Ramon Nunez. I helped his wife disappear about six months ago. He's got a history with guns, assault, and a bunch of other stuff. Last I heard, he was still in jail for assaulting a neighbor."

"Shit." He swerved around another vehicle and punched the gas pedal. "McCabe, pass that onto Egghead, then hang up with him and call 911. We need backup fast. Identify yourself as Trident and ask for the on-duty supervisor. Let me know when you have him on the line. We're going to have to coordinate a block- ade. There are too many other cars around for us to run this guy off the road." He pulled his gun from its holster, flipped off the safety, and placed it in a specially-made pocket attached to the dashboard beside the radio. This way, he still had both hands free for the steering wheel, but if he had to shoot, the weapon could quickly be drawn and ready to fire. And he also didn't have to worry about it falling out of reach if the driving got crazy. "Harper, climb in the backseat and lay on the floor. If this guy starts shooting, I don't want you visi- ble. Keep your head down unless I tell you otherwise."

Kicking off her heels, Harper did as he'd ordered. Traffic was opening up, and he continued weaving between lanes, staying ahead of the suspect's vehicle. Foster was still on the guy's tail but resisted the urge to ram the guy off the road. They couldn't take the risk since it could hurt innocent drivers or their passengers.

SAMANTHA COLE

They didn't have to worry about the Impala trying to ram Marco's truck because the car would definitely lose that fight.

When McCabe informed Marco he had the desk sergeant on the line, he noted where they were on the highway. He then estimated where they *would* be when the patrol units were given enough time to set up a roadblock. Picking an exit ramp he knew wasn't heavily used since it led to a partially abandoned industrial area, he had McCabe relay the information. They'd be there in about five or six minutes. Hopefully, that was plenty of time for units to arrive and prepare to intercept. If not, then they would have to try again somewhere else.

Things got hairy a few times when Nunez tried to ride the shoulder to get next to them. But the asshole didn't have the "oh shit" driving experience that both the former SEAL and Secret Service agent had and couldn't keep up. When they were about a half mile from where he hoped the cops were set up, Marco gave Foster a heads-up. "All right. It's the next exit coming up. Ride his driver's side and force him down the ramp. As soon as you're sure he's committed, slam on your brakes. After I pass them, the cops should throw the spike strip."

Marco had done a similar scenario about two years ago when Brody and he had been chasing a guy on the U.S. government terrorist watch list. They'd spotted him after the geek had picked Marco up at the airport. It had been sheer coincidence they saw and recognized the member of al Qaeda from the alerts they got from Uncle Sam on a regular basis. Surprisingly, the take-down had gone without a hitch, and he prayed this one had the same results.

Making it obvious he was taking the exit by slowing down a little and putting on his blinker, he hoped the idiot didn't realize it was a trap until it was too late. Hitting the ramp at about thirty miles an hour over the suggested speed limit, he was thrilled to see their backup had arrived and were all set. As soon as he passed the cop partially hidden by brush, the man stepped forward and threw the spike strip, designed to blow the suspect's tires, across the road. Marco skirted one of the patrol cars blocking the bottom of the ramp and slammed on the brakes. Just as he expected, the hole between the patrol cars closed up behind him.

"Harper, stay down until I come back for you."

He grabbed his weapon and bounded from the vehicle without waiting for an answer. In the seconds it took for all that to happen, Nunez's car had run over the spikes, blowing the tires, and the jackass lost control, slamming into the high curb, disabling the vehicle. Amidst the smoke, the cops were shouting at the suspect to show his hands while their guns were trained on their target. Marco spotted McCabe and Foster high up on the ramp where another patrol unit had pulled in behind them. Both men stayed back, letting the cops do their thing but remaining alert if needed.

One of the units on the scene was a K9 and its

handler. The dog was barking and lunging against his restraint, dying to get at the suspect, who still wasn't obeying the orders to exit the vehicle. If Nunez wanted to be stupid, then the dog would be released. Marco really wished Nunez decided to be stupid. His hopes were dashed when the driver's door finally opened, and the man stuck his hands in the air. The nearest cop holstered his weapon, confident the others had his back, and yanked Nunez out of the driver's seat until he was face down on the ground. Once the suspect was cuffed, Marco fought the urge to interfere by kicking the guy's ass and, instead, turned back to his truck and opened the rear driver's side door. "Harper, you can get out. Are you okay?"

Instead of getting out or answering him, she stared into space, wide-eyed and breathing rapidly. Too rapidly. *Oh, shit.* He forgot all about her panic attacks. He'd only seen her have one once, many years ago, and it was just as scary now as it was back then. Kneeling outside the door, he took her hand and rubbed her arm, careful not to crowd her. "Sweetheart, take it easy. Slow, deep breaths, baby. Come on. You can do it."

"Is she all right?"

Marco glanced over his shoulder and found one of the cops had come to check on them. "Panic attack. Do you have any paper bags in your car?"

"Yeah, in the evidence kit. Hang on."

The uniformed officer hurried to his nearby car as Marco tried calming Harper down. "Easy, baby. It's going to be fine. Take some deep breaths."

A few moments later, a brown lunch bag was thrust into his hand, already opened, and he brought it to her mouth. "Come on, sweetheart. Breathe into the bag. You're going to be fine. Nothing is going to happen to you on my watch."

It took a few rounds of coaxing, but finally, she seemed to comprehend him and grabbed the bag from his hand, trying desperately to take slow, deep breaths. After about two or three minutes, the excessive amounts of oxygen in her system from the rapid breathing were replaced by the minimal amount of carbon dioxide needed by her blood. Her color began to return to normal, and she pulled the bag from her mouth, taking a few gulps of fresh air while swiping at the tears rolling down her cheeks. "I—I'm s-sorry. I don't... don't know w-what happened."

"*Shhh*. It's fine, baby. It's all over, and you're okay. I'm sorry. I should have checked on you sooner." He stood and held out his hand. "Do you want to get out or stay in there?"

"O-out, please."

She exited the vehicle on shaky legs, and he held her close until she could stand alone. Foster, the only one still wearing his tie, and McCabe joined them, laughing at something. When he raised an eyebrow at them, McCabe shook his head, trying to get his words out between his chuckles. "Funniest fucking thing I ever saw. The dog's been on official patrol for only a week now. After he calmed down, the handler relaxed the leash. Damn dog took a few steps forward, lifted a leg, and peed on fucking Nunez. It was fucking classic."

Marco snorted before he threw his head back and chortled. Despite still recovering from her panic attack, Harper began giggling as well. Soon, they were all laughing so hard that more tears had to be wiped away.

When she got herself back under control, Harper turned to him. "Does this mean it's over? I mean, with his history, I'm sure the bail will be high if he isn't held without it."

"I don't know, baby. First things first. They'll take him in and book him. Murdock will have to go through a procedure to interview him since this arrest is out of his jurisdiction. Once we're clear here, I'll take you back to the compound, and then I'm sure Ian will get us permission to watch the interview."

Speaking of his boss, the man screeched his SUV to a halt beside Marco's truck and jumped from the driver's seat. Just as fast, Devon exited the passenger seat as Boomer and Brody arrived in the geek's pickup truck. It was obvious the incident had freaked them out as much as it had him. Ian was the first to reach them. "Is everyone okay?"

Marco nodded, still not leaving Harper's side. "Yeah. We're good. But I think we have to come up with a name for this takedown since this is twice it went like clockwork. Although this one had a funnier ending thanks to the canine unit."

The newcomers stared at him in confusion, then burst out laughing when McCabe explained it to them before adding, "Think we can get Kat to train Beau to do that?"

"You fucking cunt! Where the fuck is my wife?"

As he was being led to the back of a patrol car about a hundred feet away, Nunez's bellows caught everyone's attention, but none more than Marco's. "That son of a bitch."

With clenched fists, he growled and took a step forward, but his teammates quickly closed ranks around Harper and him, stopping him in his tracks. Ian spoke to him in a low voice, full of warning. "Chill, Polo. There are cameras everywhere."

He hadn't noticed until it was pointed out to him that the police activity had attracted the usual lookyloos, many of whom had their cell phones out, filming everything. Behind him, Foster took hold of Harper's arm and helped her into the backseat of the truck again, closing the door after she was in. Marco was glad the man instinctively knew to get her out of sight.

The on-scene sergeant approached the group and shook a few hands, having dealt with the team numerous times. "I'm going to need whoever was in the two vehicles to come to the station for statements."

"Can you send someone to our office for Ms. Williams' statement?" Ian asked, taking charge, as usual. "Her mother and daughter are there under our protection. Until we know for certain they're out of danger, I'd prefer to keep them all together at the compound."

"Sure, I think we can arrange that. I was told a

detective from Clearwater wants to talk to this guy about the bombing attempt the other day and a home invasion."

Ian nodded. "Yeah, Drew Murdock. I notified him as soon as I heard the tail was someone Harper recognized. We'll be meeting him at the station. Polo, why don't you ride with me? Dev, Boomer, and Egghead can take Harper back to the compound. Foster. McCabe. Follow us so that you can give your statements."

"Wait."

Glancing over his shoulder, Marco saw that Harper had rolled down her window a little and had been monitoring the conversation. He stepped closer to the truck. "What's the matter, sweetheart?"

She must have hit the button on the door because the glass lowered a few more inches. "I have to go to my office— "

"Absolutely not. You're—"

"It's important, Marco. I have to activate the alert system for Friends of Patty. I know it's highly unlikely Ramon knows where his wife is, but I have to let the contacts know what happened so they can send the alert down the line. They need as much warning as possible if they need to move her."

He shoved a hand through his hair in exasperation. While he loved that the woman was strong-willed and stood up for herself and others, it sometimes made him nuts. "Can't you do that from the compound?"

"No. They'll think I was hacked if the alert doesn't

come from my computer's IP address. It's an encrypted program."

Brody, who'd been listening to the two bicker, leaned in. "I can get you into your system, Harper, and make it look like you're on at the office. It's easy enough to do if you know what you're doing—which, of course, I do."

"Anyone ever tell you you're too freaking humble?" she asked with a sigh.

The geek grinned, making his dimples stand out. "All the time, darlin'. All the damn time." Slapping his best friend on the back, he opened the driver's door to Marco's truck and climbed in. "Your woman is in good hands. See you later."

Brody pulled away as soon as Devon and Boomer were in a position to follow while Marco watched them drive up the entrance ramp to the highway.

His woman. He liked the sound of that.

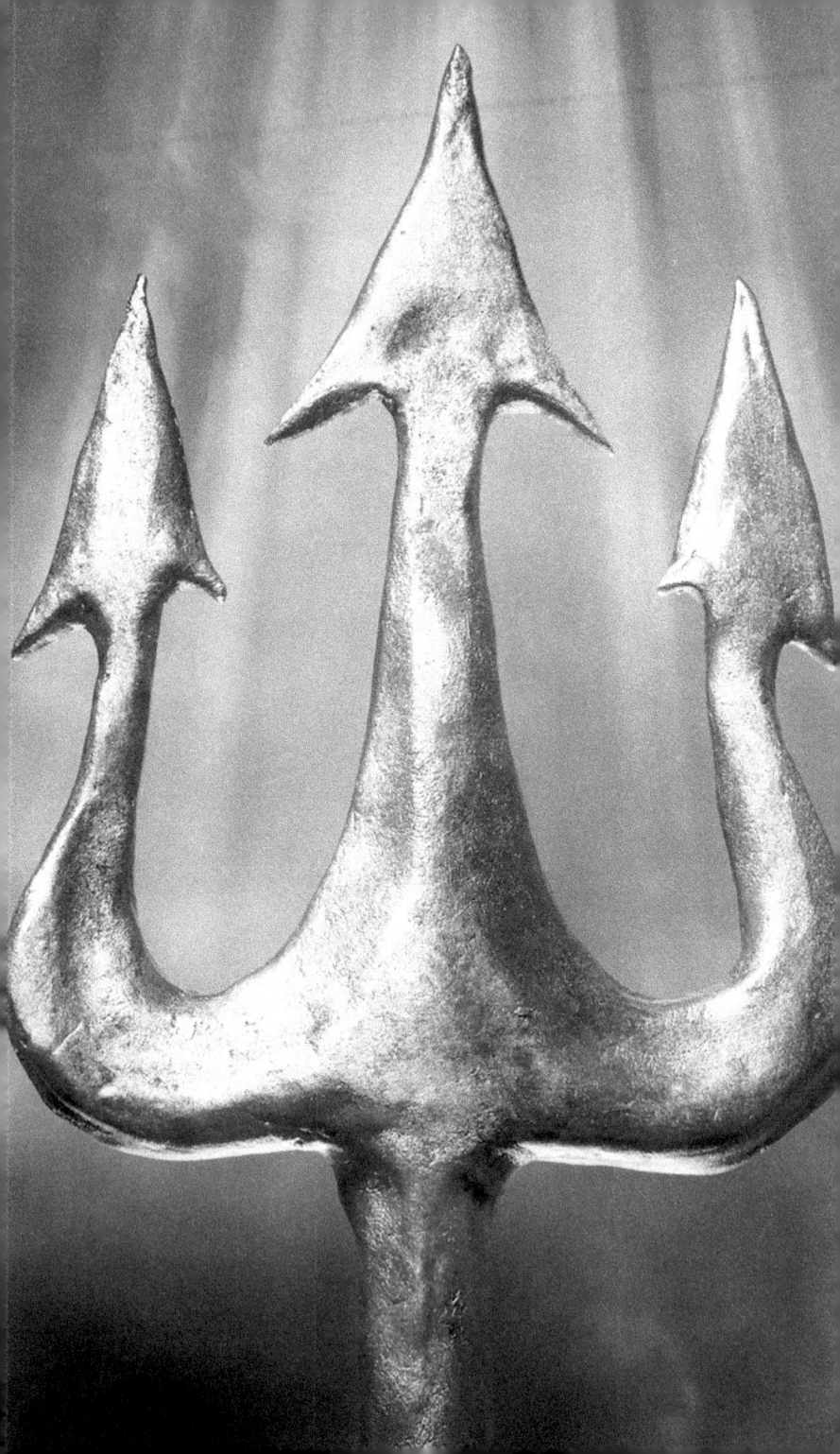

CHAPTER EIGHTEEN

Marco stared at Nunez through the one-way mirror with Ian at his side. The asshole was cooling his heels in the interrogation room, and Murdock was intentionally drawing out the wait. It was all part of Interrogation 101—make them sweat a while. A nervous suspect was a chatty one. While he understood the tactic, the delay was driving Marco bat-shit crazy.

One of the arresting uniformed officers was standing stoically in the room with Nunez who was sitting at the table drumming his fingers. Foster and McCabe were out in the detective bureau, giving their statements for the record. Marco had already given his account of what had happened, and a detective had been dispatched to the compound for Harper's statement.

The door to the observation room opened, and Murdock and a TPD detective entered. The tall Black man in a tailor-made suit wasn't someone the Trident team had worked with before, and he stuck his hand out to them as he introduced himself. "Isaac Webb. I've heard a lot about Trident. Nice to meet you, but I wish it was under better circumstances."

"Ian Sawyer. This is Marco DeAngelis, and we wish it were under better circumstances as well."

After his boss shook the man's hand, Marco followed suit. "I appreciate you letting us watch the interrogation."

Leaning his hip on the only desk in the small room, Webb nodded. "No problem. Murdock here told me what's been happening, but I wanted to fill you in on what we found before we go in there." He handed Ian the manila file he'd been carrying. "Nunez knew your bomber. Or, at least, we believe he did."

"What?" Marco hadn't been expecting that bit of info, and it was evident from his surprised expression that Ian hadn't either. "How?"

Webb pointed toward the file Ian had opened and was now scanning. "They were in Zephyrhills Correctional at the same time four years ago. Same cell block for about three months."

"Fuck! He's got to be the one who hired Rodgers."

"Easy, Polo." Boss-man was still flipping through the new information in his hands. "I'm not too sure about that."

"What? Why? He obviously blames Harper for his wife going missing—"

"Exactly." Ian glanced at Webb and Murdock, who

nodded in silent agreement, clearly understanding the other man's reasoning. "Yes, he blames Harper, but why kill the one person he believes knows where his wife is? Think about it. If Nunez was the one in Harper's house the night she was attacked, why knock her out and run? Why not threaten her to reveal where his wife is?"

Fuck! He'd been hoping they had the right guy, but Ian was making sense—especially if they added the rose and note on his truck and the phone issues and letter by messenger over a year ago. If Nunez wanted to know how to find his wife, he wouldn't get rid of the one person he thought could lead him to her. Marco ran an irritated hand through his hair before letting out a deep breath to calm himself. He was letting his anger rule his thinking, and it was never a wise thing to do. "Damn it. All right, let's find out what he fucking knows."

Murdock and Webb left the observation room and, moments later, entered the interrogation room. From behind the mirror, Ian and Marco watched the men play good and bad cop. Unfortunately, it didn't take long to realize Nunez had nothing to do with the assault and bombing attempt. While the man's hatred for Harper was clear, his body language, confused responses, and adamant denials of guilt had everyone believing he had no idea what they were talking about in reference to the attempts on her life. There were no signs of even the slightest recognition of Rodgers when Nunez was shown the other prisoner's mug shot from four years ago. After close to an hour of questioning, it was evident that, once again, they were back to where they started—with no suspects.

The two detectives rejoined them in the observation room while the uniformed officer took Nunez downstairs to a jail cell. Webb crossed his arms and addressed Marco. "Sorry, but as you saw, I doubt he's your man for the bomb and home invasion. He's a lousy liar—you could tell when he answered the questions about the gun and drugs." When the cops on the scene did an inventory of the car before it was towed, they found a 9mm under the front seat and some crack cocaine in the glove compartment. "The good news is, we have enough to hold him on for parole violations. By the way, my captain said to thank you for waiting for the backup instead of taking Nunez on yourselves, since he's already having a shit day. Although I have no doubt it saved the bastard's life since, from what I've heard, I shouldn't bet against you guys any day of the week. Anyway, with his history, the bail will probably be too high for the asshole to come up with it, if the judge doesn't just deny it in the first place. I'll give you a ring after his arraignment and let you know his status."

Marco shook his hand. "I appreciate it, thanks."

"No problem."

As Webb returned to his desk in the detective bureau, Murdock walked with Marco and Ian to the lobby, where McCabe and Foster were waiting. When

Cain saw them, he lifted his hands questioningly. "Anything?"

Pushing the door to the parking lot open, Ian shook his head. "Nope. He's not going anywhere, but he's also not our suspect."

"Fuck," McCabe mumbled as they all filed outside after the man. "Now what?"

"Back to square fucking one."

MARCO WATCHED AS HARPER PACED THE EMERGENCY room's waiting area, wishing he could set her mind at ease. They'd been halfway back to the compound from the police department when Devon had called to say an ambulance was on its way for Harper's mother. Listening to Harper give her statement to the police detective resulted in fifty-nine-year-old Karen experiencing chest pain. The quick-thinking detective had radioed into dispatch for the paramedics to be sent. After getting the news, Ian immediately changed direction, and they met the ambulance at the hospital. That had been well over an hour ago, and they were still waiting to hear from the doctor—as if Harper needed more stress today.

In addition to Ian, Harper, and Marco, several other people were waiting around. Some were with them—others were waiting to be seen or were there for family members. Foster and McCabe were stationed outside at both the ambulance and walk-in entrances. Kat and

Boomer had driven Harper over, with Abbott following them. The female sniper was now posted outside Karen's cubicle, keeping watch—Ian wasn't taking any chances with the woman's safety since they once again had no idea who wanted to hurt Harper.

"Marco?"

He tore his gaze from Harper to find Kat standing beside him, holding out a cup of coffee while balancing a cardboard tray with several other cups. "I figured everyone could use some."

As Boomer rushed over to take the tray from her, Marco took the proffered drink. "Thanks, hon. I appreciate it. I'll take one for Harper too."

Striding over to her, he stepped into her pacing path, causing her to stop short. "Here. Kat brought everyone some coffee."

She took it from him but didn't bring it to her lips. Her eyes filled, and she wiped them with her hand before any tears escaped. "I'm scared. She looked so pale when they put her in the ambulance. I was an idiot for giving my statement in front of her."

Taking the cup back from her, he placed both of them on a nearby coffee table, then pulled her into his arms. He loved how she melted into him, letting him comfort her without hesitation. "It's going to be okay, sweetheart, and it's not your fault. Your mother is a tough woman who'll be around for a long time if she has any say about it."

Her arms tightened around his torso in a quick

squeeze before she released him. "I should probably call Kristen to see if Mara is all right."

"She's fine. I guarantee it. Kristen knows what she's doing, and Devon's reading all those books you gave them. And I told him there's always YouTube if he gets stuck with anything." She snorted and chuckled as he'd hoped she would. "Trust me, she's in good hands."

"Karen Williams's family?"

They turned as the nurse's voice carried over the low chatter throughout the room. Marco took Harper's elbow and stepped forward. "Yes. This is her daughter, Harper."

The older woman dressed in scrubs gave them a reassuring smile. "You can see her now. She's stable, but the doctor is going to admit her. He'll explain everything if you follow me."

Moments later, they passed Lindsey Abbott as they entered the small room where Karen was lying on a gurney with wires and IVs hooked up to her. Overhead, a monitor beeped out her steady heartbeat and displayed the rest of her vital statistics, all of which currently appeared in their normal ranges. A nasal cannula sat on her upper lip, supplying her lungs with fresh oxygen.

Her eyes opened as she heard them approach, and she held out a shaking hand to Harper, who grasped it like a lifeline. "How do you feel, Mom? Do you still have chest pain?"

"No. They gave me some nitroglycerin pills, and

after the second one, the pain went away. How are you doing? I'm sorry about all this."

"Oh, please. It's not like you planned it. It was probably all the stress of the past ten days. It's me who should be sorry for putting you through all this. I should have insisted you go to Aunt Toni's in Miami until we figure out who is behind all this."

Marco bit his tongue instead of correcting Harper since he still didn't know if it was his past that had come back to haunt them, but he couldn't shake the feeling he was right about that. Soft footsteps entering the room had him pivoting to see who it was. An older, gray-haired man wearing bifocals and blue scrubs greeted them. "Hi, I'm Doctor Mark Schaffer, the cardiologist."

Shaking the man's outstretched hand, Marco introduced himself and then Harper.

Opening the chart he was carrying, the doctor consulted several reports. "We just got the labs and EKG results back, and it doesn't appear you had a heart attack, Mrs. Williams. However, I think you've developed angina, which is basically chest pain associated with heart disease. It occurs when the heart doesn't receive enough oxygen, and with your history of high blood pressure, it's not an unreasonable diagnosis. What we need to do now is figure out if you have stable or unstable angina."

"What's the difference?" Harper asked.

"Stable angina is usually brought on by an increase in stress or moderate to heavy activity, and we can control with medication. Unstable angina comes on at rest or with very little activity and will probably require either angioplasty or bypass surgery, but we'll discuss that if needed. I'm admitting you to the cardiac floor, Mrs. Williams, and scheduling a cardiac catheterization for tomorrow or Wednesday. That's a procedure where I'll make a small incision in the groin area and then thread a small catheter through the artery up to the heart to see if there is any blockage in the coronary arteries. It'll be done under local anesthesia and take about an hour or so. From there, we'll decide on a course of treatment. Any questions?"

Karen glanced at her daughter and then Marco. When both shook their heads, she turned back to the physician. "Not at the moment, but after this sinks in, I'm sure I'll have a few."

The man smiled. "That's usually the case, but don't worry. This is all very routine. Now, they'll take you upstairs as soon as a room is ready for you. In the meantime, just try to relax. I'll check in with you later, but the nursing staff will keep an eye on you."

They all thanked the man as he returned to the emergency room nursing station, leaving them to digest everything he'd told them. It was another two hours before Karen was transported to the cardiac unit and ordered Marco to take Harper home because she looked pale and exhausted.

Ian, Kat, and Boomer had left a while ago, and the boss had sent Knight to the hospital to join Abbott on guard duty outside Karen's room. After returning from the restroom to where he'd left Harper with her two assigned bodyguards in the lobby, Marco found her ending a phone call.

"That was Jenn," she told him. "She brought Mara back to our apartment because Kristen was having another bout of morning sickness—why they call it morning sickness when it happens around the clock is beyond me. Anyway, Jenn said everything else is fine. The baby just woke up from a nap, and she's feeding her. I asked her to order us salad and pizza because all I want to do is go home and crash."

Marco took her arm and led her out to his truck in the parking lot with Foster and McCabe flanking them. She barely spoke on the way home and almost dozed off once or twice. Back at the compound, he opened the door to Jake and Nick's unit for her and was surprised to see a furry body, with a mug that was so ugly it was cute, eyeing the new arrivals. "Hey, Spanky. What're you doing here?"

The bullmastiff was sprawled out on the living room floor and didn't even bother to lift his head, but his tail thumped against a coffee table leg in greeting. Marco knew the passive response could be deceiving in this case, because if the dog had sensed a threat to any of his favorite humans, he would have immediately gone into protective mode.

Jenn came out of the temporary baby's room with a smiling Mara on her hip. "Parker had to go to Orlando for a construction job meeting, and Shelby took off work to go with him. The meeting is early tomorrow morning, so they left a little while ago to have dinner and get a hotel for the night. I'm dog sitting until they get home tomorrow." She set the baby into a bouncer seat, next to Spanky, with little toys hanging above it to entertain her. "Harper, you look exhausted, and please don't take that the wrong way. The pizza and salad should be here in a few minutes, and the baby's been fed and had her diaper changed, so let Uncle Marco do what he does best and take care of you."

Dropping her purse and coat on a nearby chair, Harper nodded. "I will. And thanks for watching Mara."

"No problem."

Marco winked at his niece. "Thanks for everything, Baby-girl. Are you going to stay for the pizza?"

Picking up some books from the coffee table, she shook her head. "Nope. I ordered a chicken Caesar salad to be delivered for me, and also ordered extra pies for all the guards after checking with Uncle Ian. I've got a mid-term tomorrow in my child psychology class, so I've got lots of studying to do. Come on, Spanky. Let's go downstairs."

After closing the door behind the young woman and bulky canine, Marco patted Harper on the ass as she bent over to say hello to the baby. "Go lay down for a bit. I think you need the sleep more than the pizza right now. I'll heat it up for us later. Mara and I will just catch the news and see if there's a game on somewhere."

He was pleased when she didn't argue with him and

headed down the hallway after giving both Mara and him a quick kiss. "Just save me one slice to have with my salad and don't let me sleep more than an hour, please, otherwise I'll be up all night."

"No prob." Starting with the oh-eight-hundred court appearance, it had been a long day, but now, at five-forty-five in the afternoon, it was still too early for her to try to sleep straight through to the morning. As he placed his keys, wallet, and gun on the dining table, his phone rang. He glanced at the screen and then hit the connect button. "Hey, Reverend. What's up?"

"Hey. How's Harper's mom?"

Obviously, someone had called or sent a text to Jake out in California earlier. Sighing, Marco flopped into one of the two living room recliners to the delight of Mara, who giggled at him. "Looks like angina and not a heart attack. They're scheduling her for a cardiac catheterization tomorrow, if not Wednesday. She's stable and was sent to the cardiac unit. We just got back to your place a few minutes ago, and I sent Harper to bed. Between everything that happened today, and all she's been through in the past week, she needs to crash for a few hours. I think I'll plan a low-key scene for after her nap. She needs to get out of her head for a bit, otherwise, I'm worried she'll have another panic attack."

"Yeah, Egghead filled me in on what happened with the tail you had. Give Harper a hug from me." Before Marco had a chance to respond, his friend continued.

"Listen. I spoke to Todd, and he's going to do some snooping around."

Jake's snitch, Todd Wheeler, was a fallen-through-the-cracks-of-the-system teenager, who'd ended up in a few foster homes after his mother had been murdered. At sixteen, he'd struck out on his own and landed on the streets, eventually developing a drug habit to support. Catching him breaking into cars for cash, the former SEAL had befriended him and helped him get his act straight, which included sobering up and finding a job and a place to live. Now a year and a half later, the kid still repaid him with loyalty and information.

"Shit. I just hope he doesn't get himself into a jam. This asshole has already wasted one person and tried to kill Harper twice."

The sound of papers shuffling came over the line. Jake must still be at his office in the new San Diego compound Trident had purchased. "Yeah. I told him to be careful, but he's a smart kid. He knows the ins and outs of Tampa's underground pretty well, and I trust him not to do anything stupid. I gave him your number. Nick and I are taking advantage of a few days off, so we're going camping tomorrow through Thursday, and I'm not sure what the cell reception is going to be there. I told Egghead to order me some satellite phones, along with a bunch of other stuff, but they won't be in until next week."

A knock at the door had Marco rising from the chair. "I think the pizza was delivered and someone brought it up. Have fun camping, and I'll keep you posted."

"Sounds good. Talk to you later, bro."

Disconnecting the call, he opened the door to find his best friend standing there with a box and bag from the pizzeria they always ordered from. He stepped back to let Brody enter, then shut the door again. After putting the food on the table in the dining area, the geek squatted next to Mara and softly tickled her belly, causing her to thrash all four limbs and let out a little squeal. "Hey, sweet-cheeks. Where's your momma?"

"Hopefully sleeping," Marco responded, since his daughter was still only speaking gibberish. "I was just about to check."

"Mind if I stay for dinner then?"

Waving his hand over his shoulder, Marco strode toward the hallway leading to the bedrooms. "Beer's in the fridge."

CHAPTER NINETEEN

An hour later, both men had eaten three-quarters of the pizza, leaving two slices and most of the salad for Harper. Mara had made it through twenty minutes of the news as her Uncle Brody made funny faces at her while she sat in the bouncy seat he'd set on the coffee table. After she nodded off, Marco placed her in her crib, keeping with Harper's routine, and turned on the baby monitor.

The two men briefly discussed the case, then turned the subject to the news and sports. Having Brody here, with no one else around, had gotten the wheels in Marco's head spinning. A ménage was on Harper's green limit list, meaning it was something she'd done before and was willing to do again. When he'd questioned her about it, she'd told him the few times she'd participated in a threesome, it was with the Dom she'd been collared to for two years. Sometimes, another male Dominant joined them, and then other times, it had been with a female submissive. Since finding all that out, he'd been tossing around the idea of having his best friend join them for a scene. It wouldn't be a regular thing, just occasionally, but Marco knew how much pleasure they could give his sub together. And with all that was going on, he'd meant what he'd said to Jake earlier—he needed to get Harper out of her head for a bit to destress.

He was sure his teammate would be more than willing to join them since he was now aware of Harper's experience in the lifestyle. While Brody had told him point blank that he'd hit on Harper in the past, Marco wasn't worried any other lines would be crossed. They all knew the dynamics of the lifestyle very well. Brody wouldn't do anything Marco disapproved of, and he, in turn, would honor his submissive's limit list and safeword. The baby would be sleeping for a few hours, and they had the monitor on, so Marco only had to ask Harper if she wanted to proceed with a ménage tonight.

Rising from the recliner, he told Brody to stick around and he'd be back in a minute, then walked down the hallway to the master bedroom. Wearing a pink cotton loungewear set, Harper was sleeping on top of the comforter in the darkened room. Kneeling next to the bed, Marco softly stroked her hair. "Hey, Butterfly. Time to get up."

Her eyes fluttered open, and after they focused on him, she stretched the kinks out of her body. "Hi. What time is it?"

"A few minutes before seven. Are you hungry?" A growling from her stomach had them both chuckling. "Okay, that question is answered. Listen... Brody's here. After you eat, I'd like to ask him to join us, but only if you're okay with it. If you're not up to it or don't want him as a third, just tell me. But I think you will not only enjoy yourself, but it will also help you destress. It's your choice, though, and I'll respect it."

While she remained silent, thinking it over, he could see her eyes had lit up at the suggested scene. He dragged the back of his hand down her shoulder and across her left breast, feeling it immediately tighten in response to his touch. "Don't answer yet. I want you to eat first. Either way, we'll play tonight because I think you need it. But it will be your decision whether Brody joins us."

She sat up and cupped his cheek with her hand. "Thank you."

"For what?"

"For taking care of me and knowing exactly what I need. For being here for me through all of this."

Standing, he held out his hand to help her up, then embraced her. "I'm just sorry I wasn't there for you for the past year, but I hope someday you'll be able to forgive me."

"I already have. Besides, it wasn't your fault to begin with."

He waited in the bedroom while she used the toilet in the master bath before washing her face and brushing her teeth. When she emerged, she appeared more awake and rested. As she checked on Mara, Marco went to the kitchen to get her salad and reheat the pizza. He wouldn't mention anything to Brody until Harper gave him a verbal answer that she wanted the other man to join them.

After finishing her dinner and the half a glass of wine he'd poured for her, Harper stood from the other recliner, then knelt in front of him in perfect present positioning. Her gaze remained on his lap as she said, "My answer is yes, Sir."

Not expecting this turn of events, Brody raised his eyebrows at Marco, who simply gave his friend a nod, then gently placed two fingers under Harper's chin and lifted until their eyes met. "Say all of it, Butterfly. What are you saying yes to?"

"I'm saying yes to playing right now, with Master Brody being a third during the scene, Sir."

There was no hesitation in her response, which thrilled him and made his desire to pleasure her grow. "And what are your safewords?"

"Cauliflower or red."

"Good girl. Go to the master bedroom and remove your clothes. Then return here with my toy bag from the spare bedroom." He'd left it in there last night after cleaning the toys they'd used in the panic room.

"Yes, Master."

After watching her disappear down the hallway, Brody turned back to his friend. "Are you sure about this? I mean, this isn't a weekend fling here."

"Absolutely." He leaned forward with his elbows on

his knees and sighed. "She needs this, bro. And our friendship, our brotherhood, will always be good. No worries there. There're very few people who I trust with my woman, and with kicking my ass when it needs it, and you're number one on both lists."

The geek nodded, then smiled. "Okay. Then, I'm honored and will follow your lead. Anything I should be aware of?"

"Nope. She's into the usual standard play. Nothing extreme. She's done the threesome thing before, but it's been quite a while. I started with a smaller plug last night, then increased the size after the first scene we did. She should be able to take both of us without a problem. I'll make sure she's stretched enough before we double up."

"Sounds good," was the response given as Harper reemerged. She didn't have a stitch of clothing on, as instructed, and didn't seem embarrassed or shy about it. As she handed Marco his toy bag, she started to drop to her knees again.

"Uh-uh, sweetheart. Across my lap so I can warm you up with a spanking." He set the duffel on the floor next to the recliner, then sat back to give her room. This wasn't a punishment spanking—being in the lifestyle for years, Harper would know that. Instead, it was precisely what he'd said—a warm-up. It would help her get into the zone of full submission while leaving the past week's stress behind. Moving to the side of the chair, she gracefully lowered herself, belly down, across his lap and the leather armrests.

Still sitting on the couch, Brody grabbed the remote, changed the TV from ESPN to a classic rock music channel, and then settled in to watch the other two get started. Marco ran his hands down Harper's bare back and up her thighs until they met on the twin swells of her ass. He squeezed them, bringing the blood to the surface so she wouldn't bruise. "Ready, Butterfly? I want you to count out loud. I'll start with ten, and then you'll switch to Master Brody's lap to receive ten from him. Okay?"

"Yes, Sir."

He hadn't even struck her yet, and already he could feel the tension leaving her body. Lifting his left hand, he swiftly dropped it again, smacking her left ass cheek. While she'd been expecting it, that didn't stop a gasp from escaping her lips, followed by, "One."

The next one landed on her right cheek. "Two."

He slowly increased the force behind each spank as he worked the count up to ten. Not to the point of harming her, but he was learning his sub really enjoyed pain play. The last strike landed on one of her sit spots, and he could hear the cleansing tears in her voice as she rasped out, "Ten."

He rubbed the reddened flesh and asked, "Where are you, sweetheart? Give me a color."

"Green, Sir."

"Then go get the rest of them from Master Brody."

He helped her stand and watched as she stepped over to his friend. Brody held out his hand, and she took it without pause, letting him guide her across his lap. From where Marco sat, her feet were pointed in his direction, and he could see the wetness coating her pussy as she got into position.

Giving her ass a few squeezes, the other Dom repeated the earlier instructions to Harper. "Count out loud again, subbie. Are you ready?"

"Yes, Sir," was barely out of her mouth when the first strike landed on her already tender flesh. While she counted out her spankings, Marco stood and removed his shirt, pants, shoes, and socks, leaving only his boxer briefs on for the moment. Picking up his duffel, he quickly found his stash of condoms, along with the lubricant he would need to take her ass. Glancing at the couch, he decided to move them into the master bedroom as Harper announced the twentieth and final spank. The king-size bed would be more comfortable for all of them, and he was sure Jake had installed a restraint system for when Nick and he were here.

Taking what they would need with him, along with the baby monitor, he told her, "Help Master Brody get undressed, then bring him to the bedroom. I'll be getting a few things ready."

HARPER'S ASS WAS ON FIRE, BUT THE PAIN INFLICTED BY hard palms on her soft flesh had quickly transformed into pleasure. Damn, she'd missed this. Not only the D/s aspect, submitting to a Dom... her Dom... but being able to clear her mind of everything and just feel.

As Brody helped her rise again, she trembled—not from fear but anticipation. From the spanking, she was already in the zone of contentment, bordering on sub-space, and it would only get better from here. She trusted Marco with everything in her and knew she could trust the man before her as well. Her Dom wouldn't expect or accept anything less from his best friend.

When Brody stood, she tugged his T-shirt out of his pants and dragged it over his head. He ran his fingers through his dirty-blond hair as she tossed the shirt on the couch and then turned her attention to his belt buckle. He'd removed his boots and socks at some point—probably during her first spanking. Her fingers fumbled with the top button of his jeans, and she gave him a "seriously?" look when she realized the fly was all buttons. He chuckled, then hissed as she brushed against his denim-covered hard-on while undoing each one. Pushing the jeans down his slender hips and toned thighs, she was surprised to find he was going commando.

Holy crap, is he hung!

Dropping to her knees, she bunched the fabric to his ankles, letting him step out of them.

Giving her a hand up again, he swept her hair off her shoulders, then lifted her chin with his fingers until their gazes met. "Before we go any further, Harper, thank you for letting me join you. It'll be my honor and pleasure."

"And mine, Sir." She was honest with him. Her pussy was already throbbing in unison with her ass cheeks.

Taking his hand, she led him to the master bedroom, where Marco had been busy. The lights were off, but he'd lit several candles, giving the room a soft glow. The comforter had been removed from the bed, and only the sheets and pillows remained. He'd pulled out four straps attached to the bed posts, which Jake had tucked under the mattress. She'd found them while changing the linens the other morning, grateful her mother hadn't seen them —that was one question she'd no desire to answer. Two pairs of leather cuffs and a blindfold were sitting on the bed, which Marco pointed to. "Bro, get these on and start hooking her to the posts, belly up, but don't do the ankles yet. I need to grab one more thing from my bag."

"No prob. Come here, subbie."

Harper followed the Dom and stood next to the bed, where he made quick work of attaching a set of cuffs to her wrists as she held her hands out in front of her chest. In the meantime, Marco returned with the pink vibrator she'd used the night before. It seemed as if every one of her orifices would be filled tonight. Her eagerness grew along with the wetness between her legs.

After the cuffs had been attached to all four limbs and the blindfold secured, the men helped her up on

SAMANTHA COLE

the bed. A hand nudged her hip, and she scooted over to the center of the mattress. "Good girl," Marco praised. "Arms up and out."

They attached the cuffs to the straps so she couldn't move her arms. With the blindfold on, she had to rely on her other senses. Neither man said anything, but she heard them moving around. From the far end of the bed, Marco told her, "Bend your knees, Butterfly, and spread your legs."

Oh, fuck. She now knew why he'd brought the vibe in. It was going in her ass—most likely to stretch her a little more, so she could take one of the men there, and she wondered where she would be accommodating the other. While doing as ordered, she felt the bed tilt in two spots. At the foot, which she assumed was where her Master was, and to her right side. Her ass cheeks were spread, and fingers applied lubricant over her anus. At the same time, a mouth closed around her right breast, sucking and licking the nipple. Pleasure shot through her, and the hands at her ass took advantage of it, breaching her sphincter with a finger. It wasn't long before the digit was replaced with the lubricated vibe. It was eased in and out several times until, suddenly, it was turned on. "Oh, shit! Oh, my God!"

The mouth at her breast moved over to the other one just as a tongue licked her pussy. *"Ahhhh! Ffffuuuck!"*

Her loud cry was reprimanded with a smack to her

thigh. "Quiet, Butterfly. We don't want to wake the baby. Straighten your legs for me."

Following the order while biting her bottom lip, she was reduced to gasps and whimpers as the Doms licked and nibbled her flesh. The vibe was lighting up every nerve ending in her rectum, and the combination of sensations pushed all thoughts from her mind except how wonderful it felt. Just when she thought they would push her over the edge, both mouths left her. She held back a cry of disappointment and felt the bed moving, realizing they were changing positions. From what she could figure, Brody was now between her legs, attaching her ankle cuffs to the straps at the foot of the bed. The vibe was then rotated and gently moved in and out, stretching her. *But where is Marco?*

Her answer came in the form of the sudden pain, then pleasure, which shot through her as a drop of hot wax landed on her right breast. She gasped and bucked her hips before large hands held her in place, and a mouth attacked her pussy again.

"Color, Butterfly?"

"Green, Sir," she gasped, trying to keep her voice down. "Very green."

"Good." She could hear the unspoken desire in her Master's voice.

Another drop landed on her left breast, the heat sending her into orbit. It hurt briefly but quickly mutated into an indulgent feeling of electricity shooting through every cell of her body. As Marco painted her chest and abdomen with wax, Brody feasted on her, alternating with sucking on her swollen pussy and exposed clit, and playing with the vibe. The sensations became too intense, and she was reduced to begging for release at the fear of coming without permission. "Please, Sirs! I'm close! It's too much! Please!"

"Come for us, Butterfly."

With those words, another drop of wax plopped directly on her left nipple as Brody closed his teeth on her clit. Behind the blindfold, her brain exploded with Fourth of July fireworks. Darkness was overcome with sparks of white, red, blue, and yellow lights. She opened her mouth to scream, but a pillow was quickly put over her face to muffle it. Thank God, because not only would Mara have awakened, but the entire compound probably would have heard her. As her orgasm continued in waves, the men didn't let up. Pleasure/pain shot through her again when more wax struck her right tit, and her pussy was tongued relentlessly. She plummeted a second time, screeching into the pillow.

This time, they let her recover, and once her cries were reduced to quiet moans again, the pillow was removed. Marco asked, "Okay, sweetheart?"

"Oh, yes… Sir… v-very okay."

She heard both men chuckle as they unhooked the cuffs from the straps. They were far from done, she knew that, as she lay limp, waiting for whatever was coming next. Or *who was coming* next.

CHAPTER TWENTY

Marco reveled in his submissive's muffled screams of pleasure. If her skin hadn't held her together, he was sure she would have fragmented in front of them. Her body quaked with her release as Brody and he drew it out as long as they could, unsurprised when a second orgasm hit her just as hard. Once he made sure she was okay, he glanced at his friend, who rose to his knees in between her legs after removing the now inactive vibe from her ass and tossing it aside. Grinning, the man wiped her cum from his mouth and chin. "Holy shit! Too bad Shelby isn't into women because I'd love to see the two of them come together."

Chuckling, Marco finished undoing the last strap. Before the pixie submissive had been collared by Parker, the two men had tag-teamed her many times. The woman was explosive, to say the least, when she came. They had never been able to fuck her mouth at the moment she orgasmed because she had an involuntary reflex to bite down—and neither man had wanted to become detached from their manhood as a result. "I know, right? Scoot over, Butterfly. Let Master Brody lay down. You're going to ride him as I fuck that luscious ass of yours."

"Yes, Sir."

He smiled. She sounded breathless, and he wondered if it was from her back-to-back orgasms or the anticipation of taking them both at the same time. His bet was the latter. From what she'd told him, it'd been years since she'd taken two cocks at once.

After rolling on a condom he'd retrieved from the nightstand, Brody lay in the center of the bed, and then Marco assisted Harper into positioning herself over the man's hips. Brody held his hard cock in place as she slid down on it, both of them moaning as she did. With little thrusts of his pelvis, the Dom quickly filled her, then held himself deep in her core, waiting for her Master to join them. "Shit, man. Hurry up. She feels fucking incredible."

"I'm coming."

Still blindfolded, Harper smirked. "Not yet, but you will be."

Her sassiness prompted Brody to reach around and smack her ass. "Brat."

They all laughed as Marco put on a condom and then climbed on the bed behind Harper. Grabbing the tube of lubricant, he coated two fingers on one hand

and then his throbbing shaft. He thrust his fingers into her back hole and made quick work of ensuring she would be able to take him. In the meantime, his friend could no longer stay still and moved his hips as he played with her nipples. The moans coming from her mouth had Marco speeding things along. Withdrawing his fingers, he gently pushed on her back until she draped herself across Brody's upper torso. He straddled his friend's thighs, not bothered by any unintentional contact with him, as he'd gotten over any weird feelings years ago. While both of them were nothing but straight, in order to tag-team, they were bound to brush up against each other.

Lining the tip of his cock with her back hole, Marco rubbed his hand up and down her back. "Ready, sweetheart? Tell me if you need to be stretched more or if something doesn't feel right."

"Y-yes, Sir. Please, hurry. I need you."

And he needed her... no, it went beyond that. His heart clenched. *Holy shit!* It'd happened. The impossible had happened. This woman had taken his hardened heart and, without even trying, showed it how to fall in love. He was up, down, and turned around in love with her, wanting to spend the rest of his life with her. Not just because of Mara, although his daughter was the icing on the cake, but because he didn't think he could live without seeing Harper every day and making love to her every night. Once again, his sister had to be laughing at him from her grave.

A moan from Brody brought Marco back to the

here and now. Tilting his hips, he entered Harper's ass an inch at a time. It took several rounds of withdrawing and plunging until he was seated far enough inside her. As they had done for years, neither man needed prompts or instructions from the other when they began to alternate their thrusts. One was on the way out, as the other was on the way in.

The three of them grunted, groaned, and perspired as one. Despite stretching her, Harper's ass was so tight, Marco was almost seeing stars as she hugged his cock, and he felt Brody's through the thin membranes separating them. It wasn't long before the pace was increased, and his balls drew up tight with his pending release. "Hit her clit."

The other man snuck his hand between his and Harper's lower bodies and found the little pearl that would send her over the edge, taking both men with her. As soon as her orgasm hit her hard, Marco came with her, emptying his seed into the latex barrier a few moments before Brody followed. Their shouts and loud groans were a testament to the fact they'd all forgotten to keep their voices down when nirvana had overtaken them.

Marco was surprised they hadn't woken the baby up as they lay in a heap, trying to catch their breath. The monitor on the nightstand was silent. It was good to know Mara could sleep through all the commotion they'd just made. Easing from Harper's body, he left the two of them to untangle themselves as he stumbled to the bathroom to dispose of his condom and get a wet washcloth and dry towel to clean his sub. It might come as a shock to most people outside of the BDSM community, but this was the part of a scene he loved the best—the aftercare—because that was when his submissive needed him the most. It was when she was utterly exhausted and sated and counting on him to take care of her needs, which were no longer sexual or part of an emotional release. This was when he felt truly needed.

Returning to the room, he found Brody easing her to the mattress as he slid out from under her limp body. When the man noted his partner had come back, he removed the blindfold the sub was still wearing, then stood from the bed and headed to the bathroom to get rid of his condom. Marco sat next to Harper and spread her legs. He cleaned her with the cloth, then moved so he could sit with his back to the headboard and put one of the pillows in his lap.

Coming out of the bathroom, Brody stepped over to the bed and helped him remove all the cooled wax from her chest and abdomen. They then moved the woman's upper body until her head rested on the pillow. He glanced at Marco, who nodded. "Feel free to stay or go. It's up to you."

Brody leaned over and kissed Harper's bare shoulder. Reaching down, he grabbed the comforter from the carpet and opened it to place it over the submissive's body. "I'll leave you to do what you do best. And

I'm glad things are working out for the two of you despite everything going on. You deserve to be happy and in love, man. Everyone does. So don't blow it." He held out his fist, which Marco bumped with his own. "Be good. And thanks. It was an honor."

"Same here. I'll talk to you tomorrow." As the man headed for the door, Marco added, "Hey. Can you check on Mara? But after you put your clothes back on, because I really don't want her seeing her uncle bare-assed naked with his junk swinging in the breeze.

The only response he received was a middle finger in the air, and he chuckled as the bedroom door closed. On his lap, Harper sighed and cuddled closer as he stroked her back and silky blonde hair. He didn't care how long she slept since she needed it, but he would watch over her while she did as he tried to figure out how to keep her and their daughter safe. And in the morning, he'd tell them both how much he loved them.

Three Weeks Later

STRIDING INTO IAN'S OFFICE, MARCO WAS A LITTLE surprised to see Devon there too. Boss-man had called him during his Wednesday morning workout in the gym to say he needed to talk to him. After wiping off his sweat with a towel, he'd grabbed a bottle of water and hoofed it over to the offices. From where he sat behind his desk, Ian told him, "Close the door and have a seat."

Uh-oh. This can't be good. As the door clicked shut, he walked over and sat in one of the visitor chairs in front of the huge mahogany desk filled with papers and files. Devon remained where he sat on the arm of the couch to Marco's right, with his arms crossed. Marco glanced from one man to the other. "What's up?"

"Drew Murdock called— "

Excited, he sat up straight. "He's got a lead?"

Frowning, Ian shook his head, disappointment evident in his expression. "No. They've got nothing. Everything has gone cold. Same as us. With no more contact or attempts on Harper's life, things have died down. I'm sorry, Polo, but we've got to move on. We've got gigs coming in faster than ever, and we can't keep contracting them out. I need the Omega team training together so we can start utilizing them for what they were hired for."

Slumping back in the chair, Marco ran a hand down his face in frustration. When Devon opened his mouth to say something, he held up his hand to stop him. "It's all right. I knew this was coming. I'm not happy about it, but I understand where you're coming from. And I got the same shit from Harper last night. She needs to get back to her practice. Her staff has been there, but she can't continue doing things from here."

It was apparent that neither of his bosses was happy the case had been left dangling without a solution either. But who knew if the guy was just bidding his time or had been killed in a car wreck or arrested for something else within the past few weeks? They couldn't keep hiding here forever. Devon uncrossed his arms and leaned forward. "We're not saying we aren't still going to protect her, but it's going to be a lower scale. It could be weeks, months, or never before he strikes again. You two, Mara, and Karen are welcome to stay in Nick and Jake's apartment. Neither one of them will be in for at least another month, the way things stand now. And it's not like there aren't enough beds in this compound to accommodate everyone. We'll keep Blackhawk's men on a rotating assignment for any time Harper or her mom have to leave the compound." There was a pause, and Marco could almost guess what was coming. "Egghead, Boomer, and I will be heading out on Monday to do a week's recon in Belize. Keon called with some info on the white slavery case they've been dogging and wants us to check things out. He doesn't want to go through channels because he's afraid they have an internal leak. The last two times they tried to check things out, the operation had up and scrammed before they got there."

Larry Keon was the number-two man in the FBI—the Assistant Deputy Director—and Trident's primary contact in the agency. It was through him many of their contracts and missions had been acquired. Ian dropped his hand on the desk. "You know we'll do anything for Harper and you. You're family. But I can't keep handing cases off. I'm not sending you with Dev because I know you need to be close for now. So, as of tomorrow, you're back on drill instructor detail with Omega."

Nodding, Marco asked, "Anything specific you want me to start with?"

"Yeah. How to avoid a hard-on while on the princess detail."

A bark of laughter came from Devon while Marco groaned and rolled his eyes. "Seriously? Tahira's coming for a visit? For how long?"

Princess Tahira was the daughter of the King of Timasur, a small country in Northern Africa near Mali. While the king, queen, and prince were friendly and undemanding during their excursions to the family's vacation residence in Clearwater Beach, the twenty-four-year-old exotic beauty was a completely different story. Especially when it came to her unmarried American bodyguards supplied by Trident. The original team members rotated through the "princess detail" with personnel from Blackhawk Security and worked with the Timasur guards to keep her safe during the visits. There wasn't a single one of them whom Tahira hadn't hit on, and whenever they turned her down, her "revenge" consisted of hours of shopping in every boutique within a hundred-mile radius—give or take a few miles.

But whatever happened during Ian and Angie's vacation in Timasur last year, at the King's invitation, had softened Boss-man's opinion of the woman. "She's coming in next Thursday and will stay for three weeks. Nothing big is scheduled except a charity function she'll be attending. I'm supposed to be getting a fax on that later today. Two of her female cousins are also coming, but Tahira, of course, takes priority over them if anything goes down. Drill it into the Omega team's heads that I will kill anyone who can't control themselves around her—she's off-limits. Costello has nothing to worry about since, as far as I can tell, Tahira has no interest in other women, but every guy who hasn't put a ring on someone's third finger is fair game for her."

Marco grinned at Ian. "Think I can avoid the come-on if I tell her about Harper and Mara?"

"I actually think she'll be thrilled for you, but then she'll add the rug-rat shops to her list of stops." Marco gave Devon the finger when he started laughing again since as the bosses, Ian and he didn't have to rotate through the detail, unless it was an important event. "Anyway, back to the present, you might want to wander into the garage later—Babs reported for duty today."

Tempest Van Buren's handle in the Air Force had been well earned. Babs was short for 'bad-assed bitch'—a moniker she'd been given after several harrowing missions where she did some remarkable helicopter flying and saved the lives of numerous troops, quite often under enemy fire. Her last military mission didn't end as planned, though, when she had no choice but to crash land the helo. She'd suffered a career-ending injury, but somehow, the five men on board with her had walked away with a few scratches, their bells rung, and one or two broken bones. Having been on numerous missions in the Middle East, with Babs flying SEAL Team Four in and out of danger, the news of her crash had reached them quickly. As soon as Ian had heard she was retiring from the military due to her injury but could still fly, he'd called her with the job offer. On top of everything else, she was an ace mechanic, so she would fly and maintain their new chopper and their vehicles.

Marco had experience flying choppers from before his SEAL days and kept current with all his licenses and certifications. But they'd wanted a full-time pilot who would be able to stay with the bird during a mission, and Marco was too valuable a team member to be left behind. However, he would train with Babs so he could take over if needed. "Yeah, I'll check in with her now." He stood. "Then I'll go get Harper's schedule for you. She'll probably be calling to thank you since she's been chomping at the bit to return to her office."

"And she'll be guarded the entire time," Devon vowed, following him out of Ian's office.

"I know. Thanks." Taking the back door from the offices down a short hallway, he pushed through the door leading to the maintenance garage. The area took up the back half of the warehouse building and had more than enough room to work on several vehicles at once or have the bird towed in if the rotor blades were folded. Loud music blared from a nearby radio as he scanned the garage, looking for their new pilot/mechanic. A few of the company's SUVs were scattered around, some with their hoods up, as well as Ian's Audi S5 Coupe. Not seeing anyone, he strode to the radio to turn it down.

"Change that station, and we're going to have a problem."

Smiling, he only lowered the volume, then turned around to see Tempest walking toward him, with an almost imperceptible limp, from behind one of the SUVs. The brunette was about five-seven with a slender build and dressed in a new maintenance jump-suit and high-top sneakers. "Just bringing it down to a reasonable decibel. But, seriously, the Bee Gees? Are you kidding me?"

She shrugged her shoulders. "My mom loved music from the sixties and seventies. She always had it on at home or in the car, which was really embarrassing when it was her turn to carpool. But somewhere along the line, it rubbed off on me."

Marco laughed. "You're looking good, Babs. How's the leg?"

"Still missing." She stopped and pulled her left pant leg up a few inches to reveal the prosthesis she now wore after losing the limb below the knee eighteen months earlier. Someone had painted it with the American flag for her. "But I'm digging the new one. Just can't wear high heels anymore." Stepping up to him, she gave him a hug hello, which he returned. "I hear congratulations are in order. Marco 'I'm-never-getting-married-or-having-kids' DeAngelis is a dad. Go figure."

"Yeah, shocker. But I'm digging it now," he teased, throwing the word back at her. "I'll bring Harper and Mara by later so you can meet them." He paused. "Listen. I heard about your father. I'm sorry I couldn't attend the services—I was OCONUS."

A heavy sadness fell across her face. "Yeah, Ian told me half the team was in South America somewhere... and... well, committing suicide doesn't exactly deserve a big send-off."

She glanced away, clearly wanting to change the still-raw subject that had delayed her starting date with Trident, so he dropped it and gestured toward the nearby equipment bench. "I ordered the basic shit for you but figured you'd want to order your own preferences on some stuff."

"You got most of it. I'm still doing an inventory, though. Egghead said to tell him what's missing, so I'm making a list. The bird is awesome, by the way. I couldn't believe it when Ian said he'd gotten his bloody rich hands on an MH-X Silent Hawk. I love flying stealth. If you get a chance later, want to go up for a spin?"

He feigned horror. "With you? Nope. No way. Uh-uh. Your version of going 'for a spin' usually results in someone puking, even someone with experience. Call me when you want to go for a nice, steady flight."

"Chicken." Laughing, she stepped over to turn the radio's volume back up until "Play That Funky Music" was blaring.

Shaking his head in amusement, he left her to finish

hcr inventory and headed up to the apartment they were all still using. After Karen's release from the hospital with a stable angina diagnosis and new medication, she'd taken the spare bedroom, giving Marco and Harper's relationship her blessing. With Kristen and Angie's help, they'd gotten more furniture for the room, including a dresser, armoire, nightstands, and a flat-screen TV.

A semi-comfortable routine had developed for them. While one of the Trident women watched Mara, Marco would take Harper to her office for a meeting with her staff about current cases or to court. Foster and McCabe were usually the ones tailing them. After returning to the compound, Harper did what she could on her laptop, and Marco joined Brody and Boomer in checking out a bunch of dead-end leads.

They'd cleared Harper for play at the club, and Marco had paid her full membership fee, which she'd fought him on before finally giving up when he wouldn't budge. They were a couple now—D/s and boyfriend/girlfriend, even though he thought those latter terms were so high-school-ish. While he fully intended to put a ring on her finger soon, along with a permanent collar on her neck, he wanted the attempts on her life to be far behind them first, with no chance of recurrence. Only then would they be at peace and ready to start the next phase of their lives.

Scanning his hand, he pushed open the door and found Mara in her command center seat, where she could swivel around three-hundred-sixty degrees to play with various attached toys. It was on the living room floor near Harper, who was sitting on the couch going through her case files and making notes. She smiled at him and took off her reading glasses, which she only seemed to use while reading court briefs. "Hi. Done with your workout already?"

The domesticity of the scene was something he'd begun to crave each day. Coming home to his woman and child was a blessing he now knew he couldn't do without. He hoped one day soon, it would be without the worry that someone wanted to take it all away from him. "Yeah, it got cut short for a meeting with Ian and Devil Dog. Your mom's not back from cardiac therapy yet?"

She shook her head, then looked at the clock on the cable box. "Nope. Lindsey and Darius should be back with her in about twenty minutes or so. Is everything all right?"

Stepping around the giggling baby, he sat in the recliner closest to the couch. After letting out a big sigh, he filled her in. "The police have run out of leads and have to turn their attention to other cases. So does Trident. We'll be staying here until I'm more comfortable with returning home, but I've got to start training the new team tomorrow. We can't keep putting it off. Half of my team has to head out of the country this coming Monday, but I'll stay home. And you're getting your wish. Devon needs your schedule for the rest of this week and all of next week so he can set up the contract agents guarding you at the office and in court.

They'll be driving you, though. I want someone experienced in vehicle evasion if someone comes after you again."

"Okay. I can live with that. I'll draw up the schedule when Mara goes down for her nap in a little bit." She paused. There was clearly something else on her mind, and his gut clenched as she bit her lip.

"What is it, Butterfly? Talk to me."

"What… what happens when we leave here? Are Mara and I going back to our house while you return to yours?"

Moving from the recliner to the spot next to her on the couch, he took her hand and brought it to his mouth for a kiss. "What do you want to happen?"

"Honestly, I want what we have here. I don't want to go back to living in separate houses. I-I really don't want to go back to my house. I won't feel safe there anymore." Over the past several nights she'd woken in a cold sweat with flashes of the night she'd been attacked. Unfortunately, she hadn't been able to give them any information on the attacker. From what she remembered, she'd heard a noise as she entered the foyer and turned. He'd been wearing a ski mask, and she only had a quick glance at him before he swung the bookend at her. It'd struck her as she spun around to run. She didn't remember him saying anything at all.

"I'll tell you what. This weekend, we'll put both houses on the market and start looking for one for our new family… and any other kids who might join us down the road."

Her eyes widened. "Really? Are you serious?"

Chuckling, he kissed the back of her hand again, then turned it over and kissed the palm. "Yeah, I'm serious. I told you I want us to be a family, and someday soon, we'll make it official. And I can't think of a better way to start than with a new house without any haunts. Even though most of her stuff is gone, Nina's ghost is in my house. I still associate that room as the one where she died, no matter what I do to change it. I want a place that only has room for happy memories of her. Somewhere she can watch over her nieces and nephews in peace. And yes, I want more kids. I want you. I want it all."

"I think that's the most beautiful thing you've ever said to me. I love you."

He leaned in and kissed her lips. "I love you, too, Butterfly."

"Da-da." Mara's voice had them both twisting to stare at her. "Da-da."

Marco was shocked. Although the now six-month-old baby had been saying "ma-ma" for almost a week, this was the first he'd heard "da-da." "Holy shhh… ugar. She said, 'da-da!' Is that the first time she's said it?"

"I think so," Harper giggled. "But remember what I told you the other day. She probably hasn't associated it with you yet. Same as ma-ma." It'd been hysterical a few days ago when their daughter had first called Harper "ma-ma," to her delight, and then proceeded to call everyone else "ma-ma," including Tiny and Beau.

Kneeling on the floor, he pulled the play seat closer to him. "Say it again, Mara. Say da-da."

"Da-da," she shouted before blowing raspberry bubbles at him and clapping her little hands.

"That's my girl. I love you, too, sweet cheeks."

"Da-da-da-da-da-da."

He smiled, knowing he wouldn't give this up for the world.

CHAPTER TWENTY-ONE

"Fuck you, assholes! Come and get me, you pansy-assed pieces of shit! I fucking dare you!

Marco chuckled as Boomer disappeared behind the black curtain of the third-floor window of the simulation training building to go find a place to hunker down and wait for the Omega team to sniff him out. While the entire six-man team hadn't all reported for duty yet, for a couple of reasons, the four men who had —Foster, McCabe, Knight, and Mancini—were training with Abbott as an additional member for now.

Yesterday morning, the first day back on training, he'd run them through the obstacle course, various calisthenics drills, and sparring in the gym. Today had started with gun qualifications at the indoor range and the outdoor shooting gallery, which was set up like the Main Street of a town. Targets would randomly pop out of buildings' doors, windows, and alleys as a team member walked down the "street."

After lunch, Marco had set them up to begin working as a team—one unit—eventually having them functioning as a well-oiled machine. Each had worked in teams before, either in the military or law enforcement, but it would take a while for them to learn their new teammates' styles, lines of thinking, strengths, and weaknesses.

They were dressed in black combat pants and T-shirts and loaded to the gills with gear and non-lethal weapons, ready to go in and find their tango. Boomer would don protective goggles and earwear so the team could deploy a flash-bang grenade if warranted. Their guns were replaced with a new line of simulated ones, which felt, sounded, and reacted like real ones would, including a kick when fired. The differences being they were bright red for safety reasons and used lasers to shoot their targets. The "tango" and "hostage" were wearing light-weight jumpsuits and ski masks, which would register any shots that hit their mark. Boomer would feel a mild vibration anywhere he was "shot."

The interior of the building had been completely coated with a unique black paint. If the laser shots hit the walls, ceiling, or floor, a colored dot would appear when a purple fluorescent light was scanned over them. Marco would have to do that quickly after the scene was shut down, as the marks would fade after fifteen to twenty minutes until they were completely gone. But he should only need to scan one room this time. Each team member's shot would register a different color, so they knew whose went where.

After giving Boomer a few seconds to hide, Marco shouted, "All right, team! Your tango has a hostage—in this case, a blow-up doll known as Naughty Nurse Betty, with a lousy makeup job and perky tits. And Baby Boomer refuses to be taken down. Rescue the hostage without deflating her, and get your tango, dead or alive. Move out!"

As three team members rushed to the front entrance, two went around to the rear door. Marco followed the trio from a distance. He forced himself to concentrate on the "rescue" and not on Harper being in her office, out from the protection of the compound. Yeah, she had two bodyguards from Blackhawk Security on her, but he was still uneasy about it. He had to get over it, though, if they would have some sort of normalcy again in their lives. A little while ago, he'd run into Kristen, who'd been heading over to Harper's law practice. They were having a video conference with the attorney in New Jersey they were using for her asshole ex-husband's lawsuit. The local lawyer had apparently found some interesting evidence to use to fight the demand for half of Kristen's book royalties.

Taking a few steps into the building, he shut the door behind him, plunging them all into complete darkness so their night-vision goggles could be utilized. With headsets on, the team spoke quietly to each other as they cleared the rooms one by one. Marco was like the rest of them, having no clue which room Boomer had chosen. Many of the interior walls could be moved to create different setups so the teams wouldn't get complacent with their training.

On the second floor, Foster was the lead heading into a room when shouts and gunfire rang out. Within thirty seconds, the chaos died down, along with the "tango," who'd been hit in the head and chest by the lasers. The "hostage" had survived.

"Good job," Marco praised. "But next time, Boomer will shoot back at you with paintball pellets, and then we'll see how good you are." He unclipped the fluorescent light wand from his utility belt and waved it over the walls and floor. Only two dots in different colors were on one wall, but that was to be expected when firing on a moving subject. Contrary to what Hollywood wanted people to believe, it was not that easy to do under pressure despite a team being highly trained.

After ensuring everyone had removed their night vision goggles, Marco walked over to the window to let some light in. As he pulled the blackout curtain to the side, Boomer's cell phone rang. The goofball was still lying prone on the floor where he "died" and rolled to his side to retrieve the phone from his front pocket. "Yo!" There was a pause, and then he kicked Marco's leg to get his attention. "Hey! Where's your phone?"

His hand immediately went to his hip and remembered he'd left his cell on a picnic table outside the building, along with some of the equipment. His first thought was something had happened to Harper or Mara. Panic assailed him. "Shit. What's wrong?"

"Chill. It's the front gate. Jake's snitch is here to talk to you."

He hadn't heard from Todd Wheeler since the day after Jake told him the kid was doing some snooping of his own. Hoping they finally had a new lead to check out, he left Boomer to finish the scene's aftermath evaluation and jogged toward the front gate, grabbing his phone on the way. Bringing Todd into the Trident offices, he pointed toward the conference room as they passed the reception desk. "Colleen, can you send Dev and Ian in ASAP?"

"They're in Ian's office with Dr. Dunbar," she informed him.

"Then send her in too."

Todd took a seat, and Marco strode to the opposite side of the conference table, sitting across from the nineteen-year-old. "What'd you find out?"

The skinny kid leaned on his forearms on the table. "One of my old street buddies called me a little while ago. He would've called sooner but hadn't heard I was looking for info. He was at a party..." Todd paused as Ian, Devon, and Trudy Dunbar entered the room and took seats at the table in silence. "Anyway, my buddy was at a party the other night and said there was this high, drunk dude bragging about how he was going to be coming into money as soon as he offed some chick. Said they tried to blow her up, but she got lucky."

"Shit," Devon spat. "Please tell me your buddy knows this asshole's name."

Todd shook his head. "No, sorry. He never met the

287

guy before and didn't know it was important then, but does the name Paula mean anything to you?"

The name didn't mean anything to Trudy, but the three operators glanced at each other in shock. It wasn't that common a name, and none believed it was a coincidence. Ian was the first to recover. "Yeah, why?

"He started complaining about the person who hired him. Kept saying that name—Paula—and what a bitch she was. He was only putting up with it because he was going to cash out big time when it was over. He even said something about her being crazy and that she killed someone else but didn't say who or where." He paused as his head swiveled, his gaze darting from face to face. "So, who is she?"

Ian stood and dug his wallet out of his back pocket. He handed Todd a hundred-dollar bill and a Trident business card. "Someone who's going to wish she'd never laid eyes on any of us. Thanks for the info. If you hear anything else, let me know. My cell number is on the card."

Knowing he was dismissed, Todd stood, pocketed the card and money, and headed for the door. "No prob. Say hi to Jenn and Alyssa for me. I haven't seen them since Christmas." Having no immediate family, the team had invited him for the holidays after he'd given Jake information on Alyssa's father, who had been trying to kill her after abusing her for years.

Fury boiling within him, Marco barely waited until the kid was out of earshot before slamming his fist on the table. "I'm going to fucking kill her!"

"Calm down, Polo. Colleen! Get both teams in here!"

"Yes, Sir," was the startled response from the reception area to Ian's bellowing.

Checking his cell for a number, Ian pulled the room's landline phone toward him on the table, hit the speaker button, and dialed a number. After three rings, it was answered, and they could hear the squawking of police radios in the background. "What is it, Sawyer? I'm kind of busy."

Ian set his hands on the table and leaned forward. "I don't care, Murdock. I think we know who's behind the bomb and assault."

"Shit! Who?"

"A former female employee who has had an infatuation for Marco in the past." The team members started filtering in with curious looks on their faces, including Babs, who'd just come in from the garage. "She was our secretary and fired for being too fucking nosy. None of us suspected it had gone this far, though. I think she was the one who offed the bomber too."

One of the last ones to enter, Brody sat beside the very pissed-off but still stunned Marco. He leaned toward his best friend and whispered, "What's he talking about?

Ian held up his hand to silence all chatter as the detective's voice came over the speaker. "All right. Text me the info, but it will have to wait unless it's an emergency. I just pulled up on a domestic homicide. I'll send someone to pick her up as soon as possible."

"That's—"

"That's fine," Boss-man replied, cutting off Marco's intended rant as he stood, sending the chair he'd been in flying backward on its casters, causing the entire room to stare at him. "Let me know when they have her."

Despite sounding distracted, Murdock acknowledged him, and Ian disconnected the call. He glared at Marco. "Stand down, Polo. He's got his hands full, but it doesn't mean we can't go get her ourselves."

"Someone mind filling us in?" Boomer asked, clearly as confused as Brody and the Omega team were.

Too livid to explain, Marco lifted his hand in a gesture for Ian to tell them. The boss straightened to his full height and crossed his arms. "We know who's behind the attacks on Harper... Paula Leighton."

"What! Are you fucking shitting us?"

Ian rolled his eyes at the youngest member of the original Trident team. "Do I sound like I'm fucking shitting you, Baby Boomer?"

"Holy fuck." Brody's murmur was filled with the shock Marco was still feeling.

Eyeing the new team, Ian filled them and the psychologist in about the former secretary whose workplace crush seemed to have taken over what little sanity they now realized she had.

As Harper disconnected the video conference call with her old law school friend, Kristen sat back in her chair. "So, my bastard ex-husband stole money from his clients, lost it gambling—which I didn't know he was into, by the way—and is now suing me to refill the coffers before the authorities find out."

Nodding, Harper finished writing a quick note in Kristen's file. "That's about it in a nutshell. Stephanie will have her investigator bring everything to Tom's company before the day is out and then work with them to report it to the police in New York City. With all the evidence the investigator has uncovered, I wouldn't be surprised if Tom's arrested by mid-next week after they verify everything."

"So, the lawsuit will be dropped?"

Standing, Harper walked over to the mini-fridge she kept in her office to grab a can of Diet Coke. Kristen shook her head in silent refusal when she held one up to her. After shutting the door, she sat behind the desk again. "I'm afraid not. At least not that fast. He may decide to continue since he'll need the funds to finance his defense campaign. But Stephanie will keep filing motions to hold it up as long as possible." She took a sip of the cool liquid. "And if it does end up before a judge, you heard what she said. She doubts a judge would find in his favor since we have plenty of witnesses who'll state he told you to keep the little profits your books made."

Kristen snorted. "Yeah. He was pretty shocked at

the divorce proceedings when he found out how 'little' those profits were. Not."

"Speaking of which, I heard *Velvet Vixen* climbed into the top ten on the *New York Times* Best Sellers list. That's awesome since it was just released last week. Congrats."

The woman beamed and had every right to be proud because it was a huge accomplishment most authors never came close to, much less achieved. "Thanks. I think the interview I did for *Good Morning America* on the release day had a lot to do with it. Oh, and guess what?" Her eyes opened wide as excitement seemed to pour from her. She didn't even pause for Harper to answer her. "I forgot to tell you! I'm so excited. I'm going to be on *The Victoria Ashton Show*! Can you believe that? Me... on Victoria's show... I watch her every day!"

"That's great. When?"

"Next month, as long as my OB/GYN clears me to fly, which is a Devon demand. I tried to tell him there's nothing to worry about until my last trimester, but Master Devon wasn't having any of that." She glanced at her watch and stood, grabbing her jacket from the back of the chair. "Speaking of the devil Dom, I need to stop at that gourmet butcher shop he likes for some steaks. This kid has to be a boy because why else would I be craving beef for the past week? The good thing is that Devon insists on grilling them, so all I have to do is throw together a side and salad."

Harper also stood, picking up Kristen's file to give to her secretary. Her practice was on the bottom floor of a three-story Victorian house that had been converted into offices. The second floor was used by a massage therapist, who was also skilled in acupuncture, but her appointment hours varied. The top floor office was currently unoccupied, and the landlord had a sign out front advertising the available space. The building was on a quiet side street, off the main drag, and was separated from the local library by a large parking lot and about twenty yards of trees and shrubs. There were three undeveloped lots on the other side of the house before a residential neighborhood began. While she lived in Clearwater, this area was just over the Tampa border.

Opening the door to her office, they found her paralegal, Monica, had come out of her own office and was chatting with Joanie, their secretary. One of the bodyguards, Jerry, who'd driven Harper to work both days, stood against the wall next to the door. She'd tried to convince him to take a seat yesterday, but he'd refused, saying he could respond faster while standing. His partner, Lucy, was in the parking lot, sitting in their car. They rotated every half hour to let the other person sit for a while.

Harper was just about to hand Kristen's file to Joanie when the main door to the office opened. Everyone looked to see who was walking in, but all they saw was a hand come from the side and throw something into the large reception area. Before anyone could react, the room exploded with a blinding light and deafening boom. Thrown off her feet, Harper fell backward, striking her head against the door jamb to her office, and then her world went black.

CHAPTER TWENTY-TWO

"Egghead, find out where she's living now, and we'll go pay her a visit."

The geek was already way ahead of Ian's order, typing furiously on his laptop while Marco dialed Harper's cell number on his phone. She would recognize Paula if the nut job showed up at the law practice.

Damn it. No answer. She was probably still on the video call with the lawyer in New Jersey. Marco's mind was flying in ten different directions. How hadn't anyone figured this out before? "Fuck!"

Everyone stared at him when he slammed his palms on the table. "I fucking forgot all about this... shit! Back in the hospital... Harper said something about calling me a bunch of times."

"Yeah, and we found out the blocks had been put on the phones," Brody replied. "Paula had to have done it. She had all our cell numbers."

"But *after* Harper couldn't get me on my cell, she

said she called here and left several messages with the secretary. Paula was still here back then. The bitch forged a fucking letter to Harper telling her I wanted nothing to do with her or Mara."

Devon crossed his arms and leaned against the wall. "So, everything that happened back then and now is all related. She's probably the one who put the note and flower on your truck too."

"Ian?" All eyes turned to their secretary standing in the doorway. "Chase Dixon is on line two, and he says it's an emergency."

Stabbing the speaker button on the landline once again, Ian connected the call. "Chase, what's wrong?"

"I'm sorry, man." Everyone tensed at the worry and regret in the man's voice. "I got a call from my guy on Harper—"

Panicked, Marco dove across the room toward the phone. "What happened?"

"A flash-bang was thrown into the office. Whoever it was, zapped everyone with a Taser, then zip-tied them. My guy managed to get out of the zips, called 911, and then me. Harper's gone, and Dev's wife is alive but unconscious."

"Fuck!" Devon ran out the door in sheer terror, and Marco knew precisely how he felt.

Ian was obviously torn between staying and going after his brother, but he knew he was needed here—they had to get Harper back. He pointed to the door. "Batman, drive him so he doesn't crash on the way or kill anyone when he gets there. And call me when you know something!" His voice increased with each word as Darius sprinted through the office toward the parking lot. "Chase, what else?"

"Everyone else is shaken up but fine. My other guard, who was outside, said some woman pulled in and asked about the office to rent on the top floor. She caught Lucy off guard, zapped and zipped her, and then locked her in the trunk of the car. By the time she recovered and got out, it was all over. The suspect is driving a gray Honda Civic. Unknown Florida plate. She's described as Caucasian, thirty to thirty-five, five-foot-six, one-eighty, shoulder-length brown hair, unknown eye color due to sunglasses. Wearing jeans, sneakers, and an over-sized pink sweatshirt. Sound like anyone you know?"

The remaining members of Kristen's Sexy Six-Pack glared at each other. Ian answered for all of them. "Yeah. We know exactly who that is. How long ago was this?"

"Fifteen, twenty minutes tops. I'm on my way to the scene."

Brody began typing away on his laptop, hacking into the city's traffic camera feeds. However, Marco wasn't optimistic about spotting the vehicle on the system since gray Honda Civics were a dime a dozen. The only reason his feet were still in the room was that he had absolutely no idea where to start looking for the Harper and the crazy-assed bitch. What if he never saw the woman he loved ever again? What the hell would he tell Mara as she got older and wanted to know where her mother was?

"Hey." Ian's voice snapped him out of it as he placed a solid but comforting hand on Marco's shoulder. The phone call with Dixon had ended. "We'll find them and get Harper back. It's what we do, brother. You know that."

Marco nodded, hoping beyond hope his friend spoke the truth.

Ten minutes later, they were still at a loss for where to start looking. The good news was Devon and Darius had arrived at the scene just as Kristen was being put into an ambulance. She was now awake but shaken—and scared out of her mind that something might have happened to her unborn child. Devon was just as freaked, but Darius was keeping him in check. The Omega operative had also passed on that there was nothing more to add to the intel that the rest of them had already been given.

Brody hung up his cell phone. "Her last known landlord says she skipped out on the rent over a year ago, and he has no idea where she went. Everything I can find with an address for her lists the one she had when working here or older. I've got nothing on her paying any utilities anywhere in a two-hundred-mile radius for over a year. It's like she fell off the face of the earth."

Several people were on laptops and phones, trying to track down Paula Leighton's location. Marco's frustration was mounting as he racked his brains, trying to think where the bitch would have taken Harper. Trudy had tried to talk to him, but, no offense to the shrink, he wasn't in the mood to calm down.

"Ian?"

They all turned toward the door where Colleen stood, pale and her eyes wide in alarm. Ian waved her into the conference room. "What is it?"

She stepped forward and pointed to the landline phone on the table. "S-she's on the phone. Paula. She's demanding to talk to Marco and said if he doesn't get on the phone, she'll kill Harper."

Everyone froze. Then panic assailed Marco, and he lunged across the table for the phone, but Trudy stopped him from picking it up. He glared at her. "What the fuck?"

"Easy, Marco. Take a deep breath before you talk to her. She's psychotic and probably far from rational at this point. Don't yell at her or threaten her. Forget trying to reason with her. Instead, play into whatever fantasy she's in."

He glanced at his teammates—except for Brody, who'd run to his war-room to trace the call—meeting Ian's gaze last. His boss nodded gravely. "Trudy's right. Paula's obsessed with you and probably thinks you two are soulmates, so make her believe you think it too. It might be the only way to get Harper back alive."

Oh, God, help him. Could he do this? Could he convince a deranged woman he was in love with her when, in truth, he was in love with the woman he was trying to save? He closed his eyes and counted to five in his head before opening them again. "Okay, Trudy, you're the shrink, so I'll do it your way. I'll put her on speakerphone so you can help me through this. Everyone else, stay fucking quiet."

Trudy sat at the table and pulled a pen and pad of paper closer to her. When she was ready, Marco cleared his voice, stabbed the speaker button, and connected the call. "DeAngelis."

They could hear shuffling and the sound of traffic over the line, but no voices.

"Hello? Paula, is that you?"

"Of course, it's me, lover. Who did you think it was?"

He winced at the purring in the woman's voice. It was as if she was trying very hard to sound sexy, but instead, the tone only made his stomach churn. Swallowing hard, he tried to keep calm. "Well, you, since Colleen told me you were on the phone. I was... I was hoping you'd call."

"Really?" She clearly hadn't expected him to say that and sounded suspicious. "Why?"

Why? Because I want to track you down, throw you in a padded cell, and flush the key down a toilet. That is, if I don't kill you first. "I've been thinking about you since I saw you at Donovan's a few weeks ago."

Paula snorted. "Liar. You never thought about me as a real woman. I just answered the phones and brought you coffee without being asked."

Wishing he could reach through the phone and

strangle her, he tried to sound understanding and apologetic. "You're right. I didn't see you as a woman. Back then, I thought of you as a coworker, and I would never get involved with a coworker. But now that you no longer work here, it's no longer an issue, right? I mean, Harper was just a one-night stand that got out of hand." He almost choked on the lie. "So, nothing is stopping us from getting to know each other better now, right?

"Oh yes, there is. This bitch is stopping us. But once she's out of the picture, we won't have to worry about her anymore. You and I will take our baby and raise her together."

Holy fuck, the woman gave new meaning to the word insane! "Is Harper with you right now?" Trudy waved a finger at him. He growled. "I mean, the bitch."

"Yes, she is. We're taking a lovely drive together, isn't that right?"

A muffled scream came over the line, scaring the crap out of him. He leaned on his hands, closer to the phone, as if he could zip through the line like electricity or something. "Paula! What are you doing? Where are you? If you hurt or kill her, you'll go to jail, and then we'll never be together. I don't want that to happen." Bile rose in his throat, and he forced it back down. "Paula, sweetheart. Please tell me where you are. I'll come there and tell Harper it's all over between us, and you and I will take care of the baby."

"I'm not stupid, darling, and I have no intention of going to jail. Once you bring the baby to meet us, I'll let her go, and our little family will start over somewhere else where she won't distract you."

God, he wanted to vomit. There was no way he was letting Mara within five miles of this whack-job. "What do we need the baby for? You know I'm not a fan of kids. It could be just you and me together."

"And baby makes three," Paula sing-songed. "Don't worry. I'll take care of little Anna Marie. I think that's a much better name than Mara, don't you think?"

Seeing Trudy nod, he agreed, "Yeah, that's a great name. I like it a lot."

"Good. I'll take care of her, and you won't have to do anything."

He glanced at the digital clock on the wall. What the fuck was taking Brody so long? Boomer was standing in the hall, where Marco could see him, and would give the signal when they knew the call had been traced. "That... that sounds great. Where should I meet you?"

"Get the baby and start driving north on I-75. I'll call your cell phone in a half hour and let you know what exit to take."

Ian motioned with his hand to draw out the call a little longer. *Damn it, Brody, hurry the fuck up.* "Just give me the directions now, in case one of us has cell phone trouble. And it will take me a little longer than a half hour to get on the road. I need to pack a bag of clothes for me and the baby."

At the same time Boomer gave a thumbs-up signal, Paula barked into the phone. "I'm not stupid, Marco." She didn't trust him any more than he trusted her. "If I give you the address now, you'll just send the rest of the team after me. That's not going to happen. Take your truck. I put a tracking device on it months ago. Obviously, your precious team was too stupid to look for one. You better be on the road when I call you, and I'll know if you're lying. If I see anyone else but you at the destination, I'll kill the bitch, and then the brat the first chance I get."

"All right," he placated, trying to get her to ease up on the irrational rage. "Calm down, honey." His lip curled in a sneer at the sweet nickname. "I'm leaving the office now. I'll go get Mara..." Trudy's flailed her arms at him. "I mean, A-Anna Marie, and I'll be on my way... alone. Just me and the baby. I have a duffel with spare clothes in my truck, so that will do for now. Okay?"

The insane woman was purring again. "That's perfect, lover. I'll call you in thirty minutes."

The call disconnected as Brody hurried into the room. "Got her, but she's moving. Had to ping a bunch of cell towers to triangulate and figure out which way she was heading. She's on I-75 going north, just north of Wesley Chapel. Any idea where she's going?"

Marco shook his head in fear and frustration. "No. Anyone else?" No one in the room answered him. "Shit. Ian, there's no way I'm taking Mara with me!"

His boss gave him a "well-duh" look. "Didn't think you would, ass-hat. But we need the baby's car seat and blanket, a ten-pound barbell from the gym, a radio receiver, and some duct tape."

What the fuck?

Ian ignored the looks of confusion and began barking orders. "Babs, get the chopper in the air. Start heading toward Paula's current location and standby for the coordinates as soon as we get them. Abbott, it's time to impress me with those sniper skills, but hopefully, they're not needed. You're in the chopper without a spotter. With Dev and Knight gone, I need everyone else on the ground. Load up." With quick nods, the two women rushed out the door, heading toward the helipad. "Boomer, you're with the geek in the com-van. Mancini, McCabe, and Foster, take one of the trucks and follow them. I'll ride shotgun with Polo until we get close. Trudy, as much as I would like to have a shrink on this op, I'm not willing to risk having you there." The psychologist nodded in understanding. She wasn't trained for hostage negotiations. "All right, everyone, gear up—weapons, vests, headsets, the works. Let's move out."

———

LYING ACROSS THE BACKSEAT OF THE SEDAN, HARPER twisted her hands behind her back, trying to slip out of the metal handcuffs on her wrists. It was no use—they were on too tight.

When she had first started coming around about twenty minutes earlier, she thought she'd had one too many glasses of champagne the night before. It was the only thing that gave her such a wicked hangover and queasy stomach the next day. But as her throbbing head cleared, she found she was restrained with a gag in her mouth and realized a hangover would be preferable to what she was going through now.

Covered by a blanket, she'd been able to wiggle enough for it to drop down from her face. Since her head was against the rear driver's side door, she couldn't tell who was in the seat in front of her, but when the female passenger turned to look at her, Harper recognized her right away. Paula... something. Trident's former secretary and the woman Marco and she had run into a few weeks ago at Donovan's. Unable to ask what the hell was going on, she could only mumble, which had received a curt "Shut the fuck up" from Paula. Then Harper had to listen to the insane woman talk to Marco on the phone. What she wouldn't have given to hear his voice, if only for a moment. At one point in the conversation, Paula turned around and pointed a gun at her. She hadn't been able to hold back the involuntary scream, which was muffled by the bandana stuffed in her mouth and tied around her head.

Now, things were quiet again as they continued to drive at a high rate of speed. Paula had told Marco to drive north on I-75, so Harper assumed that was the road they were on. The question was, where the hell were they going?

"Get off at the next exit," Paula ordered the driver.

A male voice responded, "Where are we going?"

Good question.

"Just fucking drive where I tell you to."

After taking the off-ramp and then making a right as instructed, the driver spoke again. "Why the fuck didn't we just kill everyone back there? It would have been so much easier than tying everyone up."

Paula growled. "I told you. If we killed any of them, Marco's team would've come after me, and I would never get my hands on that baby. Since they had her protected at the compound, I had to get Marco to bring her to me since you couldn't do it. Turn left here."

"What's so special about the fucking kid?"

"She's Marco's, and she should be mine..." She looked over her shoulder at Harper. "Not yours. You don't deserve to have his baby, you slut."

It was useless to try to tell the bitch to fuck off, so Harper glared at her instead. If only looks could kill.

Laughing at her captive's predicament, Paula turned back toward the front and hit the resend button on her cell. When the call connected, she gave Marco the directions to what sounded like the middle of nowhere.

Harper felt around the seat and the space between it and the backrest, looking for anything she could stick into the slot where the handcuff key went. A few years ago, she and Nina dared Marco to let them restrain him with his cuffs to see if he could escape. After he did it in less than two minutes with one of Nina's bobby pins, he showed them how to jimmy the locking mechanism, using anything thin and handy, until it released. Both women had been able to free themselves after several attempts, and now, Harper prayed she remembered how to do it.

Her fingers brushed against something foreign between the fabric cushions, and it took her a moment to realize it was a plastic pen. Catching her fingernail on the clip after a few tries, she dragged it closer until she could grasp it. After pulling it out, she waited for her two kidnappers to start talking again, then snapped the pen in half. The inside plastic tube that held the ink was the perfect size for the keyhole. She was about to try to pick the lock when the vehicle turned onto an unpaved road and began to bounce with every dip and rock the tires hit. Harper tightened her grip on the makeshift tool, not wanting to drop it. She would have to wait until they stopped.

Paula pointed to something outside the windshield. "Pull in here and park next to that barn."

"That's a barn?" The driver sounded incredulous as he snorted. "It looks like it's going to fall apart."

"Did I ask your opinion, Lairson?"

"Where the fuck are we?" The vehicle stopped and the emergency stick, between the front two seats, was yanked. "Whose property is this?"

"I don't know or care. All I know is it's abandoned, and no one is around for miles."

The engine shut off, and both front doors opened. Moments later, the door by Harper's head swung open, and she got her first look at kidnapper number two, albeit upside down. He was a tall, skinny guy in his mid-twenties, she guessed. Sharp, angular facial features made him look gaunt, and she wouldn't be surprised to find out he was a drug addict. Grabbing her under her armpits, he dragged her out of the car until her feet hit the ground and she could stand. A glance around told her they were indeed in the middle of fucking nowhere on some old farm. What had once been a house was now a pile of burnt rubble. The pastures and areas around the barn were overgrown with weeds. Lairson held her by the bicep and pulled her along as Paula led the way into the dilapidated barn with peeling red paint covering the outside. It was darker inside, and she was shoved to the floor in what used to be a horse's stall. Taking inventory of what was around her, she spotted several loose two-by-fours a few feet away, which could be used as weapons *if* she could free her hands.

Paula sat in a chair at a card table, which she must have brought in beforehand since it looked so out of place, and then opened the laptop she'd been carrying. A mobile Wi-Fi adapter was plugged into one of the ports. Harper couldn't see the screen, but she assumed the woman was looking at a map with a signal from the tracking device she'd said was on Marco's truck.

"Good," the crazy bitch announced. "He should be here in about a half hour. Once he gets here and I make sure he has the baby, I'll get in his truck. Your money is in a duffel bag in the trunk of the car. After we leave, kill the bitch."

CHAPTER TWENTY-THREE

Paula refreshed the web page for the tracking device. Everything was going according to plan, and soon, the man she loved would be all hers. She sneered at the whore on the ground in the stall. Lairson thought he was going to kill Harper, then take what he believed was a duffel bag full of money and run. But Paula had other plans the worthless piece-of-shit didn't know about—mainly the explosives she had set up around the barn.

After their initial introduction, she'd bypassed using Lairson as a middleman with Rodgers, knowing she wanted a few more things from the bomber before she killed him. She'd had him make her several bombs, with C-4, which would blow when she turned on the remote in the pocket of her sweatshirt and then flipped the first detonation switch. Neither Lairson nor Harper would be leaving here alive.

Under the pullover, around her waist, was also a

belt of explosives—just in case Marco had any bright ideas about rescuing Harper. The second switch would send them into the afterlife together. If Paula couldn't have him and his baby, then no one would.

Clicking on the laptop's touchpad, she refreshed the screen once again, and the signal showed Marco's truck was approaching the exit he needed to get off at. It was amazing what you could buy and learn via the internet these days. Getting the gun, tracker, C-4, and anything else she needed was a piece of cake. All that had been required was Wi-Fi service and some money, which she had thanks to her unsuspecting benefactor, who was now frozen solid in the freezer in his garage.

Reaching into her pocket, she pushed the black thumb switch on the back of the remote, turning it on so it would be ready if needed. It was only a matter of time before she finally got what she wanted—to be Mrs. Paula DeAngelis. She giggled to herself. *That has such a nice ring to it.*

"WHEN YOU TAKE THE EXIT RAMP, I'LL HOP OUT AND GET in the van. Are you up for this?"

Marco nodded. "Yeah. I just hope your idea about the baby works."

In the car seat behind him, they'd used the ten-pound barbell and wrapped two blankets around it to make it look like Mara was with him. If he had to pick the carrier up, it would appear to be the correct weight.

Tucked into the fabric was the radio receiver. Brody would transmit a recording of a crying baby for effect. Marco wasn't planning on letting Paula get close enough to see it was all a scam, but hopefully, it convinced her enough for him to get the upper hand. His biggest fear right now was it was too late to save Harper. He doubted an insane woman, who'd already killed someone in cold blood, would let her hostage go —especially since she saw Harper as competition.

"Just roll the window down a bit so Paula can hear the crying. Get her talking as much as you can while we get in position. Babs will be coming in from the north in stealth mode. By the time Paula hears them, it'll be too late."

The new chopper was a military prototype they'd gotten from Sikorsky, the manufacturers of Black Hawk aircrafts, most of which were used by the U.S. government. The unique, ultramodern design helped the aircraft cruise in relative silence, making it the ideal bird to sneak up on a target. SEAL Team Six reportedly had used another MH-X Silent Hawk in the raid on Osama bin Laden's compound when the terrorist had been killed. But that information was still speculation since most of the mission was deemed classified—even to retired members of another SEAL team.

From what Egghead had found out about the property they were going to, it was an isolated and abandoned horse ranch. The satellite photos showed it was overgrown with high grass, trees, and shrubs, making it easy for the team to close ranks around the barn, which was the only structure still standing. A gray vehicle was parked near the building, and they assumed it was Paula's Honda Civic.

Marco slowed the truck to take the exit ramp as Ian prepared to switch vehicles. "Just remember... try to keep Paula calm and... well, you know the fucking deal. Get us as much intel as possible."

Stopping at the end of the ramp, Marco glanced at his friend, who opened the door and climbed out. "Just boogie and let me know when you're in position."

The whole changing of vehicles took Ian less than ten seconds. When they were on their way again, Marco let the other two SUVs pass him so they could speed up and get to the properties adjacent to the one he had been ordered to go to. It was another twenty minutes before he turned down a long dirt driveway after getting the go-ahead from Ian and Brody, each leading a three-man team. Babs and Abbott were nearby, waiting for the signal to fly in. Marco had to keep Paula on the south side of the barn to allow them to get as close as possible before she heard them. While the chopper was supposed to be silent, when it was right overhead, there was no way you'd miss it.

As he approached the run-down barn, Marco parked about thirty yards away from the Civic. There was no one in sight. Scanning the surrounding area from the driver's seat, he knew his team was out there among the overgrowth, but if he couldn't see them, there was no way Paula or anyone else would see them.

He cracked open the rear windows a few inches and the front ones even more. When Egghead hit the transmit button, a baby's cries would come over loud and clear. Moving his lips only a fraction, he whispered into everyone's headsets. "No eyes on tango, yet."

He killed the engine and opened the driver's door. As he climbed out, the sound of unoiled hinges shrieked as a door to the barn swung open.

IT'D TAKEN HARPER ABOUT TWENTY-FIVE MINUTES before she finally picked the lock on one of the cuffs. Despite her sweaty hands, she might've been able to do it faster, but she had to stop every time the greasy-haired guy leered at her or when there was complete silence to avoid her escape plan being detected. Well, she didn't exactly have an escape plan, per se, more like a hopeful partial plan. Paula was the only one with a gun, as far as she could tell, while Lairson kept playing with a switchblade. If one of them went outside, she could grab a two-by-four and hit the other over the head. She would then be able to escape by squeezing through the open boards of the wall at the back of the decrepit barn. Timing would be everything. For now, she kept her hands behind her back, giving the illusion she was still incapacitated, and whenever no one was watching, she inched closer to her intended weapon.

In the silence that had fallen over the barn, they all heard a vehicle approach. Pulling the gun out of her waistband, Paula hurried over to peek through a window mostly covered in dirt and dust. "He's here! I knew he'd come." She pointed to another window on the other side of the barn and then at two openings in the wood planks. "Lairson, check those. Make sure no one else is coming."

Her lackey rolled his eyes but did as he was told. When he announced he didn't see anyone, Paula went to the hinged door they'd come through instead of the huge sliding doors. The shriek of ungreased metal echoed throughout the vast expanse, and Harper used the noise to reach over and grab the closest piece of wood big enough to do the job. As the crazy woman stepped outside, her cohort went to the glassless window and peered out. His back was to the stall where Harper was, and she slowly stood, trying hard not to make a sound. Holding the plank like a baseball bat, she crept forward. She was almost in striking range when a floorboard squeaked under her weight. Lairson spun around, wide-eyed. Knowing her life was on the line, Harper took another step and swung with all her might.

Stepping away from his vehicle, Marco watched Paula exit the barn. The nine-millimeter gun in her right hand made him a little queasy, wondering if she'd already used it to kill Harper. His own weapon was hidden at the small of his waist. He held his hands out to the side so she wouldn't perceive him as a threat. Until he laid his eyes on Harper, he would have to play along with the façade he'd started back in the conference room at Trident. He glanced around, trying to appear nonchalant. "Talk about the middle of nowhere. Is this place yours?"

The woman rolled her eyes and pointed the gun at him. "Please. You know it's not. Lift your shirt and turn around. Toss your gun on the ground. I know you wouldn't come here without a weapon.

Or two. He had a backup piece on his ankle, in addition to a knife, which was built into his belt buckle. Reaching back, he withdrew his 9mm and tossed it a few feet away from him, but still close enough so he could dive and retrieve it again. He then lifted his shirt and slowly did a complete one-eighty. "Where's Harper?"

"Being guarded by a guy with a very big knife. He'll release her after we leave. Did you bring Anna Marie?"

Right on cue, the sound of a baby crying pierced the air from within his truck. "Yeah, but she's been crying for a while, and it's been giving me a headache. Why don't we just leave her here?"

"No." Paula shook her head and stepped toward him. Marco counteracted with a forward step of his own. He had to keep her away from the truck. "She's coming with us."

"All right. We'll take her with us. But first, I want to see Harper to tell her it's all over between us."

The crazy woman stared at him for a few moments

as if trying to make up her mind. She then raised her voice. "Bring the bitch out here."

There was no response.

"Lairson!"

Still nothing. And then McCabe's low voice came over Marco's earpiece. "Got eyes on the principal. She's running north away from the barn. Shit. Someone's on her tail. Intercepting. Stand by."

Marco clenched his teeth, trying not to react. He trusted his team to rescue Harper and keep her safe. His job now was to distract Paula. "You know what? Never mind. I really don't want to see her again. She'll just beg me to stay. Why don't we get out of here?"

The woman looked torn between leaving with him and returning to the barn to find her partner-in-crime. Marco was tempted to dive for his weapon or get closer to her to take her down, but something bothered him about her appearance. He hadn't paid attention to it earlier, but now, as she twisted to glance over her shoulder, he noticed what he had thought was just her stocky body shape was something more. The question was, what did she have wrapped around her waist? If he were over in Afghanistan or Iraq, his first thought would have been a suicide belt. But Paula wasn't that crazy... was she? *Fuck! Think*. How could he alert the team without giving away that they were out there?

"Tango down, but not out. Principal secured." The whispered update told him that Harper was safe, thank God, and while McCabe had eliminated the male threat, the former Army Special Forces' sergeant had refrained from killing him.

Paula seemed to sense something was wrong, but she surprised him by taking several steps toward him and pulling something out of her sweatshirt pocket. Pointing the gun at his chest, she ordered, "Get in the truck." When he didn't move, she barked, "Now! Or I'll blow up the barn with that bitch in there."

She held up a little black box with two silver switches on it. *Fuck!* As she lifted her arm above her head, the hem of her sweatshirt rose above her waist. There was no point in trying to be subtle anymore. "Paula, what is that? Are you wearing a suicide belt?"

A few muttered curses came over his earpiece, but he ignored them, keeping his attention on the woman's hands. One could kill him with a bullet, and the other could blow him to smithereens. She was too close now for him to escape unscathed if she flipped the switch, but not quite close enough for him to go on the offensive—not yet, anyway.

Holding his hands at shoulder height, he took a few steps backward. She stopped him as he was about to go around to the driver's side of his truck. "No! Slide in from the passenger side."

Come on, you crazy bitch. Come closer. He didn't know which switch was the one for the belt, and he couldn't take the risk that it was the one she had her thumb on. He knew the team had eyes on them, but they couldn't take a shot at her yet. Any miss or non-lethal hit could result in her jolting and flipping the switch. A headshot could cause an involuntary jerk of her hand and fingers, again detonating the device. They would have to wait until Marco was out of range or close enough to grab the remote.

The cries from the "baby" were still broadcasting, and even though it wasn't Mara's cry, Marco knew he would do anything to walk away from this alive. He had a long life he wanted to live, and it included walking his daughter down the aisle one day.

Babs' voice came over the radio as he took a few more slow steps backward. "We're coming into range. I'm going to come up hard over the barn. Can Abbott take the headshot without detonation if you get a hand on that remote? Sneeze or cough once for yes."

A sneeze was easier to fake, and Marco let one loose. The sudden "ah-choo" was just enough to startle Paula, and he lunged forward, closing his fist around her hand and the remote while knocking her gun to the ground with his other hand. She briefly screeched in a blind rage as he crushed her hand against the little black box, preventing her from flipping either switch. She struggled with all her might, and he fought just as hard to keep her from falling. He would have to drop with her, putting him in Abbott's line of fire. His heart pounded in his chest. This was the do-or-die moment —and he sure as hell didn't want to die.

The quiet of the surrounding area was suddenly broken as Babs' chopper roared over the top of the barn, sideways, with Abbott aiming her sniper rifle out the open rear door. Putting his life in his teammate's hands, he pushed Paula's body as far away from his own as possible without letting go of his grip on her hand. A high-powered shot rang out, and a split second later, Paula's head exploded with the impact. Her instantly dead body pulled him to the ground as it collapsed, and he ignored the blood splatter that hit him in the face. Within seconds, his teammates on the ground ran forward, and Boomer fell to his knees next to Marco and what remained of his stalker.

"Keep a good grip. Let me see if I can remove the belt first."

"Hurry." Marco glanced up and saw Harper running toward him, but McCabe caught up to her, grabbed her around the waist, and held her back from the blast zone. The fear in her eyes was making Marco's stomach churn more than the explosive device or the fact that his face was covered in blood and brain matter. As Boomer figured out how to remove the suicide belt, Marco looked up at Brody. "In my go-bag, get me something to wash this off. I don't want it to touch Harper when I get my arms around her."

A few minutes later, Boomer placed the belt far enough away in the field, west of the barn, so everyone was out of the blast zone. Marco refused to let go of the remote and Paula's lifeless hand until his teammate rejoined them by the vehicles. Once he did, a loud boom resonated through the air as the device detonated without harming anyone.

Brody had retrieved a towel and wet it with a bottle of water before handing it to Marco when he finally released his grip and stood. He quickly wiped his face, neck, and arms and ripped off his bloodied shirt before rushing over to where Harper stood crying and struggling against McCabe's firm but gentle grip. Marco nodded, and the man let her go so she could run into his arms.

Her body hit him with an impact that sent him back a step, but he didn't care as he crushed her to him. She sobbed into his chest as he caressed her head and back. "It's over, Butterfly. *Shhh*. It's over." His gaze went to Abbott and Babs coming around from the rear of the barn where they'd landed the bird. He mouthed "thank you" to both women, who just smiled and gave him a pair of thumbs up.

He didn't know how long he stood there, holding Harper in his arms before the sound of sirens approaching reached his ears. Ian had called the local sheriff to alert him of the situation. Paula's partner would be turned over to them, and apparently, he needed a trip to the emergency room. Harper may not have knocked him out with the two-by-four, but she did break his wrist when he threw his arm up to ward off the blow.

It would be a few hours before this was all cleared up, but he planned on keeping Harper as close to him as possible—exactly the way he wanted for the rest of his life.

EPILOGUE

Three Months Later

Holding Mara sound asleep on his shoulder, Marco watched Harper open, inspect, and close all the cabinets in the empty house's new kitchen after they'd walked through the entire place twice. They had just accepted a bid on her home while his was already scheduled for closing next month. His place was where they were living for the moment, as they packed up the belongings of both houses and donated what they didn't need double of. Between the three closings, they could stay at Nick and Jake's apartment again for a few weeks if they needed to.

This one-level, four-bedroom ranch currently belonged to Parker Christensen, whose company, New Horizons, flipped houses a few times a year in addition to its numerous commercial construction jobs. It had been completed a few days ago, and Marco was impressed by how it had turned out compared to the "before" pictures he'd seen. Because of their close friendship, Parker gave them the first shot at purchasing it at a reduced price before putting it on the market for several thousand dollars higher.

Harper spun around and walked toward where he was standing in the large attached family room. "Well, what do you think?"

Shrugging, he grinned. "You know me. As long as we install Egghead's top security system, and there's a lock on our bedroom door for when sweet cheeks here starts walking, then I'm good."

Her laugh echoed in the barren room as she approached the sliding door leading out to the back-yard, which already had an in-ground pool. It was wonderful to see and hear her carefree again. After a full investigation, the team had been cleared of any wrongdoing in Paula's death. It had been a clear-cut case of self-defense—although the local sheriff wasn't happy they hadn't contacted him about the situation before rescuing Harper.

Randy Lairson had recovered from the injuries he'd received but had been shafted and killed during a fight in prison while awaiting trial. During an interrogation at the hospital, after he'd regained consciousness, he had admitted he was the one who'd assaulted Harper in her home. He was supposed to have kidnapped Mara that night, but thankfully, the baby had been with her grandmother. Lairson had also hired the bomber, whom he'd known from the streets for a few years.

As for Paula, they'd located where she'd been living for the past year from the address associated with the license plate on her car. The deceased homeowner's body was found stuffed into a full freezer in the garage. With no known relatives, Marco had made sure the poor guy got a proper burial. Upstairs, in one of the house's bedrooms, the obsessed woman had created a shrine to Marco. Most of the pictures covering the walls were of him at various locations around Tampa and his house, taken from a distance with a high-powered zoom lens. The tracking device she'd placed on his truck had been recovered from the undercarriage on the passenger side. He had no idea how long she had been stalking his movements, but the pictures seemed to date back to when she'd still worked for them.

Shoving the unwanted memories from his mind, he focused his attention on Harper's delectable ass. The black slacks she wore perfectly showcased her curves, and she'd paired them with his favorite pair of stilettos and a blue, short-sleeved blouse. He'd bet anything that, despite the pants, she was wearing a pair of thigh-highs underneath, and he couldn't wait until he could find out later if he was right.

"Well, I love it. It's even nicer than the other one we looked at. Parker outdid himself. There's plenty of room back here for a jungle gym. I love the open floor plan too. But..." She faced him again, giving him a steamy, seductive look, which had his cock stirring. "My favorite part is that the master bedroom is on the other side of the house from the children's rooms. I won't have to have a pillow thrown over my face when you make me come."

God, he loved this woman. Her fingers went to the new collar he'd had a jeweler design for him. It was two chains braided together—one silver and one gold, since she liked to wear both depending on her wardrobe. Last week, they'd had a ceremony on the center stage at The Covenant, where he'd vowed to be her Dom—to love and cherish her and take care of her every need for as long as they had each other. She, in turn, had knelt and bestowed upon him her undying love and submission.

Last month, he'd gotten another tattoo and updated the first one. He'd had Mara's name, in script, added to the spot under Nina's angel, so his sister was always watching over her niece. The new tattoo was on his right upper arm and was an intricate design that represented Harper and his D/s relationship, with her name underneath. But the significance of the fancy Triskelion, with three intertwined pieces, would only be recognized by those in the BDSM lifestyle. Harper had gotten a smaller version of the design on her right ass cheek, with his name, so Marco would see it every time he spanked her.

Harper didn't know that her engagement ring was

in his pocket right now. She'd told him he didn't need to get her one—that she was happy enough with the collar and a future wedding ring. But, yeah, he wasn't buying that. Plus, his soon-to-be mother-in-law and the women at Trident would give him hell if he didn't get her the ring many women dreamed of receiving for most of their lives.

After swearing her to secrecy, he'd taken Jenn shopping with him to get a woman's point of view since he had no clue what to look for. In the end, he'd found the perfect ring. A platinum and gold setting with a one-and-a-half karat diamond. But his favorite characteristic was the four small stones, two on either side of the diamond—a garnet, aquamarine, emerald, and pink tourmaline—his, Harper's, Nina's, and Mara's birthstones, respectively. He'd even had a baby bracelet made for Mara with the same stones, and it was also in his pants pocket.

He smirked and shook his head at her. "Not too sure about that, Butterfly. You take sexual screaming to a new level. I think I need to start looking at ball gags for you."

"*Hmmm.*" Her eyes lit up. "Oh, my God. Thanks for reminding me. I have to get the rest of the stuff I need for the goodie bags for Kristen's shower next week. We have them separated—white bags for the vanilla guests and blue for those in the lifestyle. Definitely can't mix those up. Otherwise, there will be a lot of confused and embarrassed women out there."

They'd all been grateful when the ultrasound, which had been done in the emergency room, showed little John Devon Sawyer, or J.D. as he'd already been affectionately dubbed, had not been harmed by the flash-bang grenade or Taser shock. Last month, the happy parents-to-be had found out they were expecting a boy in about twelve weeks, and Devil Dog was over the moon about it. They had also been relieved to hear that Kristen's ex-husband's lawsuit for half of her royalties had been ruled in her favor. Tom Rydell wasn't appealing, since he had far more serious problems, such as multiple state and federal embezzlement charges filed against him.

Harper glanced at her watch. "We should get going. We don't want to be late for the ceremony."

The school where Nina had been a teacher was dedicating a garden memorial to remember the beloved educator and co-worker. The growing family from Trident was meeting them there in an hour, along with students, teachers, and other friends. Even Jake and Nick had flown in for a long weekend to attend. Carter had called with his regrets that he couldn't be there, but promised to swing by and see it the next time he was in town.

"Before we go… is this it? Are we going to tell Parker we want the house?"

Taking one more quick look around, Harper nodded. "I think so. Everything is brand new, and there's plenty of room. It's close to the compound.

Shelby and Parker live two blocks away. There's an elementary school right up the street, and it's a quiet neighborhood, so I don't think we'll find anything nicer or more ideal than this."

"Good." Reaching into the pocket of his dress pants, he made a fist around the ring and pulled it out. Making sure he had a good hold on his sleeping daughter, he went down on one knee in front of Harper, grinning when her eyes almost bulged out of her head. "I never knew what I wanted before it all fell into my lap out of the blue. I am madly, hopelessly, in love with you, Millicent Harper Williams. I know we did things a little backward, but I'd be honored if you would accept this…" He opened his hand to show her the ring. "… as a sign to the vanilla world that you belong to me. Will you marry me?"

Tears poured down her cheeks as she nodded. Clearly, her voice had deserted her. He stood and, with one hand under Mara's diapered butt, slid the diamond on Harper's extended left ring finger. He pulled her toward him and gently, and then not-so-gently, kissed her lips until the baby began to stir between them.

Reluctantly letting his new fiancée go, he glanced down to see a pair of gray eyes, which matched his own, staring up at him. Lifting Mara over his head with both hands, making her giggle, he grinned at her. "Mommy and Daddy are getting married!"

Ready to read the next installment of the Trident Security Series? Get Curt and Dana's story, *Whiskey Tribute*, today! Keep reading for a preview.

For the best reading order of the Trident Security series and its spinoffs, check out the printable list on my website - www.samanthacolebooks.-com/pages/best-reading-order.

Want to know what's coming next? Join my Facebook Group -
Samantha Cole's Sexy Six-Pack's Sirens...

Or sign up for my newsletter -
samanthacolebooks.com/mailing-list

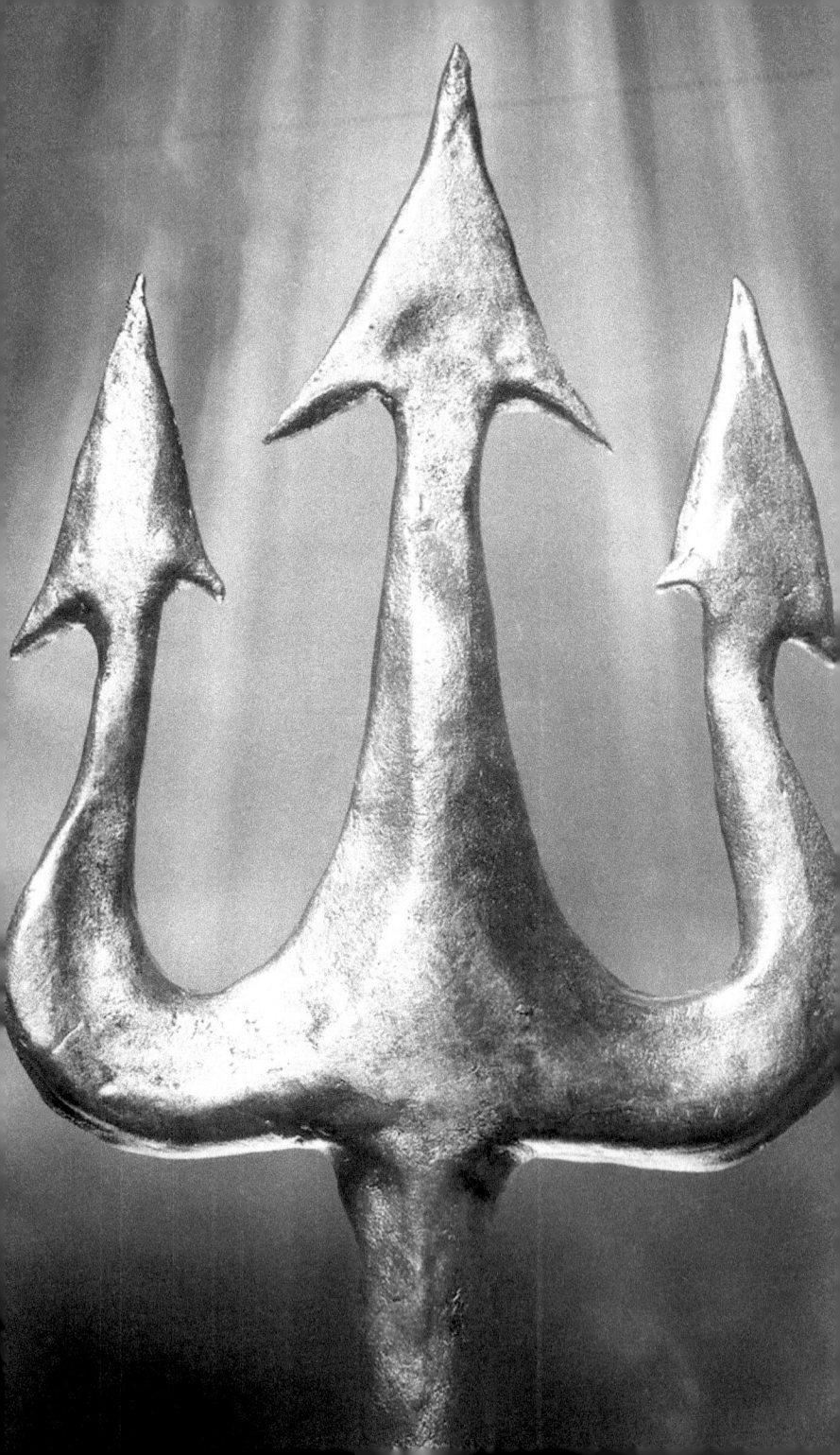

Whiskey Tribute
Trident Security Book 7

F lush against the wall of the shed separating his teammate and him from their sworn enemy, Curt "Elmer" Bannerman peeked around the corner, searching for a target. Nobody was in sight, but it didn't mean they weren't out there. There were plenty of places to hide, so the tangos could be anywhere. Glancing at his partner, standing stoically beside him, weapon in hand, he cocked his head toward their destination. "We're going to make a run for that boulder over there. Keep low. Ready?"

The response he got was a nod of the head and a muttered "yup."

"Count of three. One. Two. Three. Go!"

Zig-zagging across the expanse, they were almost to safety when he realized he'd run them right into an ambush. *Shit!* He blocked his partner with his bigger body, ready to defend with his life, and was hit dead in the chest by an exploding projectile. Stunned he'd been caught with his proverbial pants down, he grabbed his sternum and fell to his knees.

"I got you!"

Cheers were followed by laughter and giggles as the Prichard kids all came out of hiding and bombarded him with snowballs while celebrating nine-year-old Justin's successful throw, which took down the former Navy SEAL. Even his partner, six-year-old Amanda, had turned traitorous and dropped her snowball on his head.

"Ouch! Come here, you." He playfully reached for the little pixie, but she ran behind her second oldest brother, ten-year-old Taylor, for protection, squealing the whole way. Twelve-year-old Ryan and his brothers continued to pelt Curt with snowballs, so he let Amanda get away, then rolled to his feet and quickly returned fire, making sure he didn't hit anyone in the head.

Their mother, Dana, stuck her head out the back door of the old farmhouse, which was no longer part of a farm, aside from a few chickens and one cocky rooster. "Dinner's ready! Come and get it!"

The kids whooped it up in unison. Apparently, they'd worked up appetites as big as Curt's own. He knew Dana had made her famous beef stew, and his mouth was watering just knowing it was inside waiting for them. Or maybe it was the chef who was making his mouth water.

Knock it off, asshole. She's your best friend's wife and, therefore, off-limits.

While the kids ran inside, Curt ambled over to where his old teammate, Marco "Polo" DeAngelis, was stacking the last of the firewood they had cut up before the kids came out to play.

Yesterday, the two men had made the trip up to Stormville, Iowa, from Florida—Marco from Tampa and Curt from Daytona Beach. As retired Navy SEALs from Team Four, they were taking care of the family of one of their own—one of the fallen. Eric Prichard, Curt's best friend since basic training, had been murdered by an assassin over a year ago in what had originally looked like a hit-and-run accident.

Eric had been doing his evening run when he was struck and killed by an unknown vehicle. It was later learned that seven former members of Team Four had been targeted because of a mission they'd been on years ago. Three of the seven had been killed before the rest of them figured things out and the threat was eliminated. Curt didn't know all of the details, as the resulting investigation was deemed classified by the government. But his former lieutenant and Marco's current boss at Trident Security, Ian Sawyer, had discreetly let him know Eric's death had been avenged —justice had been served.

Immediately following Eric's funeral, a bunch of his

former teammates had put together a rotating schedule. Twice a month, two of them would head up here and stay at a local motel. They would then spend the weekend doing everything around the house and property Eric could no longer do for his family. A new roof had been put up, the main bathroom had been renovated, and the landscaping was tended to. If nothing pressing needed to be done, whoever's weekend it was would do something fun with the family, like camping or a trip to Six-Flags. Today, Marco and he had spent the morning making fast work of painting little Amanda's room pink and purple. She'd been making it known for several weeks she was now too big for the Winnie the Pooh theme she'd had for the past four years.

Curt approached his buddy while brushing the snow from his blond hair. "Hand me the axes. I'll put them in the shed. You're looking a little hypothermic there, Polo."

"Ya think?" the man snorted, his Staten Island accent coming through. "It's colder than a witch's tit out here. I knew there was a reason I moved to the Sunshine State."

Chuckling, Curt bent over, pulled one of the axes out of the old tree stump they'd used, and then took the one Marco handed him. "I could get used to it again. You forget—I'm from Montana. This is nothing—a tropical heat wave."

"Yeah, well... why don't you stop ogling the merry

widow, tell her how you feel, and then you can live in the Tropics of Iowa all year round."

Even though his cheeks were red from the cold, the six-foot-four, two-hundred-twenty-pound man blushed. Was it that fucking obvious he had a hard time keeping his eyes in his sockets when Dana was around? *Shit.* And when the fuck had that started? Yeah, she was attractive... hell, she was hot—always had been. Even though she still carried around some of the weight she'd gained during her four pregnancies, her body still rocked. He loved curvaceous women, and she had an awesome hourglass figure. *Shit*. Not wanting to admit his friend was right about the ogling, he lied. "What are you fucking talking about? I'm not interested in Dana."

Crossing his arms, Marco rolled his eyes. "Please. Don't give me that. You get a goofy, fucking grin on your face every time she walks into the room. Probably a fucking hard-on, too, but I have no desire to confirm that by taking a look at your junk. Every time someone can't make it up here for their weekend, you've been filling in. And don't tell me it's because Eric was your best friend."

"He is... was... damn it." Scowling, Curt turned and strode toward the shed, but Marco followed on his heels. *Damn it.* Why couldn't his buddy just drop it? Curt had no business lusting for his best friend's wife. He was here to do right by Eric's family. Nothing more.

"I know he was." Marco's voice was stern but also filled with sympathy. "But you know better than I do he'd want you to have a good life without him. The same goes for Dana. I've seen the way she looks at you sometimes. And the kids and you get along great—so what's the problem? It's been almost a year and a half since he was killed. Get off your fucking ass before someone steps in and snatches her up."

What? Curt saw red and whirled around so fast that Marco almost got hit in his cold cock with an ax. "Who's going to snatch her up? Someone else been eyeing her?"

The bastard had the audacity to smirk. "Thought you weren't interested."

"Don't fuck with me, Polo. Who the fuck else is interested in her?"

Clearly finding amusement in Curt's demeanor, the other man shrugged. "I don't know for sure, but Egghead mentioned the Sheriff seemed to be sniffing around a lot when he was up here two weeks ago." Brody "Egghead" Evans was Marco's best friend and teammate at Trident Security, as well as a former member of Team Four, and was the biggest computer geek in the world—or close to it.

"Fuck that shit." His gaze went to the house's rear entrance, and the thought of Dana in another man's arms had his blood boiling. He should have known she was going to have guys chasing after her someday, but not this soon. Years ago, he'd promised Eric that if anything happened to him, he would watch over Dana and make sure she and the kids stayed safe and protected. And it was a promise he intended to keep.

Marco slapped him on the shoulder before taking

the axes from him. "So, you gonna man up and tell her how you feel?"

Curt nodded, his eyes never leaving the backdoor. If it kept the other sharks at bay, he'd do what he had to. "Damn, fucking straight."

"About fucking time."

But the moment he stepped into the country kitchen and saw Dana ladling the stew into bowls for everyone, his courage fled. Eric was still here—in every picture, every expression on his children's faces, and in every beat of Dana's heart. He couldn't do it. He couldn't lust after his best friend's wife. Not now... and not even ten years from now. All he could do was keep everything platonic and be her go-to guy when she needed help with anything. It sucked being a man who always did the right thing.

"UNCLE CURTSY, CAN YOU READ ME A BEDTIME STORY before you leave?"

He ignored Marco's smug grin at the nickname Amanda had been calling him since she'd first been able to say his name. It was embarrassing sometimes, but when his goddaughter looked up at him with her big brown eyes, he just melted. "Sure, sweetheart. Go brush your teeth like your momma told you, and then pick out a book."

Smiling, she ran to the bathroom. The boys were playing video games in their bedrooms as the two men finished putting the last of Amanda's furniture back where it belonged. Dana had put the new sheets and comforter on the bed and planned to hang the new curtains tomorrow. At the moment, she was doing another load of laundry. It amazed him how many clothes four kids could go through in a matter of days.

"So you chickened out, huh?"

He'd been wondering when his friend was going to say something. All through dinner, his guilt had been eating at him. He was an asshole, lusting after another man's wife... and not just any man, but one who'd saved his life on a mission gone FUBAR—fucked up beyond all recognition—in Afghanistan. "Shove it, Polo. She's not ready, and even if she was, I can't get past the fact she belongs to Eric."

Marco sighed heavily. "Belonged, man. Past tense."

Curt pushed a white, straight-back chair under its matching desk and scowled at the other man. "You know, you're the last person I expected to hear shit from about this. Mister I'm-never-getting-married-and-having-kids."

The man's childhood had been shitty, and the only family he truly had, besides his brothers-in-arms, had been his sister, Nina, who'd passed away of cancer over a year ago. Marco had taken it really rough, and it was good that his teammates had been on his six, watching his back and getting him out of his funk.

"Hey, just because I don't want it for me doesn't mean I don't want my friends to find someone to love." He glanced out the bedroom door to ensure no kids were lurking about and lowered his voice a little. "But that's what I like about the lifestyle. I can get my rocks off, have a temporary relationship with an end date, and give a woman the care she needs and what I need to give. Nothing drastic, and then I move on. But that's not you, man. You're missing out on something real here. Just because I'm not walking down the aisle doesn't mean I don't recognize when two people belong together."

Curt knew all about the BDSM lifestyle his buddy was talking about, but it had never been for him... or Eric. While neither of them had a problem with some of their teammates going to clubs like that and even owning one, they hadn't felt the draw to it the others did. Vanilla sex, with the occasional slap and tickle, was fine with him. He just didn't get into the whole Dominant/submissive thing. "Yeah, well, I get the feeling there's some chick out there that's going to turn your world upside down and slap-shit forward. And I'm going to laugh my ass off when it happens. As for me and Dana... never mind—"

He dropped the rest of the conversation when Amanda came skipping in and hurried to her bookshelf. Picking a book, she handed it to him and jumped into her bed, climbing under the fresh sheets. Marco slapped him on the back as he headed toward the door. "I'll see if Dana needs anything else done before we leave. Night, Amanda."

"Night, Uncle Marco." Hugging her favorite stuffed rabbit, she moved to the inside of the twin bed to give him room and then patted the spot next to her. "Sit here, Uncle Curtsy."

Doing as he was told, his elbow accidentally knocked over the 5x7 frame on her nightstand. After setting it right, he stared at the photo of Eric with his then four-year-old daughter on his shoulders. Curt's gut clenched a little. Damn, he missed the guy.

Don't worry, my friend. I'll take care of them.

Ready to read the next installment of the Trident Security Series? Get Curt and Dana's story, *Whiskey Tribute*, today!

A PROMISE BETWEEN BEST FRIENDS...

Curt never thought he'd be forced to keep a pledge to watch over Eric's family, but an assassin made that vow a harsh reality.

Eighteen months later, he's still keeping an eye on them, but his feelings for the pretty widow have shifted somewhere along the line.

Dana had been both a mother and a father to her children during her husband's multiple deployments, but once he retired, she'd thought those days were over... she was wrong.

While his SEAL teammates have been there for her,

one stands above all the rest— the man slowly invading her dreams.

They started as friends, but now, both want more. Can they move past the feeling of betraying a dead man by wanting each other? Or is Eric always going to stand between them?

For the best reading order of the Trident Security series and its spinoffs, check out the printable list on my website - www.samanthacolebooks.-com/pages/best-reading-order.

OTHER BOOKS BY
SAMANTHA COLE

***Denotes titles/series that are only available on select digital sites. Paperbacks and audiobooks are available on most book sites.

***THE BID ON LOVE SERIES

(WITH 7 OTHER AUTHORS!)

Going, Going, Gone: Book 2

***THE COLLECTIVE: SEASON TWO

(WITH 7 OTHER AUTHORS!)

Angst: Book 7 (M/M)

SPECIAL COLLECTIONS

Trident Security Series: Volume I

Trident Security Series: Volume II

Trident Security Series: Volume III

Trident Security Series: Volume IV

Trident Security Series: Volume V

Trident Security Series: Volume VI

ABOUT SAMANTHA COLE

USA Today Bestselling Author Samantha Cole is a retired police officer and paramedic who now writes heart-pounding romance in multiple forms—MF, MM, and ménage. From military heroes to rugged cowboys and small-town heat, her stories blend passion, loyalty, and danger in perfect balance.

Awards:

Wannabe in Wyoming (co-authored by J.B. Havens) won the bronze medal in the 2021 Readers' Favorite Awards in the General Romance category.

Scattered Moments in Time won the gold medal in the 2020 Readers' Favorite Awards in the Fiction Anthology category.

Where the Broken Bloom (formerly *The Road to Solace*) won the silver medal in the 2017 Readers' Favorite Awards in the Contemporary Romance category.

Sexy Six-Pack's Sirens Group on Facebook

Website: www.samanthacolebooks.com
Newsletter: samanthacolebooks.com/mailing-list

facebook.com/SamanthaColeAuthor
instagram.com/samanthacoleauthor
bookbub.com/profile/samantha-a-cole
goodreads.com/SamanthaCole
amazon.com/Samantha-A-Cole/e/B00X53K3X8
tiktok.com/@samanthacoleauthor
youtube.com/@SamanthaACole-bp6yu